M000222144

ANDREW G.
NELSON

GLASS CASTLE

ANDREW G. NELSON

GLASS CASTLE

Copyright © 2019 by Andrew G. Nelson

Cover Design Copyright © 2019 by Huntzman Enterprises

Published by Huntzman Enterprises

First Edition: September 2019

ISBN-10: 0-9987562-7-X
ISBN-13: 978-0-9987562-7-1

Printed in the United States of America
1 3 5 7 9 10 8 6 4 2

DEDICATION

They say that writing is a solo adventure, but that is not true. While authors spend an enormous amount of time in their *minds*, creating worlds, characters, and plots, the path from idea to print is not accomplished without help.

This book would not exist without the love, support, and constant encouragement of my wife, Nancy. From the beginning she was my biggest fan, and without her the tales of James Maguire, and his numerous friends and foes, would have remained an *idea* locked away in my brain. Thank you for always believing in me.

And I would be greatly remiss to not acknowledge God, through whom all things are possible. My life can be summed up in one word: Experience. Some of them have been high points in my life while others have taught me lessons, but during all of them He has been a constant and faithful companion.

Other Titles by Andrew G. Nelson

ACKNOWLEDGMENTS

Writing a book is a personal journey, but it is not one that you accomplish alone. Life brings people and events that mold and shape you. It is through those experiences that you are blessed with the foundation to write.

In my twenty years with the NYPD I was honored to work alongside some truly great men and women and I consider myself blessed to have had the opportunity.

To my brothers and sisters lost in the attack on September 11th, 2001, and all those who lost their lives in the years before and after, you are never forgotten.

Fidelis Ad Mortem.

The gleaming fortress sat atop the highest hill in the land, overlooking the sea. A masterpiece of unparalleled opulence; designed to impress even the most discerning visitor. But when the winds of war finally came, it was revealed to be just an elaborate illusion; a castle of glass, constructed in peace and prosperity, which offered no protection from the enemy at the door. – The Glass Castle

CHAPTER ONE

Manhattan, N.Y.
Saturday, October 25ᵗʰ, 2014 – 6:21 p.m.

The young woman was lying on the bed; her back toward the unseen pinhole camera. Her upper body was resting on her forearms, as her long slender legs crisscrossed back and forth playfully, providing an occasional peek of her rather curvaceous ass. She hadn't changed positions in nearly an hour, as she read the book splayed out in front of her.

"That must be one hell of a page turner," the man watching the computer monitor said, as he leaned back in his chair and rubbed his weary eyes.

Covert surveillance was a tedious job, even when the subject under observation was an attractive woman. Once you got past the initial voyeuristic rush, it all became mundane. There was nothing *titillating* about watching someone devour a sandwich, as they watched the evening news, or engage in other private activities. That being said, he had to admit that this particular target did have her moments.

He averted his eyes for a moment, as he stretched his neck, rotating it left and right, trying to ease some of the fatigue. He rubbed his hands against his face, feeling the stumble that had formed.

For the past three days he had been cooped up in the apartment and he was becoming restless. Surveillance was never easy work, but it could be downright torturous when you were doing it solo.

The woman was young, and she kept a rather irregular schedule, so it was difficult to develop a pattern on her, but judging from her current behavior it was clear that *something* would happen soon. He looked down at his watch and then stood up. The night was still young and he needed to make sure he took care of his needs before any activity began to happen.

Walking over to the adjacent kitchen, he opened the refrigerator door and peered inside. The shelves were filled with a variety of half empty containers from several of the local takeout joints. He lifted the cardboard lid on the pizza box and removed the last slice, placing it on a paper plate, and then tossed it in the microwave for thirty seconds. While it was spinning around getting nuked, he grabbed himself a coke and popped the top.

You're definitely gonna pay for this when you get back into the gym, he thought, taking a drink.

A moment later the microwave turned off and he removed the pizza, watching as the cheese slowly bubbled up top. He fought the temptation to take a bite, saving the roof of his mouth from a second degree burn.

He made his way over to the sliding patio door and stepped outside.

A cold wind was blowing in off the Hudson River and a steady rain fell. Despite the inclement weather, the view from the forty-third floor was stunning. The heavy, gray cloud cover reflected the brilliant lights of the skyscrapers, giving the scene an almost surreal look, as if it had been pulled from some futuristic sci-fi movie.

The cool weather worked like a charm and after a few moments he could safely take a bite of the pizza, as he peered down at the city scene below. For a kid from San Diego, the sights were almost surreal. The bright lights of Times Square lit up the 7th Avenue thoroughfare, as taxis and pedestrians all vied for the same limited real estate.

This is a hell of a way to make a living, he thought.

Well, to be fair, he'd had certainly had much worse assignments than doing opposition research on *perverted* people.

He had sold his soul a long time ago. It made things so much easier. Having a conscious, especially in politics, was often considered to be a liability. If there was anything that came close to encapsulating the concepts of good and evil, government work was it. Generally speaking, most people entered it for the right reasons, but that didn't last long and the quaint naïveté got a very rude wake-up call.

If a candidate was serious about winning, they'd have to bring in a seasoned campaign manager who would sit them down and set them straight. Campaigns cost a lot of money to run properly and the people willing to fund them always expected something in return. Normally that took the form of favors or access. The concept of *quid pro quo* was something you learned pretty quickly in politics 101.

Of course, getting elected was only the beginning. Once they were in the spot, whether at the local, state or federal level, they spent the rest of their time trying to stay there. The people might have elected them, but the party leaders kept them in office. As a result, they demanded loyalty. If, God forbid, someone had the audacity to vote their conscious, they would most likely find themselves in a fierce primary battle with a well-funded opponent, but it rarely ever made it to that point. The trappings of office were enough to convince most elected officials, especially those at the federal level, to simply go along with the program and *play the game*.

Since the founding of the Republic, Americans had always had a healthy skepticism of the concentration of power, and rightfully so. After shedding the mantel of a repressive monarchy, the framers of the Constitution took great pains in establishing a political system of checks and balances, which they hoped would prevent not only a disproportionate accumulation of influence in any one branch of government, but also a disproportionate accumulation of privilege. That lasted right until the time that the politicians realized they could reward themselves with the people's money.

The very comfortable salary provided to legislators, far beyond that of the average worker they represented, was only one of the numerous perks. Others included lucrative pensions, insurance coverage, and global travel junkets. There was also the fact that lawmakers often crafted exemptions and immunities from financial issues which was not afforded to the constituents they represented.

During tough economic times, while many families faced a decline in their household worth and struggled to make ends meet, most politicians fared pretty well, often seeing an increase in their bottom line. As the divide, between representative and represented, grew wider, so did the detachment. Many realized that staying loyal to the party was much more beneficial. In fact, the higher on the political ladder you traveled, by getting coveted committee positions, the better you did financially. So it behooved most politicians to hold the party-line vote, all while blaming their *esteemed* colleagues across the aisle for the ensuing gridlock. It was all just part of the game; a grand cycle that which repeated no matter which side was in power. In the end, the only ones who suffered were the folks that paid their taxes and kept the government running.

When they were done with public office, or if they somehow got defeated, most of them transitioned to the lobbying sector. Once there, they would use their considerable insider knowledge to push whatever agenda was willing to pay the going rate, even while collecting their sizable congressional pensions.

In a way it made sense. A tremendous amount of time, money and effort went into *oppo-research*, because it was a highly lucrative business. The people in power wanted to stay in power and they only wanted to share it with like-minded people. If there was dirt on a political candidate or opponent, you wanted to know about it. Not that it meant you wouldn't deal with them, but knowledge was power and it was always nice to have leverage when the need arose. Folks tended to be much more accommodating to your *requests*, when they knew you had an unfavorable dossier on them.

Is there a dossier on me? he wondered for a moment, before acknowledging the stupidity of that question.

Hell, his probably looked like a goddamn thirty-two volume encyclopedia set. In fact, it would be a lot easier to come up with a list of the things it *didn't* include, as opposed to all the fucked up stuff he had committed. This line of work was insidious. It started with the most innocent of tasks, but soon spiraled out of control. One day you were rummaging through someone's garbage bags, the next you were breaking into a computer to search it for blackmail material. Eventually the lines blurred to where you slip-slided across it into the realm of *physical work*. You became the blunt instrument that was sometimes needed to get a point across.

It was all just a slippery slope that you traversed and before you knew it, there was no turning back. With each assignment, you traveled deeper down the rabbit hole and you eventually became no different from your prey. Each of you had a dossier; each of you had vulnerability. You lied to yourself, arguing that your *minders* would never turn on you, but you were only really safe as long as you were producing results.

He wasn't alone in this field; he heard of a few others, but operators of his stature were becoming rare. Not because of the work itself, but because of the physical and mental toll it took on a person. Most wrestled with what they were doing. Soon they began to drink away their issues, some even used drugs. At that point they became unreliable; a *liability*.

Some would drive their car off a cliff, in an alcoholic stupor, while others would die from an *accidental* drug overdose; a smaller number even committed *involuntary* suicide. Such was the price to be paid when you knew too many secrets, especially when it came to who controlled the money.

He had figured out a long time ago that the only way to last in this business was to keep everything professional. Not that he lacked empathy; he just no longer weighed himself down with it. He felt that anyone in the political field had made a choice and was therefore fair-game. If they had a family, *oh well*, they should have thought about that sooner. He had no intention of losing himself over their choices. He just did his job with ruthless efficiency.

His introspection was cut short by the soft *ping* in his earpiece, indicating activity in the apartment next door. He turned around and headed back inside, once again taking his seat behind the computer screen.

"Showtime," he said, as he took the last bite of his pizza and watched the activity on the monitor.

CHAPTER TWO

"Isn't it amazing what a difference two years can make?" Mayor Alan McMasters asked, eliciting a round of raucous laughter from the guests, in the hotel's capacity filled ballroom.

"Two years ago many of you were gracious enough to throw your support behind me, in my bid to become mayor of the greatest city in the world, I wonder how many of you still think that was a good idea?"

Again the crowd broke up in laughter.

McMasters had proven to be a very adept politician. He had parlayed his good looks and military service into a successful bid for the state senate a few years back, and then made the leap to city hall, even when many savvy analysts gave him little chance for success.

But what the political science wonks didn't count on was a man who spoke from the heart. They had underestimated his ability to connect to those he came in contact with along the campaign trail. McMasters had that rare ability to speak to people in such a congenial way that you couldn't help but like the man, regardless of what side of the political spectrum you were on. That didn't mean that folks would go against their interests, but they still liked him and believed that he wanted everyone to do well.

"However, much to the chagrin of many, who said the city's glory days were long gone, we not only stemmed the tide of decline, but we changed direction. I am honored to proclaim that the Big Apple has its shine back."

This time the room erupt in energetic clapping that grew into a standing ovation.

If it was one thing the folks in this room had in common, it was an appreciation for the turnaround the city had experienced under McMasters.

Upon coming into office he had gathered the best and the brightest, then gave them the green-light to do what needed to be done. Many questioned the risk of such folly, for an already financially strapped city, but McMasters never budged. He stepped forward and took full responsibility for what he was doing. Many in the media laughed and began writing his political eulogy, but it seemed the reports of his death were *greatly exaggerated*.

Despite the direct attacks, the city had endured and a sense of resiliency had grown amongst the residents. They came together in a show of unity that seemed to put the brakes on any potential downward spiral. While some community activists, and their lap-dogs in the media, complained of heavy-handedness, on the part of police, order was soon restored to streets where chaos had once reigned.

As safety began to flourish, the city began to prosper. Once poised on the brink of another credit downgrade; businesses now began to return *en masse*. A fear of being left-out in the *financial* cold caused them to compete with one another, for highly coveted real estate, which sparked a bidding war. Everyone wanted in and they were willing to make all types of concessions, with city hall, to get in on the ground floor.

Soon enough, formerly empty store-fronts were being adorned with the latest in goods and apparel from around the world. Times Square was once again the crossroads of the world and America's favorite *rodent* welcomed guests from faraway lands. It also propelled McMasters to the cover of many magazines which posed the question: *What's next for America's boy-wonder?*

Which was the reason he had been scheduled to speak at tonight's event.

"When I outlined my vision on the campaign trail, many said we were being too ambitious. They said any change would take years, if not decades, to bring about, but I felt differently. I knew that with great risk comes great reward. This isn't Chicago, or Detroit, or Oakland. We don't bury our heads in the sand, we figure out the problem and we conquer it," McMasters said, as he stared out into the crowd.

He had them on the edge of their seats and he knew it. They were the leaders of every sector of American life from Wall Street to the West Coast. They had all come here tonight with one desire; to be rallied to the cause, and he was leading them on that charge.

"They said it couldn't be done," he continued, pounding his fist on the podium for dramatic effect, "and we said watch us!"

Another round of applause erupted from the gallery, as they once again rose to their feet.

"I did it here in New York City and I can promise you, that if you elect Eliza Cook your next president, she will do it for America! Thank you and goodnight."

The crowd broke out into a chant of *Cook, Cook, Cook,* as the guest of honor emerged from behind the black drape curtains. She was smiling and waving to the crowd, as she approached the podium.

She paused for a moment to give McMasters a hug and a kiss on the cheek, before he took his leave to another round of applause.

"*Wow, wow, wow,*" she said, joining in the clapping. "I don't know about you folks, but I'm ready to jump into the ring with Apollo Creed right now."

The crowd laughed lightheartedly, as they resumed their seats.

"Seriously though, Alan exemplifies the can-do spirit that we desperately need in government these days; especially considering the malaise that has gripped our nation's capital under the current administration."

McMasters slipped behind the curtain, listening to the woman speak. It had been a great day and an even greater night. As much as he didn't want to jinx himself, he couldn't help but wonder what lie ahead for him.

"Well, that was inspirational," a voice called out from behind him.

McMasters pivoted to see his police commissioner, James Maguire, seated in a chair, off to the side of the small holding room.

"Christ, you scared the crap out me," McMasters said.

"You're surrounded by a hundred hired guns," Maguire said with a laugh. "What do you have to fear?"

"The truth is that I don't enjoy being the only one without one."

"I can appreciate that," Maguire replied, as he got up and walked over to grab a bottle of water from the serving table. "Speaking of hired guns, I heard you had a private lunch up on the twenty-first floor."

"Good news travels fast," McMasters replied, helping himself to one of the water bottles.

"The only thing that travels faster is bad news, but after that little rousing speech, I don't think there is much of that in your future."

"Let's just say that it was productive."

"Was it productive enough that you would give up running the city?" Maguire asked.

McMasters raised an eyebrow, as he took a sip of water.

Information was a valuable commodity in this city; hell it drove just about damn near everything, but the real key was being aware of it soon enough so you could act upon it. McMasters knew that Maguire's fiancée, Melody Anderson, had her finger on the pulse of D.C., so the fact that he knew something was up didn't shock him. The real question was what did he know? Now was his chance to see just how plugged-in Ms. Anderson was.

"What have you heard?" he asked cautiously.

"Scuttlebutt is you're being considered for secretary of defense," Maguire said.

Damn, good news does travel fast, he thought.

"I can neither confirm nor deny that rumor," McMasters replied.

"Fair enough, but would you consider leaving city hall?"

McMasters pulled a chair out from under the table and sat down. A moment later Maguire joined him.

"To be honest, James, I'm done with all the petty bullshit from those blithering idiots on the city council," McMasters said.

"That's understandable."

The mayor was the titular head of the executive branch of city government. His office oversaw all city services including public agencies and property. He was also responsible for police and fire protection, along with the enforcement of all city, state and federal laws within **New York City**, but it was the fifty-one member city council that acted as the legislative branch for the city. They were responsible for drafting local laws, ordinances, resolutions, rules and regulations.

While the positions of public advocate and comptroller were the number two and number three, in terms of the line of succession, most considered the city council speaker to be the second most powerful person in city government. Unfortunately for McMasters, he and Speaker Nydia Flores had a history, and it wasn't good.

The first time they had crossed paths was a few years back, when McMasters was a newly elected state senator. He had voted against a spending bill that had been earmarked to deliver one hundred and fifty million dollars for a new, state-of-the-art laboratory that would have brought a multitude of long and short-term jobs to Flores' district. To be fair, it wasn't a personal shot against her, but the correct vote against a bill which was laden from top to bottom with extravagant earmarks, but she took it that way.

Strike *One*.

The next event occurred when Flores endorsed Esteban Real, a local attorney and community activist, for a spot on the city council. The seat was being vacated by the current holder, whom McMasters had selected to become the new director of the Office of Special Enforcement. McMasters had thrown his support behind, Jessica Baines, a former Army lieutenant and Iraq war vet, who campaigned on combatting corruption. Things got nasty and information soon surfaced about alleged kickbacks Real had gotten while representing a local community center. In the end, Baines won handily.

Strike *Two*.

The final nail in the coffin came after McMasters was elected mayor. There had been a lot of behind the scenes political wrangling, brought about through the contentious primary battle, with many of the political deal-makers looking to heal the party. Flores had been seen as a strong contender for deputy mayor of operations, but McMasters had gone against the recommendation in favor of the late Tippi Fisher. Unlike his history with Flores, McMasters and Fisher had shared one that had been much more pleasant.

Strike *three*.

It might not have been personal to McMasters, but it was for Flores. She dug in her heels, much to the consternation of her political advisors, and became a political thorn in McMasters' side. Anything she could do to thwart his agenda became her number one priority. The party had seen McMasters' election as an opportunity to consolidate power, but the ongoing rift between the mayor and council speaker shattered that dream.

"The truth is Flores is bat-shit crazy," McMasters said. "We're all supposed to be on the same team, but I can't even stand being in the same room as her. It would be one thing if she was just standing on principal, but she just seems completely vindictive at times. I have had to come to terms with the fact that, despite all the positive changes we have made in the city, I am left with the impression that we have reached the point of diminishing returns."

"I can't say that I think you're wrong," Maguire replied, "but I think if you leave it will be a done deal."

McMasters looked over at him and Maguire could see that he was waging some internal struggle as to how he should proceed with the conversation.

"I like you, James, so let me be honest with you. We've made a lot of positive changes and folks in the party have reaped the rewards, but good times bring apathy and now they seem willing to indulge Flores' folly. It's like we broke our balls to fix things and now they are considering tearing it all back down. I'd be lying to you if I said I didn't have higher political aspirations, so this might be the right time for me to bow out, while I am still on top, before things turn into one big cluster fuck."

"So is this your way of telling me I should begin looking for a new line of work?" Maguire asked.

"You and I both know that you wouldn't be on the market thirty seconds before someone offered you a high-end six figures to come work for them."

"I think Melody would counter with seven just to have me home at a respectable time for dinner," Maguire said with a laugh.

"If things continue in the direction they're going, and I step down now, the public advocate is next in line. Jack Barone is a good man, and he's also very smart. We've had a brief, *hypothetical,* discussion about things and I have shared with him my belief that there is no one better suited for the P.C.'s slot than you. So I don't think it's a stretch to say that your position is safe."

"For now," Maguire replied, "but there will be a special election and I don't imagine a scenario where Flores is not running."

"No, she'll run," McMasters replied, "and she'll be a rather formidable opponent, but Jack has something she doesn't and that's a very deep financial war-chest to draw from."

"Don't you mean that his wife, Arianna, has a very deep financial war-chest to draw from?"

"Well, like they say, behind all great men....."

"....Is a woman with a great chest," Maguire replied.

Both men laughed at the double-entendre, but the reality was that Arianna Grant-Barone had both.

A former teen model and Columbia Law School graduate, she possessed a keen intellect to go along with her good looks. She also came from a New York political family dynasty that traced its roots back to the infamous Tammany Hall. It was said that her family's wealth originated with her great-great-grandfather, Skylar Grant, who had grown rich through politics and real estate. Unlike many before and after him, who only focused on material wealth, Skylar Grant had the foresight to gain *favor* across the entire spectrum. When the hammers began to fall on the corrupt political system, none even came close to him. It was easy to overlook the elder Grant, because he was never in the limelight, choosing to remain hidden in the shadows, but rarely did anything move within the political machine without his tacit approval or endorsement.

The marriage of Arianna Grant to John 'Jack' Barone had been seen as a modern day political love story. Many in the media had speculated that Jack Barone could one day claim the political mantel of another famous Jack, that of John Fitzgerald Kennedy. Unlike JFK, Barone didn't have the war hero status, but he had served as a helicopter pilot for the United States Coast Guard. He was also politically astute and extremely handsome.

Flores might have had the backing of the party's more progressive wing, but behind the scenes many viewed Barone as the preferred candidate. He was much more moderate in his political stance, much more so than McMasters was, and he wasn't the lightning rod for conflict that Flores seemed to be.

It was believed that Barone was more *manageable* and that he could forge the alliance with Flores that the party had so wanted from the beginning, but that was only if they could manage to survive the primary battle that would take place. Barone might have been preferred, but no one was counting out Flores to be the last one standing either.

In her last election campaign, Flores had engineered an extremely success voter registration drive that focused on the cities higher education system. They were fertile fields and her popular progressive message fell on ears that were prepared to hear it. Her approval in that community had not waned and it was expected that she would continue to enjoy her outreach there.

"What odds do you give him?" Maguire asked.

"If rumors of my departure take form, then I would speculate that Jack can most likely stave off any attempt to unseat him, at least for the rest of my term," McMasters replied. "It would catch many off guard. I mean this isn't commonplace; there have only been two mayoral resignations in over a century. I can't see them spending a whole lot of money battling for a spot that would amount to only a year. No, the smart money is that everyone will take a step back, get all their ducks in a row, and then throw the kitchen sink at the next election."

"Makes sense," Maguire replied, "but then again this is politics."

"So always have a plan B, right?"

"*Hooyah*," Maguire replied, hoisting his water bottle up in a mock salute.

"You ever miss those simpler days?" McMasters asked.

"Yeah, I do, although I'm not sure the Navy of today is the same one I served in."

"You were in combat, right?"

"I can neither confirm nor deny that, sir," Maguire replied.

McMasters smiled knowingly. "Well, if by chance you *had been* in combat I think you'd agree with me that things were much simpler."

"You mean knowing who your enemy was?"

"Precisely," McMasters said, tapping his index finger on the table top for added emphasis, "and, more importantly, knowing how to get rid of them."

"Yeah, well I think they'd frown upon that approach on the streets of New York."

"That's unfortunate," McMasters replied. "Sometimes just the threat of violence makes folks a whole lot more agreeable to work with."

"Mr. Mayor?"

McMasters turned around to see his aide, Robert Gideon, standing there.

"Yes, Bob?" McMasters asked.

The man made a show of tapping his watch, "You're running behind for your next meeting."

McMasters let out a soft sigh, as he and Maguire both stood up.

"Duty calls," McMasters said, as he shook Maguire's hand.

"You're putting in long hours today."

"It never ends, James," the man replied.

"No rest for the wicked, sir."

"If that ain't the truth," McMasters said with a laugh, as the two men turned and headed toward the door.

CHAPTER THREE

Sheraton Times Square Hotel, Manhattan, N.Y.
Saturday, October 25th, 2014 – 7:53 p.m.

Maguire adjusted the collar on his overcoat, as he watched the mayor's motorcade pull away from the curb and begin making its way south down 7th Avenue.

The heavy rain had begun to dissipate, but the wind had picked up considerably. As a result, it felt as if his exposed skin was being stung by a torrent of tiny needles.

"Hey, boss," a voice behind him called out.

Maguire turned around to see one of the members of his security detail, Detective Luke Jackson, walking toward him.

"What's up, Luke?"

"Operations just called," the man replied. "We've got a shooting up in the Four-Four."

"Are there any injuries?"

"One D.O.A., one on their way to Saint Barney's in serious condition."

"What happened?" Maguire asked, as they made their way over to the waiting Suburban.

"The initial guess is that it was most likely a drug deal gone bad," Jackson replied. "Scene is a known narcotics location, and the deceased is a frequent flyer."

"Who's heading up there?"

"Chief Barnes was notified and is on her way up to the scene."

"Okay, call Chief Fong and tell her I want some Community Affairs folks up there just in case," Maguire said, as he got into the back of the SUV. "I don't want any of the rabble-rousers trying to instigate anything for the cameras."

"Will do, boss," the man said, before he shut the door.

Maguire reached into his pocket and removed his cell phone. He scrolled through the numbers and selected the one for Sandra Barnes, his Chief of Detectives.

"Good evening, Commissioner," she said, when she answered the call.

"I'd hate to hear what you think a bad evening is, Sandy," he replied.

"I try to be positive."

"What can you tell me about our shooting up in the Bronx?"

"Came over as a radio run," she replied. "Uniforms on the scene found Marcus James D.O.A. and an unidentified male shot. According to witnesses the two men had been arguing prior to the shots being fired. Two guns were recovered next to the bodies. At this point it looks like a drug deal that might have gone south. James is known to the local cops and has an extensive drug related rap sheet."

"I guess we are looking at another honor student cut down in his prime."

"Let's just say he was in the running to be the valedictorian of the school of hard knocks."

"Any update on the other guy?"

"He's in surgery right now, but from what they tell me it doesn't look good."

"Okay, I will hang out here till the event is over," he said. "Keep me updated as to what is going on and if I need to take a ride up."

"I doubt it will get much media traction," she replied, "but I'll let you know more when I get up there."

"I sent word to Cam Fong to have a couple of her blue jackets head up that way to monitor the situation. This way if Reverend Archie decides to put in an appearance, and turn it into a media circus, we will be prepared."

"I thought he was facing some kind of federal tax charge?"

"He was," Maguire replied. "At least until he got himself a Presidential dispensation."

"How the hell does that happen?" Barnes asked.

"Well, if you don't pay taxes, you have enough disposable cash to donate to the right people who can make things go away."

"Yeah, that's so not corruption."

"Nope, it's just business as usual in D.C., Sandy."

"I can't wait till the day I retire and become a rock farmer in Maine."

"You and me both," he replied, "but till then I guess we have to keep paying the bills. Keep me posted and let me know if I need to head up."

"Will do," she said.

Maguire ended the call and leaned back against the leather seat. He rubbed the palm of his hand against his weary face, as he stared out the window.

Being a rock farmer sounds great, right about now, he thought.

He caught site of a uniformed officer standing near the entrance to the hotel, doing his best to stay warm and dry, which was never an easy task for a foot cop. Everyone just expected them to be out there, whether it was in the baking sun or the freezing cold. They became nothing more than a regular fixture of the city; seen, but not seen.

Maguire remembered walking a foot post as a rookie. It didn't last very long, just a few months, but it made him feel part of a proud, long-standing tradition. The days of twirling a wooden nightstick were over, but the image of the New York City police officer walking his post still endured.

How long before they do away with that? he wondered.

Progress, and the need to adapt to policing needs, had stripped away a lot of traditions, but he knew that some things needed to be maintained.

His trip down memory lane was interrupted by the sound of the cell phone buzzing in his hand. He glanced down at the number and answered it.

"Good evening, Chief," he said. "How are things in paradise this evening?"

"Well aren't you just the cheerful little fucker tonight?" his old partner, Alex Taylor, replied. "Did they give you a raise or fire you?"

"Nope, I'm still poor," he said, "and I'm pretty sure that no one else wants this job."

"Yeah, you're about as close to being poor as I am to being a virgin," she said sarcastically. "And I wouldn't say that no one wants your job. Did you catch the interview they did last night with good old *Billy-Boy*?"

"Yeah, not very flattering, was it?"

"Only if you enjoy being compared to an incompetent buffoon," Alex said.

The political season had spilled out nationally and, with New York City's mayor being seen as a pivotal player, one of the cable news networks had paraded out a former police commissioner, Dr. William Thornberry, to give his take on the issues. Thornberry seized on the opportunity to get his name back in the spotlight. He went on a long-winded, and self-aggrandizing, diatribe assailing McMasters and his appointments, including Maguire's stewardship of the NYPD.

That his tenure with the Department, which had been as turbulent as it had been short-lived, was overlooked by the media hadn't surprised him. The pundits were only seeking to gin up their ratings with salacious talking points, which the man was all too eager to provide. The irony also wasn't lost on those who knew Thornberry's past.

He had been brought in as an *outsider*, someone who would shake things up. Many believed that because of his strong ties to academia, that he would be an innovator; someone who would challenge the *status quo* and bring about change. Instead, his administration was plagued by a micro-managing malaise that brought things to a standstill. Unlike his cool, laid-back outward appearance, behind closed doors Thornberry had a short-temper and he didn't trust anyone within the Department. He viewed all the problems as originating beneath him in the organizational chart and insisted on overseeing everything. As a result, the chiefs of the various bureaus opted for a do-nothing approach and began flooding his office with paperwork, where it just sat.

As a result, crime stats soared, summons activity dropped, and vacancies through retirements were left unfilled. It became a case of *paralysis through analysis*. In the end, he was quietly shown the door and his time in the Department was viewed as a debacle by both political parties.

"Well, sometimes I wonder if I might be a tad bit incompetent," Maguire replied.

"Hey, back the fuck up there, rookie. I'm the only one that gets to insult you. I earned that right."

"Yeah, you did at that," he laughed.

"Besides, Thornberry isn't one to talk," Alex replied. "If memory serves me correctly that asshole was so useless he couldn't have organized an orgy in a whorehouse without help."

"Well don't hold anything back," Maguire said.

"Hey, I'm not *Willy Fucking Wonka*. You know I don't sugarcoat shit."

"Are you drinking again, partner?" he asked.

He hadn't detected any slurring of her words, but she seemed even *more* animated than normal.

"I wish," she said, "but sadly the answer is a resounding *no*."

"Yeah, but that's a good thing, right?" he said. "That means you're dealing with stuff."

"Yeah, yeah, whatever," Alex replied, taking a drag on her cigarette. "Now you sound like my accountability partner. He tells me all the time that alcohol isn't a solution to my problems. I don't want to get *too* technical on his ass, but according to chemistry alcohol is a *solution*, so....."

"Well, I'm still proud of you," Maguire interrupted her.

"Let's see how proud you are when I go postal and wipeout the idiots on the board up here."

"I guess some things never change, just the locale. So what's going on up there?"

"Oh just your typical small town nonsense," she replied. "One of my guys got called out to a noise complaint and caught one of the board member's kids partying with his friends. He tried to keep it hush-hush, but then one of the other parents pitched a bitch to a friend of theirs who is also on the board. Unfortunately that board member is from the other party, so they are feuding and now my cop is the one who is in trouble."

"No good deed goes unpunished."

"Yeah, but you know it's just stupid politics," she replied.

"Of course it is," Maguire replied. "You and I both know how you can get jammed up doing the right thing. Remember the license plate incident?"

"Don't remind me," she said.

"We were just lucky Lieutenant Fernandez went to bat for us, or the captain would have shoved that complaint up our asses *sideways*."

"Yeah, Fernandez was always a good guy," she replied. "Tough, but fair. Hey did I ever tell you I ran into that bimbo who made the complaint a few months after you left the Seven-Three?"

"No, what happened?"

"I caught her smoking crack behind the chicken joint on New Lots. They revoked her parole and shipped her ass back to Bayview."

"You've got to love it when that karma train pulls into the station."

"Yeah, *choo-choo*, and I can't wait till some of these fuckers up here get their ticket punched."

"So what will happen with your guy?" Maguire asked.

"Oh I'm gonna have to spank him," she replied, "but I'll do it with a kiss. He's a hunter, so I'll wait till hunting season rolls around to let him start his week of penance without pay."

"You're such a pushover."

"Bite me," Alex replied sarcastically. "So how are you doing?"

"Thinking about the future," Maguire replied. "You have any job openings?"

"Wait, weren't you offering me a job recently? Some *Deputy Commissioner of This or That* bullshit?"

"I think that was Deputy Commissioner of Strategic Communications," he replied, "but you didn't take it. Now I am hearing rumors of a possible change down here."

"Ooh, trouble at city hall?" she asked.

"No, not trouble," he said. "At least not in the near term; long term however might change."

"Well, why don't you just have you're *sugar-momma* buy you a department to play with."

"That's hilarious," he said. "I was thinking about getting away from the hustle and bustle of the city."

"What? So now you want to work for me?"

"You have any job openings?" he asked jokingly.

"Well, I could always use a right-hand man," she replied. "You know, someone who could hang with me and cover my ass when the fuckery begins. So are you interested?"

"Maybe, how are the pay and the benefits?"

"Pay sucks, benefits are as bad, and the work is boring, but at least the boss is easy on the eyes."

"Yeah, but I heard she's a task master," Maguire replied.

"Who are you kidding; you love it when I ride your ass, rookie."

"In your dreams," he said.

"Maybe once or twice," Alex said matter-of-factly. "But that was back when I was drinking."

Just then he was interrupted by a knock on the door.

"Hold that thought, Alex," he said, as he lowered the window to see Detective Peter May standing there.

"Sorry to interrupt you, boss, but Secretary Cook just finished up her speech and she's heading back up to her room," the man said.

"Thank you, Peter," Maguire replied. "I'll be right out."

He returned to his call, as he raised the window back up.

"Well, you've given me a lot to think about, but I have to get back to my *paying* job now, chief."

"Don't work too hard and be sure to give my *love* to Melody."

"I will," Maguire replied, ignoring the not so veiled jab, "and you make sure to do the same with Dr. Bates."

"Whatever," he heard her say before the phone went dead.

Maguire chuckled, as he opened the SUV's door. He could always count on his *always* irreverent, *slightly* acerbic, and *never* politically correct, old partner to make him laugh.

CHAPTER FOUR

Manhattan, N.Y.
Saturday, October 25th, 2014 – 9:41 p.m.

She felt an ache develop in her hands, her knuckles turning white, as she gripped the edge of the bed tightly for support. Her body was being rocked back and forth violently with every thrust.

"Oh God yes, that's it, harder, baby," she encouraged him. "Take me."

In response, she felt his thrusting increase.

Men were so easy, she thought, as she buried her face into the pillow and moaned loudly for effect.

Not that he was bad at sex; it's just that it had become a routine for her. To her it was one of those tasks she needed to perform, like washing her hair. But while she was *very* good at, it was still nothing more than a mundane chore. On a few rare occasions she might even get off during it, but most times she just laid there going through the motions and faking it. This wasn't about her pleasure, but his.

To help with the experience, she said all the important things like: *fuck me harder, oh baby you're the best I've ever had,* and *it's so big I don't think it's gonna fit.* If he thought she was lying, inflating his ego, it still sounded good and he never complained.

In the end, no matter how you looked at it, it was all just a well-rehearsed act. He was here for the sex and she was eager to provide it.

Well, at least he has some decent stamina going for him, she thought.

Her moment of contemplation was cut short by the intense feeling of her head being jerked back by her long auburn hair.

Here it comes.

The man groaned loudly, and she felt him ejaculate inside her.

"No, don't," she screamed, her body thrashing about, as she felt wave after wave of his hot seed erupted inside her.

She tried to fight, to pull away, but she knew it was useless. He was just too strong. A moment later he released her hair, and she felt his body collapse onto hers.

"I'm sorry, baby," he said breathlessly, "I just couldn't help myself."

"I know," she replied, "Don't worry; I'm sure it will be okay."

She felt his body slide off of her, as he laid down next to her.

"It's just that you are so damn amazing I just can't control myself."

"You say that like it's a bad thing," she replied, as she raised herself up on her elbows and looked over at him.

"God, you are so beautiful," he said.

"Compliments *after* the sex," she replied. "I'm shocked."

"You know I love you."

"No, you just *lust* for me," she corrected him.

He reached over and brushed a wayward strand of red hair to the side. "Love, lust, they don't have to be mutually exclusive."

"Oh really?" she asked, as she rolled over onto her side and gazed at him with her emerald green eyes.

He felt his body shudder, as a chill ran through it.

"So you don't think those feelings of *love* have anything to do with the fact that you know you can do anything you want to me?"

He thought about her question, while his eyes wandered along the curves of her naked body. Her flawless, pale complexion gave her skin the appearance of delicate porcelain, but he knew that was a lie. For as pretty and fragile as she appeared to be, he knew that she was as tough as nails.

"What's wrong with loving you for all the wonderful things you let me do?"

"I don't want you to love me," she said seductively, while she slowly raked the nails of her left hand down the center of his chest. "I want you to lust for me."

"I thought all women wanted to be loved?"

"Do I look like all women to you?" she asked, as her hand came to a rest on top of his flaccid manhood.

"No," he said, gulping hard, as he felt her hand begin to grip him tightly. "You don't."

"Mmmm," she purred. "I don't want the ring, baby. I just want everything else."

Her hand began to slide lazily up and down his shaft. Before long, he felt himself begin to get aroused again under her practiced touch.

"You can have *anything* you want," he replied.

"Be careful," she said, as a mischievous smile flashed on her face. "I just might take you up on that."

He was about to reply, when the cell phone lying on the night-table began to ring.

"Hold that thought, princess."

He rolled over and picked up the phone.

"This had better be important," he said tersely.

The man listened half-heartedly to the voice on the other end, as her hand continued to stroke him.

"When?" he asked.

She saw his jaw clench firmly and she knew the news wasn't good.

Play times over, she thought, as she released her grip and got up off the bed.

She walked over to the dresser and picked up a pack of cigarettes; casually listening to the one-sided conversation, as she lit one up.

"Okay, thank you," he replied and ended the call. "I have to go."

"No, don't leave," she said with a pouty look on her face.

"Sorry, my love," he replied, as he stood up and began getting dressed, "but duty calls."

"Sometimes I really hate your job," she said, as she slipped into her robe.

"You and me both."

She took a drag on her cigarette, and then set it in the ashtray before walking over to help him get dressed. She took the time to make sure his tie was knotted properly and then stood back to make sure nothing was askew.

"How do I look?" he asked.

"Like you should undress and get back in my bed," she replied.

"If only it was that simple."

"When can I see you again?" she asked.

"Wednesday," he replied, as the two of them made their way out of the bedroom and down the long narrow hallway, "perhaps even Tuesday; if I can clear some things up on my schedule."

"How about both?"

They paused for a moment at the door and he leaned down to kiss her one more time.

"We'll see, greedy little girl," he said with a smile.

She opened the door and watched him leave, closing it behind her.

She felt her shoulders sag, as she headed back to the bedroom.

It was all so draining sometimes, she thought, as she picked up her cigarette and took a drag. *Heck, maybe it wouldn't be so bad to be loved.*

A shiver coursed through her body at the thought.

"Who are you kidding?" she said, as she took a final drag and crushed the cigarette out in the ashtray.

She made her way back over to the bed and laid down. In her mind she knew that she wasn't *that* kind of woman. Not that she had anything against the women who sold themselves for love; it was just that she had a *much higher* price tag.

Even though she was young, life had shown her that there was much more to get, if you were willing to put in the hard work. Women who got married often traded *living* for security. She was determined to make her own way to the top and sex was the vehicle that would take her there.

She didn't want to be the wife; she wanted to be the side-chick; the one who got all the toys, all the perks, with none of the emotional commitment. She'd proven that she could give him everything he wanted while still being discreet.

She rolled over onto her stomach, then slid her hand beneath her, reaching down between her legs and began pleasuring herself. This was her time now; she knew exactly what she wanted and how to get it. She began thrusting her hips back and forth, feeling the wetness envelope her fingers, as she imagined her hair being jerked back. She loved it rough and got off on being manhandled.

So close, she thought.

Suddenly she heard a noise behind her and she smiled. She'd been so caught up in her little fantasy that she hadn't expected him to come back.

"Did you come back for more, baby?" she asked smugly, as she rolled over onto her back.

In an instant, her arrogance was replaced with fear, as she saw the black clad figure hovering above her. The scream that had begun to form never made it past her lips, as he dropped onto her, his glove-clad hands wrapping around her neck.

Her green eyes went wide in terror, as her body began to thrash about wildly, but it was all for naught. He was as practiced in his trade as she was in hers and her death was already a foregone conclusion. She could feel a stinging sensation on her neck, as the custom-made gloves, with the nylon braid infused fingers, tightened around her throat.

He stared into her eyes with resolute detachment. There was a brief moment of understanding, a moment of surrender, where he could see that she knew what was coming. He held firm, and watched as the fire in her eyes turned into a flicker before it was finally extinguished.

When it finished he exhaled deeply, as if exorcising the demons that had brought about her demise. He removed one glove and checked her for a pulse. He knew it wasn't necessary, but amateurs got tripped up by ignoring the minor details. When he was satisfied she was dead, he stood up and retrieved the burner phone from his jacket pocket.

"It's done," he said.

"Make sure it's sanitized," was the reply.

"Of course," he said, and then heard the phone go dead.

He took a deep breath and frowned, as he stared down at the woman's lifeless body.

It was the little things that annoyed him; the inference that he had to be *instructed* to clean things up.

How many did this make? he wondered.

Certainly more than he could remember, and at no time had he ever performed a half-assed job. In a way he felt like an auto-mechanic who was being told how to fix a problem by someone who'd never even driven a car.

He chased the thought from his mind, as he settled down to the task at hand. First up was taking the time to re-arrange the body. People saw what they wanted to see, so he made sure to give them the illusion that they were looking for. Once that was complete, he began searching the apartment, room by room, securing some items, while leaving others. It was all a well-choreographed endeavor, and he made short work of it.

When he was done, he took one last look around the room before heading back out the way he'd come in, through the unlocked patio door. He carefully scaled the rain-slicked balcony rail and slipped back inside the apartment he was using. It took less than a half hour to breakdown all the electronic equipment and patch up the small pin-holes in the wall used by the cameras. As he was leaving, he grabbed his backpack and took the staircase down to the basement where he disappeared out the back door.

CHAPTER FIVE

Midtown South Detective Squad, Manhattan, N.Y.
Sunday, October 26th, 2014 – 8:31 a.m.

"South Squad, Detective Martinez."

"Hey Julio, it's Almonte down on the T.S. I just got a call from the patrol supervisor; they have a D.O.A. that they're asking you to respond on."

"Where is at?" Martinez asked, as he opened his notepad and began taking notes.

"1411 B-way," Almonte replied. "Entrance is off W 40th. The apartment is number twenty-three on the thirty-second floor."

"Do we have any identification on the victim?" Martinez asked.

"Nope, nothing yet," the man replied. "Just that it is a female in her early twenties."

"Ok, thanks," Martinez said, setting the phone back down on the cradle.

What a great way to start a Sunday, he thought, as he got up from his desk. "Hey partner, we got a call."

"Already?" Detective Olivia Russo asked. "I haven't even had my second cup of coffee yet."

"Well drink fast," Martinez replied, as he put on his overcoat.

"What have we got?"

"D.O.A. in an apartment building."

37

"Please let this be an easy one," Russo said, as she got up from her desk and grabbed her coat. "The Giants are playing this the afternoon."

"Does that matter?" Martinez asked, as he held the squad room door open for her. "They will be watching the Super Bowl from the same place you are this year; on the couch."

"Shut your lying mouth," Russo said with a laugh.

The drive was only a half dozen blocks, but it still took twenty minutes to get there. There was always traffic in Manhattan, and it never took a day off, not even on a Sunday. The delay was caused when they got caught mid-block and watched, as a crane jockeyed positions in order to remove a water cooling unit from a flatbed.

It was just after nine when they pulled the unmarked Impala up to the building. After checking in with security, they rode the elevator up to the thirty-second floor. Finding the exact apartment was easy enough, as it was the only one with a uniformed cop standing outside.

"How's it going, Derrick?" Martinez asked, as they approached the cop.

"Doing good, how about you?" the man replied.

"Could be better, could be worse."

"You're one up on her," the man replied, hooking a thumb back toward the apartment door.

Russo pushed open the door, as she and Martinez stepped inside the apartment. A sergeant was sitting at the kitchen table, doing some paperwork, along with another uniformed officer.

"Hey, boss, what have we got?" Russo asked.

"Hey, good morning," he said, standing up and motioning them to follow him toward the bedroom. "Sorry to drag you out here so early."

"No problem, I'd rather be going to these calls then be on the receiving end," Russo replied.

"True enough," the man replied, as he entered the bedroom.

Martinez and Russo paused in the doorway, taking in the scene that confronted them.

"Our victim's name is Amber Skye," the sergeant said, looking through his notes. "At least that was the name on the maintenance ticket that was filed last Friday. She said she had a leaky faucet in the bathroom and when they showed up, they found her like this."

The naked woman was on her knees, her body canted slightly forward, at about a thirty-degree angle, with her arms dangling down at her sides. A nylon rope was wrapped snuggly around her neck while the other end ran back to a hook on the bathroom door, holding her in place. Her once pretty face now had a *purplish* complexion. A long, slender vibrator lay on the floor about a foot from the body.

"Once they realized she was dead, they backed out and called 911. We got an initial statement from them, but they seem genuinely spooked by what they saw. We told them not to leave the building until you guys spoke to them."

"Okay, thanks," Russo replied.

When the sergeant left the room, Martinez looked over at his partner, and then motioned with his hand toward the body, "What the fuck is this shit?"

"*Autoerotic asphyxiation*," Russo replied matter-of-factly, as she opened her notepad and began writing.

"*Que*?" Martinez said.

"They use it to get themselves off."

"Wait a minute," Martinez said incredulously. "You're telling me this is a *sex thing* and that this chick did this to herself?"

"Yep," his partner replied. "The idea is to intentional restrict the flow of oxygen to the brain. They say it enhances a person's sexual pleasure."

"Aw hell no," Martinez said with a laugh. "Now I've heard it all. Offing yourself is enhancing sexual pleasure?"

"Actually, there is a lot of truth to it, Julio. When you restrict the carotid arteries, you cut off oxygen to the brain and create a build-up of carbon dioxide. When that happens, you enter a lucid, semi-hallucinogenic state called hypoxia. Combined with an orgasm, they say the resulting rush is equal to using cocaine and is quite addictive."

"So you're saying she thought she was *coming*, but she was actually *going*."

"Pretty much," Russo replied. "Although I doubt that was her intent."

"This really is something you women do?"

"Historically it dates back to around the 17th century when it was originally used as a treatment for erectile dysfunction. So, yeah, thank you, men."

"I must live in a bubble," Martinez responded.

"It's just unusual to see a female *vic*," Russo said.

"Why's that?"

"Well, most victims are men," she replied. "It's a *secret* thing they do, when no one is around, and they only get found out *after* they accidentally off themselves. Women do it just as much; they're just smart enough to have a *spotter* around to save them, should things should take a turn for the worse."

"Sounds like a smart idea."

"Yeah, it's called *thinking things through*. It's why we outlive you poor bastards."

"So do you want to tell me why you know so much about this?"

"No," she replied curtly.

"Olivia, don't you know that partners should never have secrets?" Martinez asked.

"I'm just trying to protect you from any undue psychological trauma."

"I don't know whether to be turned-on or terrified."

"Probably a little of both," she said, with a devilish smile, "but for now let's focus on trying to positively ID our little *strang-u-bator*."

"Shouldn't be too hard," Martinez said, looking around the starkly furnished room. "It doesn't look like there's a lot of shit to sort through."

"I'll check here if you want to search the living room," Russo said. "We can meet back in the middle and compare notes."

"10-4," her partner replied, before turning and walking out the door.

Searching the apartment proved to be easier than either of them had thought. Despite appearing lived-in, the place was actually devoid of any tangible items.

There were some clothes, but just a very limited selection. There was food in the refrigerator, but it was only primary foods and not the staple condiment items like butter, syrup or mayo. They found a few magazines, but these were all store bought ones without mailing labels, and there was no sign of any actual mail. A check of the bathroom revealed the essentials, like a toothbrush, toothpaste and deodorant, but not tampons, make-up or any of the million other things women relied on.

For all intents and purposes, the apartment appeared *occupied*, but not lived in.

"You find anything?" Martinez asked, as he walked back into the bedroom.

"No," Russo replied.

"Don't you find that strange?"

"I find that a *lot* strange," she replied. "There's no pocketbook, no ID, no cell phone……. Honestly, what young girl doesn't have a cell phone these days?"

"Maybe she does and we just haven't found it yet."

"Hey, you guys done in here?"

Martinez and Russo turned to see the precinct's evidence collection officer standing in the doorway.

"Yeah, we're done," Russo said. "Grab the sheets, I'd like to know if there is any DNA."

"Sure thing," the cop said.

"Well, what shall we do next?" Russo asked

"Well, since we're already here, how about we canvas the neighbors and see if they saw or heard anything unusual?" Martinez asked. "When we're done, we go talk to our traumatized maintenance guys."

"Lead the way," Russo replied, with a flourish of her hand. "It doesn't look like I will make it back in time for the kick-off this week."

"Eh, just do what I did and boycott them. Like George Carlin once said, *let them go about losing, then, when they improve, get back on board and enjoy their success.*

"You're a shitty fan," Russo said.

"Damn straight I am," Martinez replied. "I don't need that kind of negativity from a sports team in my life; especially when the fuckers are making six and seven figures to routinely disappoint me."

CHAPTER SIX

"I knocked several times, but when I didn't get an answer, I just opened the door with my pass-key and walked inside," Duane Townsend explained, as he took a drag on his cigarette and then tapped the ash out with a trembling hand.

Even after four hours it was clear to both detectives that the man was still visibly shaken by what he had seen. Death came so naturally to them that they sometimes forgot how visceral it could be to the average person, especially one as *unnatural* as this.

"Then what happened?" Martinez asked.

"I called out Ms. Skye's name a few times, but there was no response," he continued.

"Was that unusual?" Russo inquired.

"No, not really," he replied. "Most of our tenants work, so we do the bulk of our calls while they out."

"That's a lot of trust," Martinez added.

"Most of us have been here for a decade or more," Townsend said. "I'd say just about every resident here knows us on a first name basis. They also know that we have all gone through a background check. Building management doesn't tolerate any nonsense. You screw-up once and you're gone."

"So what happened then?" Russo asked.

"Me and Luis left our cart in the apartment's doorway and headed to the bathroom to see what the problem was," the man replied. "That's when we found her."

A grimace appeared on his face as he relieved that horrific moment.

"Did you do anything else?" Russo asked.

"Oh hell no," he replied. "Luis and I damn near tripped over ourselves, and then the cart, as we fought to get the hell out of that apartment. I didn't even call down to security until we had the door shut."

"How did you know she was dead?" Martinez asked.

Townsend's face took on a look of disbelief, and his eyebrows arched, as he stared at the detective.

"Did you *see* her?" the man asked. "The only time I have ever seen anything close to that was in one of those horror movies my wife loves. The one thing I know is that it *never* ends well for the brother."

Martinez and Russo did their best, but they could not stifle the laugh, following the man's candid admission.

"I like my job, but they don't pay me enough to deal with that shit. I got the hell out of there."

"So you touched nothing?" Russo asked.

"No, nothing," he replied. "Just the door knob to get into the apartment."

"Okay, Mr. Townsend, thank you for your time," Martinez said, closing his notebook. "If we need anything else from you or Luis, we will be in touch."

The man nodded and got up from the chair.

"Hey, can I ask you a question?"

"Sure," Russo replied.

"I heard one cop talking about this being an accident," he said. "Is that true? I mean she did *that* to herself?"

"The investigation is in its infancy," Russo said. "It's much too early to say whether this was an accident or not."

"Which means it could have been," he replied, shaking his head. "Man, you really don't know what folks do behind closed doors."

"You don't know the half of it," Martinez said.

"I don't think I want to," the man replied, as he walked out the door.

"Well, now what?" Russo asked her partner.

"Let's go have a chat with security," Martinez said. "Hopefully they can shed some light on who frequented our vic's apartment."

The two detectives made their way up from the basement maintenance office to the security station near the front entrance.

It was one of those grand lobbies; the expansive ones with the polished marble floors and large, fluted-columns that would have been equally at home in the Roman senate. The columns acted as a room partition. On one side was an extravagant seating area, where potential guests could sit in front of a fireplace, as they awaited approval to take the elevator to their destination. On the other side was an ornate marble and wrought-iron staircase that led to the 2nd floor administrative offices. Directly in the center of the lobby, situated under a massive chandelier, was the security desk.

It was the kind of place that, when you walked into it, you knew whether or not you could afford it. Neither detective was under any illusion that they could, which also made them wonder how *she* did.

"Can I help you, detectives?" the security man asked.

"Yeah," Russo said, "What information do you have on file for the resident of apartment 3223?"

The man tapped a few buttons into an unseen keyboard.

"Let me look," the man replied, as he scrolled through the directory. "The only resident I have listed for that apartment is Ms. Amber Skye."

"Do you have any contact listings?" Martinez asked. "Perhaps a *who to call* number; in the event of an emergency?"

"No," the man said. "No emergency contacts and the only number I have on file is her cell phone number."

Martinez looked over at Russo and gave her a smile.

"Can we have that number?" Russo asked.

"Yeah, sure."

The man removed a pen from his pocket and wrote the number on a piece of paper, then handed it to Russo.

"I'll try it," she said, stepping away from the desk.

"Can you tell me anything about her?" Martinez asked, turning his attention back to the security man.

"She was one of the nicer residents," he replied. "I'm sure you can imagine, but a lot of folks here tend to be on the obnoxious *prick* and *prickette* ends of the spectrums."

"You don't say," Martinez said with a laugh. "So what made her so different?"

"I don't know," he replied. "She was just young and always happy. I don't think I ever saw her without a smile on her face, and she was a great tipper around the holidays."

"Do you know if she worked?"

"Not sure. She came and went at all different hours. I work twelve-hour shifts and I never saw any pattern to her movements. Sometimes I wouldn't see her for days, even weeks at a time, then other times she'd be in and out a half dozen times in one shift."

"How about any visitors?"

"That I can't tell you," he said.

Martinez looked around the lobby, taking mental note of all the discrete security cameras positioned on the ceiling.

"You guys could monitor a lost mouse in this place and you mean to tell me you don't know who visited her?"

"Listen, I'm not trying to be an asshole, but this is my job. The residents here expect a certain level of privacy and sometimes even absolute anonymity. If you want that kind of information you will need to talk to the boss."

At that moment, Russo rejoined them.

"Number went straight to voice mail," she said, "but the message confirmed that it was Amber Skye's number."

Martinez nodded and then turned back to the security man. "We spoke to most of the neighbors on the floor, but there was no answer at 3221. Can you tell me who lives there?"

The man began typing and scanned the computer screen.

"Nope, I can't," he replied.

"More privacy concerns?" Martinez asked.

"No, that apartment is vacant."

"Well, then I guess our work here is done, for now," Russo said. "Thanks."

"Anytime," the security man said.

"Our work here might be done," Martinez said, as they turned and walked toward the lobby door, "but that just means the DD-5 parade is about to begin."

"Julio, you of all people should know that the real fun in police work is in the report preparation."

"You know, Olivia, I'm thinking you have some strange ideas about what makes up *fun*."

"Hey, detectives," a voice called out from behind them.

Martinez and Russo turned to see Police Officer Jenna Linder, one of the precinct evidence collection officers, walking toward them.

"What's up, Jenna?" Russo asked.

"I thought you might want to look at this before I seal it up," the cop replied, handing Olivia a plastic evidence bag containing a book.

"What's this?" she asked, as Martinez donned a pair of latex gloves.

"Looks like a romance novel," Linder replied. "We found it behind the bed, while we were removing the sheets. One of the corners got snagged on the bedframe and we had to pull the mattress back to unhook it."

Martinez retrieved the book out of the bag and began leafing through the pages.

"I guess it slipped down between the mattress and headboard," Linder continued.

"Bingo," Martinez said.

"What did you find?" Russo asked.

"A clue," he said, as he held open the back cover to show the library mark.

CHAPTER SEVEN

Sheraton Times Square Hotel, Manhattan, N.Y.
Monday, October 27th, 2014 – 9:41 a.m.

Eliza Cook held the cell phone snugly between her ear and shoulder, as she continued reading the briefing paper in front of her.

"Jason, I didn't give a rat's ass what Senator Batemen thought, when I served with him in the senate, and I couldn't care less about what he thinks now."

Eliza turned the page, as she continued to listen to the man on the other end prattle on.

"That's fine," she replied, "but you tell him I said, when he runs for the presidency he can make all the decisions *he* wants, but this time around *I* am making them. You can also remind him that, even in my *advanced* years, I still have an excellent memory and I will remember the choices he makes now, especially when he comes up for re-election. I would hate to think that some well-funded, but as yet *unknown,* candidate would give him a primary run, but these things happen."

Cook glanced up, as she heard the door open and watched as her assistant, Emersen Lee, peeked inside.

"Madam Secretary, I'm sorry to bother you, but Melody Anderson is here."

"Thank you, Em," Cook replied. "Please show her in."

A moment later the door opened and Melody Anderson walked inside. She paused for a moment, when she realized Cook was on the phone, but the woman smiled and waved her forward.

"Yes, Jason, you're right, I do have *some set of balls*, they're just bigger than yours so God had to put them on my chest. Now handle Bateman or I'll ship you ass back to Des Moines and find someone who can."

Cook cut off the call and closed the folder. Then she stood up from the couch and walked over to greet her guest.

"Madam Secretary," Melody said, extending her hand. "I hope I didn't interrupt anything important."

"Not at all my dear, just inter-party politics at its finest," Cook replied dismissively, as she brushed aside Melody's hand and hugged her instead. "And please, call me Eliza. Everybody seems to love to stand on ceremony, but I find it can be more of a detriment at times. I prefer informal. I want people to talk with me and not to my title."

Cook motioned Melody toward the chair across from the couch, as she sat back down.

"I'll try, *Eliza*," Melody said, as she took a seat, "but you and I both know that the odds are fairly good that soon your title is about to change dramatically and there is no *informal* version for that one."

"Please, let's not put the cart before the horse. We'll cross that bridge when we get to it," Cook replied, "Coffee?"

"Yes, please, black is fine," Melody replied.

"Besides, there are always exceptions for public and private occasions, my dear," Eliza said, as she poured two cups from the carafe that sat on the table between them. "And the President is not God, despite what the current occupant believes. Besides, you're no slouch when it comes to titles either."

"You're much too kind," Melody replied.

"No, I'm not," Cook shot back. "I'm a cold, ruthless bitch who tends to be brutally honest and has a knack for identifying talent, like you."

"And here I thought you just wanted to have coffee and chit-chat."

"Oh, I'm always up for a good chat," Cook said, setting a cup in front of Melody. "So how's business?"

"For the most part it is going okay."

"*For the most part*?" Cook asked with a raised eyebrow. "Are you telling me, with the way things are around the world, that things *aren't* good with GDL and international arms sales?"

"No, overall things are fine, but we're still encountering some speed bumps with the Armed Services Committee."

"Let me guess, Dragon's Breath?"

"Yeah, after that unfortunate incident with Wilson Pope, a few members have pulled back their support."

"Anyone in particular?"

"Belinda Jones," Melody replied.

Cook rolled her eyes at the mention of the name.

"How that woman ever made it onto the Armed Services Committee continues to amaze even me, but smart money says that the path she took passed directly under the Speaker's desk. I am sure that her *sea-change* just amounts to following his marching orders."

"Her sudden reluctance struck me as odd," Melody replied, as she stifled a laugh. "Especially considering how supportive she had been of the program in the beginning."

"I'm sure that they will come back around after the Bureau finishes up its investigation, but until then they'll play hardball with you for *show and tell*. They don't want to risk being seen as too cozy until after the case is closed. I'll talk to Vernon and make sure he gets things back on track right after the FBI issues their *all-clear*."

Melody nodded her head, as she processed the information.

She knew that the FBI investigation, into Wilson Pope's leaking of classified information pertaining to the Dragon's Breath program, was intensive, but it seemed as if they were now dragging their collective feet.

In the beginning, she and Gen had developed a good working relationship with the investigators; making GDL as transparent as possible, but over the last few months the investigators had become more distant. A part of her concern was that they had expanded their investigation to other areas of GDL, but now it was as if Cook was letting her know, in a round-about way, that things were coming to a close.

"I would appreciate that, Eliza."

"Not at all," Cook replied. "I understand what an important asset Dragon's Breath can be to our military. The world is becoming increasingly more dangerous, in no small thanks to this administration, and I am fully committed to giving our armed services the tools they need to restore global order."

"I agree one hundred percent," Melody said. "So, now that we have gotten the *chit-chat* out of the way, why am I here?"

"I'll be completely honest with you, Melody. I've been watching you closely for several years now."

"That's very flattering, but why?"

"To be honest, considering how long I have served in politics, I'm not one to get too excited by people. I have dined with presidents, popes and porn stars, along with just about everyone in-between. In this line of work most people, including every single one of my colleagues on the Hill, are clamoring for the spotlight and what better way than to be seen with the powerful and beautiful. They crave it in the same way an addict craves their fix. If they are being truthful, many will tell you that being in a *political office* can sometimes feel like a drug."

"But I'm not in political office," Melody said, taking a sip of her coffee. "I'm just a girl from Queens who happened to like economics."

"It's true that you're not a politician, but you're not detached from it all either."

"What do you mean?"

"I have watched with considerable interest at the way most people, even politicians, gravitate toward you. You have a certain *je ne sais quoi* about you, which seems to make them willing to surrender the stage, just to be in *your* presence, and yet you remain unfazed by all of it. I find that all to be a bit remarkable."

"I'm not so sure about all that," Melody said. "I'm a businesswoman. If people want to be around me it's because they either need or want to sell me something."

"That's all very self-effacing, dear," Cook replied, "but let's cut the crap, shall we? Tell me, Melody, when you walk into a boardroom, or appear before a committee, do you ever find that you are measuring yourself against those around you?"

"No."

"Of course you don't," Cook replied. "And why would you? You're confident in your abilities and confidence isn't about thinking you're better than everyone else; it's about knowing that you don't have to compare yourself to them in the first place. The petty folks will claim that you got to where you are only because you're rich and beautiful, but you know better. You know the work that went in to getting where you are; all the sleepless nights and the non-existent weekends. Those without the work ethic can only bitch about your success, so wear it like a badge of honor."

"Okay, so what is it you want from me? You know that you already have my support."

"When I first tossed out your name to be a convention speaker, I got several approving nods. That wasn't much of a surprise, considering your *bona fides*, but you would have thought I had lost my mind when I said that I wanted you to be a prime time speaker on the night of the nomination."

"To be fair, I was kind of thinking that myself," Melody replied.

"I was testing my theory that people are drawn to you," Cook said. "That's why I insisted on giving you that spot. I sat in the holding room, watching the crowd's reaction on the live video feed, and I couldn't help but believe that I proved myself right."

"They were there to see you," Melody protested. "I was only playing to the base. I'm sure the folks over in the other camp weren't that impressed."

"I don't care what the politicians thought of it. My only interest was in what the *people* would think. Our internal polling showed that outside of the beltway your speech was a home-run. You hit an eighty percent approval rating among *all* likely voters and that tells me that the people trust you."

"Yes, but the other twenty percent are the same beltway politicians that you will need to govern."

"It's true that my *esteemed colleagues* are a different story. Congress is a pack of rabid wolves and, truth be told, some of my more disagreeable colleagues enjoy making sport of tearing people apart; especially some of the prettier ones. I guess that's how they make themselves feel superior to the *rabble* they represent, but in all your visits to the Hill, I never saw you buckle under the weight of the bullshit they threw at you."

"I seem to recall a rather *hard* grilling that you gave me once," Melody said.

"Did you still have an ass when you left?"

"Yes, but I'd be lying if I didn't admit that it was a bit *thinner*."

"If it was still there, it was only foreplay," Cook said with a grin. "But I seem to remember hearing about a few of the good old boys giving you the most endearing nicknames. She-devil, blonde bitch, and my all-time personal favorite, cunt, come to mind."

"Thank you, I didn't know I was so highly revered."

"Does that bother you?"

"No, not at all," Melody replied. "I learned early on that this is a blood sport and that I needed a tough skin if I had any hope of being successful. The harder they come at me, the more effective I know I am."

"Well, you proved that success during your speech."

"Yes, but people are fickle," Melody replied. "I might be popular today, but fortune can change in the blink of an eye. You should see some of the hate mail that I get from the *tolerant masses*. Besides, if you're going to be successful, you will need those politicians that I may have rankled over the years."

"Oh, I'm not worried about getting political support," Cook replied. "I can buy or bully them into submission. The one positive about being in politics for as long as I have is that you learn where all the bodies are hidden. No, what I need is someone who can go out there and connect with the people. My gut tells me that person is you."

"Well, I would be more than happy to help you out in any way that I can."

As successful as she already was, Melody understood that the key to maintaining that success was to stay connected to the right people. She knew that she had earned a reputation in the halls of Congress, but that wasn't a bad thing. Not being able to bully someone might have irked a few of the representatives or senators, but there was also a grudging admiration that came along with it. They knew she never took things personal and that she always handled herself with aplomb. But, while it was always nice to have the folks up on the Hill in your corner, the prospect of having the next President there as well was very appealing to her.

"I like that attitude, Melody," Cook replied. "Hold on tight to it, because you will need it for your confirmation hearing."

Melody had not only heard the *words*, but she'd also felt them. Like a thousand pound wrecking ball right to the solar plexus. She swallowed hard, fighting to maintain a neutral expression, as she waged an internal struggle with herself over what she thought Cook had said.

Surely you must have misheard her, she admonished herself.

"Confirmation hearing?" Melody asked hesitantly.

"Yes," Cook replied. "I want you to be my secretary of state."

Melody felt her heart beat faster, in response to the rush of adrenaline that was now coursing through her body.

Time seemed to stop, as the two women locked eyes.

"Sec….. secretary of…. of state?" Melody stammered. "As in *the* secretary of state?"

"Yes," Cook replied with a smile. "*That* one. You didn't think I had you go through all of this because I wanted you to do some fundraisers for me?"

"Maybe," Melody replied, with an almost frantic look.

"I have more people looking to throw money my way than a stripper at an accountant's convention, my dear. No, I need you for your *other* talents."

"Madam Secretary, surely there is someone who is significantly more qualified than me."

"If there was, they would have given the speech and not you," Cook said, as she took a sip of her coffee.

"It's just that you were the secretary of state and before that you were a senator. I can't compete with that kind of political experience."

"I don't expect you to, Melody," Cook said. "I'm not picking you because of your political discernment, but your business one."

"What do you mean?"

"You and I both know the current administration has screwed the pooch when it comes to the financial health of this country. He's so busy trying to be *liked*, that he's been doling out money and sweetheart deals to anyone willing to take a *selfie* with him."

"How do you think I can fix that?" Melody asked. "I mean I understand that I'm a businesswoman, but we are talking about an entire country and not just a corporation."

"Stop making excuses. There might be a few more zeros at the end of the bottom line, but you know that they are fundamentally the same."

"I could see treasury or commerce, but state deals with the global issues."

Cook shook her head, as she dismissed Melody's argument.

"No, I have other folks that can oversee printing money and make rousing speeches, filled with meaningless platitudes, but what I really need is a *she-devil* with business shrewdness. Have you looked at the amount of foreign aid this county doles out annually?"

"No, but I'm sure that it is a lot," Melody replied.

"The voters have no clue as to just how *dire* things are. If we don't get a grip on our financial house, this country will end up as a colony again. Tell me, Melody, who is GDL's biggest threat?"

Melody considered the question for a moment before she answered, "I would have to say Allied-Hastings."

"How would you like to write them a check, for twenty million dollars, as a gift?" Cook asked.

"That will never happen in this lifetime."

"Then all I can say is you are in for one helluva shock when you become secretary of state," Cook replied. "The amount of money we spend, on people that hate us, is nauseating."

"Why not just cut it off?"

"Because there is a certain amount of tactical advantage in keeping our enemies close," Cook replied, "but in the past we used aid as the carrot while we locked up the stick. I need someone who isn't going to be bullied by some smarmy prime minister, sand-lot sultan, or the occasional *dear leader*. The world needs to accept that if they will stand in line for a payout from us, then they better damn well be dressed in their Sunday best and say *thank you*."

"So you're telling me that apart from the economic imbalances there are also a lot of military issues to consider?"

"Yes, there are," Cook replied. "Right now the world is in a state of upheaval, as both good and bad actors compete for chairs at the table. We have that limp-dick in the Oval Office to thank for that. Not only has he reduced our military, and significantly degraded our capacity to kick ass and take names, but he's also been asleep at the wheel in terms of global military expansion. I doubt he could even tell the difference between the bullies and the good-guys, if the former fired an ICBM, that we paid for, up his ass. This attitude has shaken all of our allies and it has them thinking we don't carry that much clout anymore. Come January that is all going to change rather quickly; as long as I have anything to say about it."

"And you think I can do that?"

"I know you can do it," Cook replied. "Let's be honest, we both know this will not be a cake-walk. If it was, I'd have chosen someone else. On day one you will have a lot of *un-fucking* to do and I expect you to deal with it quickly. Let them saber-rattle all they want to their political bases, but I want both friend and foe alike to know that I'll put foot-to-ass on the first one that crosses a line without asking, '*mother, may I?*'"

"Wall Street is a far-cry from geopolitical stuff," Melody protested. "If I screw-up, or insult someone in the boardroom, they don't start world war III."

"Then I strongly suggest that you not screw-up," Cook said with a smile. "But in all seriousness things are already broken. What the current administration, and the ones before it, never seemed to grasp was the fact that, as much as we wanted our products to be in other countries, those countries wanted us to be there as well. But instead of finding a fair balance, we just gave away the proverbial farm to get there. Now we have to level the playing field."

"I can't argue with you."

"I don't want you to argue with me; I want you to help me fix it. Bring the tenacity that you're famous for into my administration. I will have my hands full dealing with enough issues here at home. I want to know that when I send my representative to Germany or Qatar or Beijing that she's going to not only properly represent the United States, but me. The problems facing us right now include financial, as well security issues."

"And you're sure you want me for that role," Melody asked, "and not a more politically savvy person?"

"No, no, it's time for a change," Cook said, shaking her head dismissively. "I know for a fact that they have no respect for politicians. For years we have sent career diplomats to send a message and, while our friends and foes nod obligingly, they laugh the moment we turn our backs."

"I thought you were rather effective at representing us around the world."

"I was," Cook confessed, "right up to the time it came to back up the words with actions and then the administration folded like a cheap suit. It was more frustrating than dealing with the nit-wits up on the Hill."

"And you think going with a *harder* approach is the better way to proceed?"

"Whether or not the pundits and politicians agree with it, the United States holds a significant place in the world hierarchy. Yes, our friends and enemies may bitch about it in front of the cameras, but don't let them fool you. When America is at its strongest there is a peaceful *status-quo* that everyone enjoys. However, under this administration, we have abdicated that position. Instead of being at the top of the food chain, we have become part of a collective, *global community* and our voice has gotten lost. As a result, our enemies are tear-assing through the backyards of the world while our *community* is acting like some pedantic home owners association bitching about the color of window trim. My fear is that we will ignore the little things that will eventually lead into much bigger things; like a shooting war. So we will take a page out of history and embrace Roosevelt's policy of 'speak softly and carry a big stick.'"

"Yes, but like you already pointed out, the extensive military cuts over the years have left us rather depleted. I fear that big stick is more like a *tiny branch* at this point."

"For now, but not for long," Cook replied. "I have a few tricks up my sleeve to change all that and I plan on giving the next secretary of defense the same marching orders I am giving you: fix it."

"I don't know what to say."

"*Yes* is what I expect to hear you say."

"Do I have time to think about it?" Melody asked.

"Sure," Cook replied. "You have until the close of the business day tomorrow to disappoint me, but I will give you till the end of the week, to get all your affairs in order, when you officially tell me *yes*."

"No pressure, huh?"

"*That,* my dear Melody, comes after you accept my offer."

"Thank you, Eliza."

CHAPTER EIGHT

Manhattan, N.Y.
Monday, October 27th, 2014 – 10:29 a.m.

Claire Knight was sitting at her desk, going through the stack of work orders, vendor invoices, and new tenant applications, when she heard the melodic tones of the door chime.

She glanced over at the security monitor, which showed a middle-aged man and woman standing on the other side of the frosted glass doors.

Great, just what I need, another freaking interruption, she thought, as she reached over and pressed the intercom button.

She made a mental note to have security shut down the direct elevator access to her floor.

"May I help you?" she asked.

It was the man who spoke first.

"Yes, we're detectives, ma'am," the man replied. "We'd like to speak with someone about an apartment over at 1411 Broadway."

Claire grimaced. She'd already gotten a call from the head of security, alerting her that the cops might stop by. They certainly *looked* like cops, but it was always better to be safe than sorry.

"Can I see some identification?" she asked.

Knight watched as they fumbled in their pockets and produced two black leather cases, which they opened up and held toward the camera. She zoomed in to see the gold detective shields and official looking police ID's.

It's not like you even know what you're looking at, she chided herself. *They could have bought those at a tourist shop in midtown.*

She sighed, as she reached over and hit the button that unlocked the door. Life was so much simpler in Des Moines.

She watched as the door opened and the two detectives entered the office.

"How can I help you?"

"I'm Detective Russo," the woman said. "This is Detective Martinez. We're from the Midtown South Squad."

"I'm Claire Knight. I'm the account manager for Universal Holdings."

"We were hoping to get some information about one of your apartments, Ms. Knight," Russo said.

"Is this about the woman who died?" she asked. "Ms. Skye?"

"Yes, it is," Martinez said. "Do you have any information on her?"

"Not really," she replied. "I checked first thing this morning, when security called to notify me. The only thing I have on file for her is her name and cell phone number."

"Isn't that unusual?" Russo asked. "How did she pay her rent? What about an emergency contact?"

"The apartment wasn't rented to her; she was just listed as an approved user."

"An *approved user*?" Russo asked. "What does that mean?"

"Well, the apartment is leased to a company called Home2Home Rentals."

"Wait, don't you guys rent the apartments?" Martinez asked.

"Yes, we do, for most our buildings," she replied. "But we also bulk lease blocks of apartments to other companies."

"And this Home2Home leases that apartment?" Russo asked.

"Actually, they lease several apartments in our Broadway building; all up on the thirty-second and thirty-third floors, great views."

"Any idea why?"

"Is this on the record?" Knight asked.

"Only if it has to do with apartment twenty-three," Martinez said.

"Most of the companies that lease from us, like Home2Home, cater to what I would call an upscale, high-end clientele. Most of them are celebrities, singers or corporate folks."

"Any particular reason?" Russo asked.

"Many are in town for brief periods either doing appearances, shooting films, doing recordings or financial dealings. For most of them the hotel scene is a bust because too many employees will sell the information to the tabloids. These apartments give them a sense of normalcy while maintaining their anonymity."

"Makes sense," Martinez replied, "but how does our victim fit in? She wasn't any of those things."

"That I can't tell you. Like I said, we didn't rent to her."

"So what *can* you tell us about, Amber?" Russo asked.

"Not much, I'm sorry," Knight said. "According to the records she's only been an approved user a little more than a year, but I can tell you that there were no violations listed."

"What would normally cause a violation?" Martinez asked.

"Oh, any number of things," Knight replied. "We have apartment inspections. If there was any indications of property damage, illicit activity, that would generate a report. Likewise if there were security concerns or complaints from the other residents."

"And there was nothing on file?"

"No, by all accounts, Ms. Skye was the model tenant."

"What about security?" Russo inquired. "Do they keep a record of who visits the tenants? An unofficial *guest book* maybe?"

Knight frowned at the question.

"Detective, Universal Holdings prides itself on *discretion*. The only way to enter the building is by permission. There is a phone in the vestibule. If a visitor calls and gets buzzed in, then we assume they are wanted. Security is there as a deterrent for any *unwanted* guests, and to watch over the tenants as they come and go. We treat them as the responsible adults that they are and don't judge."

"Don't judge?" Martinez said. "What does that mean?"

"Let's just say that, hypothetically speaking, if a certain celebrity A-lister, who happens to be married, is in town for a film shoot, we just assume that the nineteen-year-old who comes to visit them is just a niece *or* nephew."

"*Very nice*," Martinez said sarcastically.

"Like I said, we don't judge."

"So what can you tell us about Home2Home?" Russo asked.

"We've been doing business with them for quite some time. They lease about a hundred apartments from us on both coasts."

"Have you had any problems before with their approved users?" Martinez asked.

"I can't get into specifics," the woman replied, "so I will just say that when we have had the occasional *incident*, they have always been quick to address it."

"And if you had an incident who would you notify?"

Knight scrolled through the Rolodex on her desk, till she found the card with Home2Home's information, and then wrote the number down on a piece of paper.

"It goes to an answering service," she said, handing the card to Martinez, "but they are very prompt at getting back to you."

"Thank you for your time, Ms. Knight," Russo said, handing the women one of her business cards. "If you can think of anything else, *unofficially* of course, please call me."

"I will," she replied.

Russo and Martinez turned and headed for the door, but Martinez paused midway.

"One more question, Ms. Knight. You said that you assumed that the visiting nineteen-year-old was there to see a family member, but just how many family members come visiting nineteen-year-old residents?"

"I don't have the answer to that question, detective," Knight said with a knowing smile. "That's something you must ask Home2Home."

CHAPTER NINE

1 Police Plaza, Manhattan, N.Y.
Monday, October 27th, 2014 – 11:13 a.m.

"Police in the Four-Four Precinct say that a gunfight erupted on this very corner when the suspect, Ajani Trammel, got into an altercation with the deceased, identified as Marcus James, over an alleged narcotics transaction. According to witnesses, both men pulled weapons and a running battle erupted along the Grand Concourse, sending terrified residents fleeing for cover. According to one woman, it was like a scene out of the *Wild West*. Fortunately, no one else was hit." The woman said, as she stared into the camera. "This is Mindy Guzman, reporting live from East Clarke Place and the Grand Concourse. Now back to you in the studio."

Maguire reached up and hit the power button on the remote.

"Dodged a bullet on that one, didn't we, Tony?"

Chief of Department Tony Ameche nodded his head in agreement.

"I've been getting regular updates from Chief Fong in Community Affairs and so far things have been quiet," the man said.

"Yeah, that's only because *we* weren't involved," Maguire replied. "If Reverend Archie found out that a sector car was anywhere near the scene he'd have three hundred people outside the command protesting day and night."

"Some days I wish his fat ass would end up in the middle of one of these disputes," Ameche said with disgust.

"Never gonna happen," Maguire replied. "Reverend Archie may be a man *of* the people, but he doesn't live *with* the people. Any emergency he responds to will have at least a forty-five minute wait time; twice as long if the bridge is backed up."

"Well I guess we should be honored that he leaves his gated-community to be with us."

"The only gated-community he should be in is the one run by the Bureau of Prisons."

The conversation was cut short by the buzzing of Maguire's cell phone.

Ameche took his cue and got up from his chair.

"I'll let you go," he said. "If I hear anything more, I will let you know."

"Thanks, Tony."

Maguire picked up the phone and hit the answer button, "Hey, angel, so how'd your meeting go?"

"Oh, it was, uhm,...... *Interesting*," Melody replied.

"Really?" Maguire asked. "Was it interesting good or interesting bad?"

"Interestingly scary."

The call sound was a bit off, almost muffled.

"Where are you?" he asked.

"Fourteen."

"Fourteen where?"

"Fourteenth floor, I'm getting off the elevator now."

As if on cue he heard the melodic chime of the elevator doors opening in the background.

"You're here?!?" he asked.

"I will be in a moment, *ciao*."

Maguire heard the phone go silent, as she ended the call.

A moment later he could hear the outer office come to life in a sort of quiet chaos.

"Boss?"

Maguire looked up to see Detective Amanda Massi standing in the doorway.

"I know, Amanda," he said, with a smile. "Show her in."

He closed the case folder he'd been reading, just as Melody walked through the door.

"Hey, sweetie," he said, getting up from the desk and walking around to meet her. "What brings you to my humble *kingdom of insanity*?"

"Hold me," Melody said, as she felt his arms wrap around her in a hug.

"Are you okay?" he asked, in an alarmed voice.

"Yes,... no,... I don't know," she replied, as she rested her head against his chest. "I think I'm just feeling overwhelmed at the moment."

"Come here, sit down," he said, motioning her over to one of the leather chairs in front of the desk. "You want some coffee?"

"Yes, please," she said, as she set her purse on the desk and took a seat.

He returned a moment later and handed her the coffee.

"I'll be right back," he replied.

Maguire walked over to the doorway, "Amanda, hold my calls."

"Yes, sir," she replied.

"Okay, so what's going on?" Maguire asked, as he closed the door behind him and took a seat in the chair next to her.

"I'd don't even know where to begin," she replied, cradling the coffee cup in her hand, as she stared out the window behind his desk.

"Was it the meeting with Cook?"

"Yes," Melody said.

"Well, what did she say?"

"I don't know what I was thinking, James," Melody blurted out. "I thought she was just going ask me to head a committee; maybe be on a business council or something."

"What does she want you to do?"

Melody turned to look at him, "State, James. Eliza wants me to be her secretary of state."

Maguire's body slumped back in the chair, as his brain tried to wrap itself around what she'd just said, "Holy shit."

"Exactly."

"What did you say?"

"Nothing," Melody replied. "I have till the end of the business day tomorrow to turn it down."

"Babe, you can't turn it down."

"Can't I?" she asked.

The words came out more pleadingly, than in the form of an actual question, and Maguire realized the true extent of her predicament.

"Well, you can do anything you want, angel," he replied, "but can I ask you what you're so nervous about?"

"James, I was just asked to be the secretary of state, I think that alone qualifies for something to be *nervous* about."

"Well, yeah I guess I would be nervous too," he replied. "If I didn't have your qualifications."

"My qualifications?" she asked. "You can't be serious?"

"I am and don't sell yourself short," he replied. "Let's be honest, your resume is pretty damn impressive."

"Now you sound like Cook."

"Listen, I may not know everything, but I do know that, when it comes to politics, Eliza Cook is like the grand master of

Washington, D.C. If she wants you, then that should tell you everything you need to know."

"Thomas Jefferson was secretary of state," Melody replied. "I'm no Thomas Jefferson!"

"No, you're not," Maguire said. "Then again, not everyone who has sat in that chair has been a Thomas Jefferson. In reality, looking at the condition of the world we live in, I'd say a lot of them were more likely to be on par with *George Jefferson*."

That remark elected a laugh from Melody and seemed to defuse the tension she was feeling.

"Do you have any idea how this will impact things?"

"Like?" Maguire asked.

"Oh, I don't know, our lives for one," she said sarcastically. "I don't think they allow you to *tele-commute* when your secretary of state."

"So? I'm sure you can find a place in D.C."

"What about us?" she asked, with genuine concern.

"I'll move down there with you," he said.

"I don't think they allow the police commissioner to tele-commute either."

"This chair was only temporary, angel," Maguire replied.

"No, it's not," Melody said indignantly. "That's your chair."

"It was Rich's chair, babe. I wouldn't be here if it wasn't for him."

"But here you are," she replied. "And you have a responsibility to his legacy, and to the men and women who work for you, to stay here and keep the ship steered in the right direction."

"I thought I was supposed to be giving you the pep talk?"

Melody sighed and leaned back in her chair, her head coming to a stop on the leather head rest as she stared up at the ceiling.

It was moments like this, when exterior façade was pulled away, that Maguire fell in love with her all over again. At this moment she wasn't the powerful corporate CEO, she wasn't the rich girl, she wasn't even the beautiful socialite. She was just Melody, the same *girl-next-door* he'd fallen in love with over two years ago.

"You're staring," she said, maintaining her gaze up at the ceiling.

"You're beautiful."

"That's a stupid ceiling," Melody said, choosing to ignore the remark, as she contemplated the white concrete squares, above her head, replete with harsh, utilitarian lighting fixtures recessed between their beams. "I mean, did *any* design thought go into this stuff?"

"It's over forty years old," he said.

"That's no excuse," she replied. "It has no character, no charm."

"I think they refer to it as brutalist architecture."

"It's brutally ugly," Melody remarked. "It's like they put it together with *Lego* blocks."

"Are we changing the subject, Madam Secretary?" Maguire asked.

Melody's head snapped, as she turned to face him.

"That's not funny."

"It's a little funny," he said.

"You're an ass."

Now it was his turn to ignore the remark.

"So what are you going to tell Eliza?" he asked.

"You know they will crucify me at the confirmation hearings," she said, giving him his answer, in a round-about way.

"Let's be honest, it wouldn't matter who was in the hot-seat, babe. The way politics are these days anyone who gets nominated will have to go through the whole dog and pony show routine."

"Yeah, but how do you not take that shit personally?" she asked.

"The same way you deal with the assholes on the corporate boards," he replied. "Half of them will cheerlead for you, the other half is pissed off that you're in *their* chair. At the end of the day they'll get their punches and kicks in while they can, because when it is all over, you'll be the secretary of state."

"So you think this is real?" she asked. "You honestly believe that I will get confirmed?"

"Oh, I know you'll get confirmed," Maguire replied. "Like I said, Cook knows exactly what she is doing. I don't think there was a snowball's chance in hell that she would have asked you, if she believed there was even the slightest of doubt over your confirmation."

"What makes you say that?"

"She will be the first woman President of the United States. If you think you have a target on your back, believe me when I say it's nothing compared to the one on hers. Half the *country* might cheer for her, but there are many people who want her to fail, including some within her own party. The way things are shaping up she will have a divided Congress, which means she knows that she is going to have to do a lot of wheeling and dealing. Fortunately for her she has the *cojones* for the job, and I'm sure that she has already secured enough nods to ensure confirmation of her top picks. I doubt she'd risk taking a black-eye, on such a high-profile position, right out of the gate. Maybe she would roll the dice on secretary of the interior, but not on state."

Melody nodded her head, as she processed what he was saying.

"So this is gonna happen?"

"Unless she gets caught shooting a person on live television, then yeah, it will happen."

"And if she does?" Melody asked.

"Judging from the polls it would still be even money and my bet stays on her."

"I guess I have a lot of work to do in the coming months."

"Can I say I am proud of you now?"

"Just promise me that this won't come between us," she said, as she got up from the chair.

"I promise," Maguire said, getting up.

He reached out and took her by the hand, pulling her close to him. "If things get too crazy, I will pull the pin here and move down to D.C. with you."

"Thank you," Melody said, as she leaned in and kissed him. "Why don't you just find yourself a first deputy? Perhaps then you can spend more time with me and not with all this paperwork."

"Yeah, yeah, I'm working on it," he replied.

"Uh huh, I keep *hearing* that."

"Do you want to go grab some lunch?"

"I wish I could, but I don't think I could eat right now. Besides, I need to start looking into what I need to do to get things ready."

"When does Gen get back?" Maguire asked, as they walked toward the door.

"Tomorrow," Melody replied. "Between this and getting Dragon's Breath rolled out, we will be burning the candle at both ends for the foreseeable future."

"You think you can get it done in time?"

"I'm not sure," she said, pausing in the doorway. "I'd like to think I can, but that will depend on the FBI."

"Want me to make some calls?"

Melody considered the offer for a moment. She knew that James had access to the right people, and could get the wheels back in motion, but it just didn't feel right. She'd never asked him to get involved before and considering Cook's recent offer, she didn't think it would be proper. She would have enough issues to deal with, should she find herself in confirmation hearings, so causing her own potential *conflict of interest* scandal didn't sound very appealing to her.

"No, cowboy," she said, "but thank you. What will be will be."

"You're the boss."

Melody leaned forward and kissed him, "Don't you ever forget it."

"Never," he said with a smile.

"See you tonight."

Maguire watched, as she turned and walked away.

"You got a minute, boss?"

Maguire looked over to see Detective Angelo Antonucci sitting at one of the vacant desks.

"Sure, Ang," Maguire said. "Come on in."

Maguire walked back inside the office and sat down at his desk, as Antonucci walked in and shut the door behind him.

"What do you have for me?"

"Well, I think I've identified the *Rosary Bead Killer* leak," Antonucci replied.

"You're kidding me?"

"Nope."

A few months earlier, Maguire had created a one-man unit, known as Special Services, and tasked Antonucci with conducting a discrete investigation into whom within the Department had leaked information on the high profile murder investigation. Now it appeared that the digging was about to pay off.

"So who was it?"

"Deputy Chief Miguel Acevedo."

"The X.O. of the Detective Bureau?" Maguire asked, a shocked look appearing on his face.

"Yep," Antonucci replied

"Okay, take me back to the beginning."

"Well, I did as you asked me," Antonucci said. "I got a printout of everyone above the rank of deputy inspector and began looking at their Department cell phone records for the last several months."

"Sounds like a daunting task," Maguire said, as he tapped the edge of his fountain pen against the desktop.

"It would have been," Antonucci replied, "but I have a friend who is a *computer whisperer.*"

"Are they trustworthy?"

"Absolutely, but I never said what I was doing; I just told her what I needed. She wrote a program that allowed me to take the raw data and create searchable fields. Once I could sort through them, I could dismiss the normal Department lines. There were a few that went out to City Hall, but they came from folks assigned to units like Intel and Public Information, so I ignored them for the time being. I did however find one number that had about two dozen incoming and outgoing calls."

"Acevedo?"

"Uh huh," Antonucci replied. "But what really piqued my interest was the fact that there were also several text messages between the two numbers on the night of August 10th. So I looked back on the case folder and realized that was the night they'd identified the latest victim."

Maguire recalled getting a number of calls that night concerning the Rosary Bead Killer's latest victim, Leah Blumenthal, who was the sister of Ari Blumenthal, a member of the City Council. Maguire had wondered how news had traveled so quickly and now he had his answer.

"Who did the number go back to?" Maguire asked.

"You're not going to like it, boss," Antonucci said.

"I already don't enjoy being stabbed in the back, Angelo."

"It's the personal cell phone for Nydia Flores."

"Jesus H. Christ," Maguire said angrily, bouncing the pen off the desk. "Are you positive?"

"One hundred percent," the man replied. "I got copies of their text messages."

"How you manage that?"

"What can I say, I have friends in low places," Antonucci said, as he retrieved a sheet of paper from the case folder and slid it across the desk.

Maguire picked the paper up and began reading through it, the scowl on his face growing more intense with each line.

(917) 646 – 2XXX: *Hey, did you hear about the murder in Sheepshead Bay this morning?*

(347) 423 – 7XXX: *Yes, is it important?*

(917) 646 – 2XXX: *The victim is Ari's sister.*

(347) 423 – 7XXX: *You're shitting me?*

(917) 646 – 2XXX: *Nope.*

(347) 423 – 7XXX: *Who knows?*

(917) 646 – 2XXX: *No one yet, we literally just got the ID.*

(347) 423 – 7XXX: *You're going to make one heck of a PC one day, Miggy.*

(917) 646 – 2XXX: *You know I'm just looking out for you.*

(347) 423 – 7XXX: *I know, sweetie. Keep me posted on anything else you think I need to know. I gotta go make some calls.*

Maguire laid the paper down on the desk, and when he spoke his voice was icy cold. "What else can you tell me about these two?"

"I started looking into their background for a mutual connection. It looks like they grew up in the same neighborhood as kids and were in the same high school. I assume they kept in contact over the years."

"Personal lives?" Maguire asked.

"Acevedo is married with two kids, Flores is divorced with none. Rumors abound as to what her actual preference is and whether her marriage had been one of political convenience. She dismisses the rumors and says that she sacrificed her personal life for her political one in order to serve the people of New York."

"How *absofuckinglutely* magnanimous of her."

"Well, she is a politician, boss," Antonucci replied.

Maguire leaned back in his chair, pressing the tips of his fingers against one another, as he contemplated what Antonucci had said. He wanted to respond negatively about politics and politicians, but the comment hit a bit close to home; considering the conversation he'd had just before this one.

He also had to remind himself that the police commissioner was itself a political position, and this game was a full-contact sport. You either played to win, or you ended up a victim. There were no second place winners.

"What do we know about the husband?" Maguire asked.

"Not much, his name is Enrique Flores, but everyone calls him Rico. Some in the media tried to coax him into spilling the beans, but he refuses to discuss the matter. He worked as a teacher for the Board of Education, but after their divorce he ended up with a lucrative union job. I assume his silence comes with the paycheck."

"I want you to stay on this," Maguire replied. "I need to see if there is anything else going on. Flores is political astute. I doubt she'd be reliant on only one source for her information. If she has any other friends on speed dial, I want to know."

"I'm only one person, boss," Antonucci said. "If you want me to cover all the bases, I will need help and I also wouldn't mind having someone around to watch my back."

"I need not remind you that this matter has to be *close hold*, Ang," Maguire said soberly. "It's your investigation, so I'll let you pick your partner. Give Chief Martin the name of who you want and we'll get them transferred."

"Thank you," Antonucci said. "Excuse me for asking, sir, but isn't this something Internal Affairs should be looking at?"

"Perhaps in due time," Maguire said, "but for the moment I am less interested in discipline and more inclined to find out who is looking to undermine the Department for their own political advancement."

"Isn't that an everyday occurrence in this building?"

"Yes, but it's also not every day that the mayor is involved in an upcoming presidential election."

"Do you believe McMasters is heading out the door?"

"If the polls are correct, then January could be a very interesting month for all of us."

"So you think Acevedo is making a preemptive move with Flores?"

"I will say that I think the chief is hedging his bets."

"You know, when the big chief's start shooting their arrows at one another, it's usually the little Indians who get hit first," Antonucci said cautiously.

"Then we'd better make sure we shoot first and our aim is true," Maguire replied.

CHAPTER TEN

Columbia University Library, Manhattan, N.Y.
Monday, October 27th, 2014 – 1:26 p.m.

Detective Martinez made a right turn off Amsterdam Avenue, onto the pedestrian walkway at W. 116th Street, and pulled up to the Columbia University security booth, watching as the public safety officer approached the unmarked car.

He was an older man, probably in his late fifties or early sixties, with receding gray hair and weary looking face that said he'd seen a lot, in his time on earth. The dark blue *commando-style* sweater he wore fit snuggly around his ample midsection.

"Where are you guys heading?" he asked, as Russo held up her shield through the open passenger window.

"We're looking for Butler Library," she replied.

"That's an easy one," he said. "Head straight down this road; once you get past the trees, it'll open up and you'll see the building on your right."

"Thanks," Russo replied.

"I'm supposed to tell you that, per administration rules, you can't park there, but just throw your placard in the window and no one will bother you."

"Were you on the job?" Martinez asked, noting the man's use of the word *placard* to describe the unmarked car's vehicle ID plate.

"Yeah, Bobby Molinari, I retired out of the Two-Eight," the man replied.

"You survived the Two-Eight and you're working here?" Russo asked.

"I've got two kids to finish putting through college, so I'm doing the security gig for the tuition reduction until they're done; then it's goodbye New York and hello South Carolina."

"Smart man," Russo replied.

"I'm done with the cold and the damn snow," he replied, glancing around to make sure no one was within ear-shot range, "and these goddamn liberal pricks."

"Are they really that bad?" Martinez asked.

"I can deal with the kids," the man replied. "They're just ignorant, but the administration and the teachers are *true believers*. They screw with these kid's heads, pretending that they are educating them, when what they are really doing is inculcating them in their Marxist ideologies."

"The future leaders of America," Russo scoffed.

"These kids are lucky they can make it from the classroom to their dorm and back without someone holding their hand. I watch them head out of here on the weekends and all I can think of is that they look like walking 61's."

Martinez and Russo laughed at the NYPD complaint report reference; meaning that the kids would most likely end up being victims of a crime.

"Job security, baby," Martinez said.

"Amen," the man replied, tapping the roof of the car. "I'll tell the folks working not to respond to any complaints about the car."

ANDREW G. NELSON

"Thanks," Russo said.

"Stay safe," he replied, before turning around and heading back to the booth.

"Have you ever considered working security when you retire?" Russo asked, as she rolled up the window.

"Aw, hell no," Martinez replied. "Once I pull the plug, I'm heading to Florida. I plan on spending the rest of my days enjoying marlins, mojitos, and sweet *mamacitas*."

"You're going to be that dirty old man, sitting on the beach in a speedo, aren't you?"

"You know it, baby," he replied, as he pulled the car behind a delivery truck.

"Ain't that some shit," Russo said, as she pointed toward the truck. "Isn't it amazing that they have no issues with snack vendors parking on their property, but bitch about the police?"

"You really want an answer?" Martinez asked, as he got out of the car.

"No," she said. "Nothing surprises me anymore."

"And they wonder why tuitions are so damn expensive," he said, as the two of them made their way toward the impressive, neo-classical design, stone building with its fluted column façade.

"In their defense, this building has been around for nearly a century," Russo replied. "Faculty salaries are what you should be pissed at."

"How much do you think they make?" Martinez asked, as he held open the library's door for his partner.

"Two hundred, maybe a quarter mil," she replied.

"Are you fucking serious?"

"Like a heart attack," she replied.

"We are in the wrong line of work. We should be teachers."

"No one here is going to pay to hear the truth and have their little bubble burst, Julio."

"And they wonder why I'm jaded."

A moment later they stood before a small wooden counter, behind which sat a young girl, her brown hair pulled up into a ponytail and wearing a pair of vintage cat-eye glasses, who was tapping away at a computer keyboard.

"Hello," Russo said.

"What do you need?" the woman asked brusquely, without ever looking up from the screen.

Russo tapped the metal edge of her shield against the top of the counter, several times, until the woman glanced up.

"Information," she replied.

"About?" the woman asked, unfazed by the police shield.

"We're trying to identify who signed this book out?" Martinez asked, handing the woman a photocopy of the book cover and page showing the library information.

The woman examined the papers, then turned her attention back to the computer and continued her typing.

Russo and Martinez shared a *what the fuck* look, and were about to say something when the woman remarked, "it's overdue."

"Do you know who it is overdue by?" Russo asked.

"I don't know if I can tell *you*," she replied.

"You're not their lawyer and you're certainly not their priest, so unless you want to get your ass dragged into a court case, and have to spend a week or two waiting to to testify, just give me the damn name," Russo said angrily.

The young girl took in a deep breath and exhaled sharply, as if trying to convey just how *annoyed* she was.

"Fine," she replied. "The computer says it checked out to Mikala Stevens."

"Any other information," Martinez asked, as he wrote the name down in his notepad.

"It's overdue," the woman said tersely. "Anything else and you need to speak to student services."

"Thank you," Russo replied sweetly. "You've been so *helpful*."

If the young woman sensed the sarcasm in Russo's reply, she ignored it, as she returned to her data entry.

"What a little fucking bitch," Russo said, as they walked out of the library.

"Shhhhhh," Martinez replied. "You'll trigger someone's safe-space alarm."

"We didn't have any damn *safe-spaces* up in the Four-Oh," she said dismissively, as they stepped out into the chilly afternoon air. "These kids do not understand just how good they have it."

"I'm not gonna argue, but you're wasting precious oxygen if you try to explain it to *them*," Martinez replied, as he hooked a thumb back in the direction of the library.

"Florida is sounding better and better."

"I like where your heads at partner," he said, as he reached out and grabbed a kid, who was walking by with a book bag in his hand.

"Can you tell me where Student Services is?" Martinez asked.

The kid looked at Martinez quizzically, but and pointed toward a large, red brick building that was diagonally across from where they were standing, "It's in Kent Hall."

"Thanks," Martinez said, releasing his grip on the man's arm.

The two detectives made their way over to the building and located the Student Services' office.

"Can I help you?" a woman asked, as they approached the counter.

"I'm Detective Martinez, this is Detective Russo. We're from the Midtown South Squad. We're trying to locate a student named Mikala Stevens."

"Is there a problem?" the woman asked.

"That's what we would like to find out," Russo said.

"Hold on," the woman said, as she got up from her chair and walked into an adjoining office.

"Here we go," Martinez said softly, as he turned toward his partner.

"What? You figured this would be easy?" Russo said with a laugh.

"Hi, is there a problem?"

The two detectives turned around to see a tall, middle-aged woman, with long blonde hair and wearing a dark colored business suit.

"I'm Annette Thompson," she said, extending her hand out. "I'm the administrator here."

Russo shook the woman's hand as she introduced herself and Martinez.

"Is there somewhere we can talk, Ms. Thompson?" Martinez asked.

"Sure, follow me."

The woman led them to her office and the three of them stepped inside.

"So what's this all about?" she asked.

"We were hoping to get some information on one of your students," Russo replied. "Mikala Stevens."

"I am sure you know that we do our utmost to protect the personal details of Columbia students."

"We can appreciate that," Martinez replied, "but we're investigating a homicide."

"And you think a student was involved?"

"We believe the student might be our victim," Russo said.

A look of shock gripped the woman's face and she let out a gasp.

"Now you can understand why we need this information." Russo said.

"Sure, okay,……." Thompson replied, as she struggled to process the information. "What,….. What do you need from me?"

"Can you provide us with a photo of Ms. Stevens?" Martinez asked.

"Yes, I can do that," she said softly, as she began typing into the keyboard on her desk.

They heard the electronic hum of the printer, as it came to life, and a moment later Thompson reached over and removed the paper from the tray.

"Here," she replied, and handed the paper to Russo.

The oversized identification card photo showed the image of a young girl with shoulder length auburn hair, large almond shaped green eyes, and an inviting smile. She was wearing a button down, red checkered shirt that gave her an almost *girl next door* appearance. It was a far cry from what she had looked like in the apartment.

Martinez leaned over, looking at the image, and then glanced up at Russo.

"It's her, isn't it?" Thompson asked.

"We can't say for certain, ma'am," Russo said, validating her question without actually confirming the woman's suspicions, "but we will need whatever information you can give us about Ms. Stevens."

Thompson swallowed hard and turned her attention back to the computer.

"Mikala just started her junior year," Thompson said, as she scanned the information on the screen in front of her. "She's majoring in journalism and has a 3.5 GPA."

"Do you have a residence listed for her?" Russo asked, as she recorded the information in her notepad.

"She lives here on campus," Thompson replied.

The two detectives shared a looked.

"Here?" Martinez asked.

"Yes, over at Wallach Hall."

"Could we take a look at her dorm room?" Martinez asked.

"Yes, of course, just let me call security."

A few minutes later they met up with Bobby Molinari outside Wallach Hall.

"Fancy meeting you here, Bobby," Martinez said.

"I'm like a bad penny, I turn up all over," Molinari replied. "Actually, I got relieved when the call came over, so I figured I would pick it up since I was so close."

"These detectives need to access one of our student's dorm rooms," Thompson said. "We'll need to make out a report for the school."

"Yes, ma'am," Molinari replied, as they entered the building.

Despite it being midday, the dorm was buzzing with activity, but that came to a halt as one by one the students scattered as the four of them walked down the hallway.

"I don't think we were expected," Martinez whispered to Russo.

"The *Po-Po* is seldom expected and never wanted," she replied, as they approached a door.

"Here we are," Molinari said, as he knocked on the door.

They waited a minute, with the man knocking one more time, before he removed a set of keys from his pocket and cautiously opened the door.

"*Campus Security*," Molinari said loudly.

They entered the vacant room and began to take everything in.

It was a large, well lit room which was clearly used by two people. There were two sets of beds, desks, dressers and night tables that looked as if someone had gone on a *Kullen* shopping spree at the local Ikea.

Both desks were cluttered with an assortment of papers, textbooks and other items which showed they were each being used. The walls adjoining each of the beds were adorned with personal items, frames and photos. There were several plants scattered throughout the room, which appeared well cared for.

"Any idea which one belongs to our *vic*,..... I mean Ms. Stevens?" Martinez asked.

"No," Thompson said. "It's first come, first serve. Please remember to keep this limited to just Ms. Stevens area. We have to protect the privacy of the other students."

They split up and began examining the room.

"This is her bed," Russo said, as she looked through the dresser.

"Got her desk," Martinez replied.

They spent the next twenty minutes looking through everything, in an attempt to get more information on who Mikala Stevens was, but it was all in vain.

Despite the well lived-in dorm, there was nothing that could be described as *personal* to help them. There were no photos, no letters, nothing of an intimate nature that would give them another lead to explore; just assorted clothing, text books and notebooks.

"Well, we're back to square one," Martinez said.

"We never left square one," Russo replied.

"What's going on?"

Everyone turned to see a young, Asian woman standing in the doorway.

"Are you Mikala's roommate?" Thompson asked.

"Yes," she replied. "Is there a problem?"

"These are detectives; they're looking for information on Mikala."

"Is she okay?"

"I'm Detective Martinez, this is Detective Russo. Do you mind if we ask you a few questions, Ms...?"

"Eng," the woman replied. "Jenny Eng."

"When was the last time you saw, Ms. Stevens?"

The woman thought for a moment.

"Thursday," she replied. "It was early in the morning; around ten o'clock. I was heading to my Latin class, and she told me she was taking off for a long weekend."

"Did she say where she was going?"

"Mikala never said where she was going."

"Did she ever talk about her family?" Russo asked. "Did she have any boyfriends, girlfriends, significant other?"

"No, none that I know of," Eng replied. "I mean she was nice, she talked about a lot of stuff, just nothing personal."

"Did she spend a lot of time here?" Martinez asked.

"Yes and no. She spent most of her time during the week here, but by Friday afternoon she was gone. I wouldn't see her till Monday afternoon when I got done with classes,"

"And she never said where she was or who she was with?"

"Nope," Eng replied.

"Did you get the impression she was a partier?"

The woman scrunched up her face, cocking her head off to the side, as she contemplated the question.

"Listen, Jenny," Russo said, "trust me when I say that we're not interested in any underage drinking or stuff like that."

"I *think* she did," Eng admitted. "I mean I never saw her fall down drunk, but sometimes she'd go out during the week and would come back buzzed."

"Did she ever say where she was going or who she was going with?"

"No, like I said, she kept the personal stuff to herself."

"Did she have any friends here on campus?" Martinez asked.

"None that I was aware of."

"Okay," Russo said, as she slipped a business card out of her jacket pocket. "If you can think of anything, even something you're not sure is important, please call us."

"Okay," she said, staring down at the card. "I will."

Martinez and Russo joined Thompson and Molinari out in the hallway.

"Looks like we're done here," Martinez said.

"No problem," Molinari said. "I'm gonna head back to the office and write up the report."

"Okay, thank you," Thompson replied. "Please make sure I get a copy for the file."

"Yes, ma'am," Molinari replied, before turning around and heading back down the hallway.

Russo turned to face Thompson, "Thanks for all your help."

Thompson took a deep breath and exhaled slowly, "I think there's something I should tell you, detectives."

CHAPTER ELEVEN

1 Police Plaza, Manhattan, N.Y.
Monday, October 27th, 2014 – 4:37 p.m.

"We have a major fucking problem."

Maguire looked up from the report summary he was reading to see his Chief of Detectives closing the door to his office.

If it had been anyone else coming through the door so abruptly, Maguire would have been rightfully pissed off, but it wasn't just anyone. Barnes was about as tenacious as any cop he knew and she wasn't prone to exaggerated outbursts. He'd watched her handle several major crises at once with aplomb, so for her to be this agitated was cause for alarm.

"How big of a problem?" he asked cautiously.

"Career ending big," she said, walking over and taking the seat across from him.

"Then I guess you had better start at the beginning," he said.

"The Midtown South Squad handled a DOA call over the weekend. It was for an apparent accidental suicide."

"An *accidental* suicide?"

"Yeah, at first look it appeared to be a case of autoerotic asphyxiation," Barnes said. "The vic was found naked in her apartment with a rope around her neck. Theory was that she was having a bit of fun and pushed the boundaries a little too far. Passed out and never regained consciousness."

"Tragic," he replied, "but hardly earth-shattering."

"Agreed, however, when she went under the knife, the medical examiner, Dr. Fredrick Godwin, found injuries which he felt were inconsistent with the alleged manner of strangulation, so he classified it as a homicide."

"So he believes it was staged?" Maguire asked, leaning forward and resting his forearms on the top of the desk.

"Looks to be that way," she replied. "From what I've been told, *practitioners* of this type of activity will normally use a scarf, or something similar, to achieve their sexual high, but in this case it was a rope. The M.E. is of the opinion that the ligature marks, caused by the rope, were used to mask the real cause of death."

"Okay, so someone was around to make sure this trip was her last, but at one point does the *career ending* train pull into the station, Sandy?"

"Our victim's name is Mikala Stevens."

A quizzical looked appeared on Maguire's face, as he struggled to place the name and failed.

"And that would be who?" he finally asked.

"She's the daughter of Arianna Grant," Sandy replied, a dour expression on her face.

Maguire leaned back in his chair, exhaling deeply as he grappled with the sudden realization of the gravity of the situation.

"Arianna Grant? Jack Barone's wife?" Maguire asked. "But they don't have any kids."

"*They* don't, *she* does. Technically it's his step-daughter."

"Please tell me you're not serious?"

"I wish I wasn't," Barnes replied. "The original case listed the victim as Amber Skye, which we now know was an assumed name. They chased down a lead from the apartment, which led them to Columbia University, and they made a positive photo identification for Mikala Stevens."

"There's no way they made a mistake? We've confirmed it's her?"

"It's her," she said. "I got the news direct from Billy Walsh."

Maguire couldn't contain the frown that grew on his face. Deputy Chief William Walsh was the commanding officer of Detective Bureau Manhattan. Maguire had never worked for him directly, but they had both served in Brooklyn North. Walsh had cut his teeth as a detective in Brooklyn North Homicide. He had an impeccable reputation as a *cop's cop* and was considered one of the Department's top investigative minds. If he said that the woman had been positively identified, then, as far as Maguire was concerned, the matter was closed; not that it made him happy.

"Why is the last name different?"

"Grandmother's maiden name," Barnes replied. "Walsh told me that once the detectives made the ID, the head of student services pulled them to the side and informed them of who she really was. The story they pieced together was that Arianna got knocked up in her senior year of high school and the family kept her pregnancy in the closest. She gave birth in August and left for law school in September. Apparently Arianna's parents didn't want to ruin her chance at a stellar future, so they raised Mikala and told anyone who asked that she was their niece."

"Helluva ruse," Maguire replied.

"Helluva family," Barnes countered, "Oh, but wait, there's more."

"It gets better?"

"The squad thinks that our little budding investigative journalism student was matriculating by day, but turning tricks by night."

Maguire's brow furrowed and his jaw clenched, as the words, *career ending big,* repeated in his head.

Delivering the news about someone's death was never an easy thing; delivering the news about someone's death, who was potentially involved in illicit sex, to a politician-parent was like being the captain of a sinking ship; you knew where you were heading and there wasn't a damn thing you could do about it.

"Who else knows about this?"

"On our end?" Barnes asked. "You, me, my X.O., Billy Walsh, the detectives, and the squad C.O. On the Columbia side it would just be the school administrator. The detectives made it clear to her that, this being an active investigation and that no *positive* identification had been made, she was not to divulge the information to anyone, including the family."

"Do you think she'll play ball?"

"Sooner or later everyone talks," Barnes said coolly, "Besides, the grandparents are Columbia alum, so I imagine that our administrator's allegiances are being tested and she will cave."

"I'm going to hope that it's later rather than sooner, but I'm pretty sure it is also safe to assume the window of secrecy is closing quickly. I want you to stop by her office and impress upon her the need for absolute discretion in this matter."

Barnes nodded her head in acknowledgment of his request.

"I will have to read McMasters into this," Maguire said, "but I will need more than just a *belief*, before I sully the name of the public advocate's step-daughter."

"The apartment building is owned by a firm called Universal Holdings. They own several buildings, commercial and residential, throughout the city, but there are no red flags on them. They do however, lease out blocks of apartments to various entities. Our victims apartment was leased to a company called Home2Home Rentals."

"What kind of operation is that?"

"According to the investigators, Home2Home provides high-end apartments to celebrities and corporate big-wigs visiting the city. They started out in Los Angeles back in the late eighties and gradually began branching out. Now they operate globally, in just about every major city that boasts a financial center or an entertainment industry. Their main office is in midtown."

"So was our victim *visiting* someone in one of these apartments?" Maguire asked.

"No, *she* was listed as an authorized user of the apartment," Barnes said. "At first, when the detectives looked at the company who leased it, everything seemed legit, but that was until they ran across a certain name."

"Who?"

"You're a little young, but does the name Devin Ackerman ring a bell?"

"I may have read a story or two about him," Maguire replied.

The reality was that the name Devin Ackerman was synonymous with the bawdy days of New York City. Back when Xrated theaters lined the Times Square area and Studio 54 was *the* nightclub to be seen at.

Ackerman had grown up in the Hell's Kitchen section of Manhattan's west side. It was a rough and tumble neighborhood and Ackerman's Jewish roots made him an easy target. He learned early on that he would either have to accept the frequent beatings or learn to fight back. It wasn't long till he earned a reputation as a brawler and got a healthy dose of respect that came with it. It was a role that Ackerman took a liking too and he soon parlayed that skill into a job as a doorman / bouncer at *Johnny Oh's*; which was one of the more notorious burlesque houses on Eighth Avenue.

It was while working at the club one night that Ackerman made the acquaintance of Harry Hall, at the time a well-known Hollywood actor who was appearing on Broadway, who had a penchant for underage girls. While doing the rounds one night he saw Hall come staggering out of a utility room, his clothes in disarray and blood streaming from a large gash on the back of his right hand. Ackerman pinned the man against the wall with one hand, while he opened the door with the other and peered inside to see Jesse, a familiar young girl, unconscious and splayed out on the floor.

Ackerman pulled Hall back inside the room and threatened to call the cops. The terrified man claimed that the girl had recognized who he was and tried to rip him off. When he tried to leave, she pulled a knife and cut him. He claimed that he hit her in self-defense. Regardless of whether or not it was true, Hall knew he was fucked if the cops were called. More importantly, Ackerman knew it as well.

Jesse was a regular at Johnny Oh's and, even though she *claimed* to be 18, Ackermann, along with everyone else at the club, knew she had just turned 16. No one needed that kind of heat, not Hall and certainly not management. At the time there was an uneasy relationship between the sex clubs and the police.

The less interaction they had with one another, the better things were. So Ackerman bandaged up the man's hand and got him into a cab, along with the promise that he would personally *take care* of everything.

True to his word, Jesse disappeared that night, never to be heard from again. Whenever anyone asked about the girl, the rumor that she'd left town to go out west was repeated. Everyone just assumed that *out west* meant she had gone to Hollywood; which was the dream destination for most of the woman at the club. It wasn't a lie, although Jesse's western adventure ended in a landfill in East Rutherford, New Jersey.

A few nights later, Ackerman arrived at work to find an envelope with two front row tickets to the show Hall was starring in. Ackerman showed up alone, sending a message to the man that they needed to talk. After the show, Ackerman was escorted to Hall's dressing room, and the man was deeply appreciative of the way he had handled things. For his part, Ackerman played the role of a sympathetic listener, as Hall tried to explain away his rather deviant proclivities. In the end, Ackerman proposed a rather unique solution. Instead of Hall going out *blind* to find someone, Ackerman would instead bring them to Hall. He would also ensure that there would be no repeat performance of the other night. Hall would get his choice of girls and the discretion he required.

Hall thought about the proposal for a moment before asking, "What's in it for you, Devin?"

"Why, just your friendship, Harry," Ackerman replied with a wry smile, "and a little access."

Hall smiled and extended his hand to Ackerman, "Deal."

It was a handshake that began Ackerman's meteoric rise from Hell's Kitchen ruffian to celebrity A-lister. He became known as the *go-to guy* for all of their needs.

But unbeknownst to Ackerman, and most of the NYC party scene, the feds had taken a keen interest in some of the sordid activities going on behind the gilded doors of the club scene. While Ackerman was hobnobbing with celebrities, musicians and athletes, the FBI's New York City field office was conducting covert surveillance and wire-tapping. It wasn't long till the music stopped and the warrants were served.

The feds had played their cards right, scooping up the most criminally vulnerable and the ones most likely to sing like canaries. Each new day brought another round of damning headlines, as one by one they fell like tin soldiers. An eerie pall fell over the frequent party scene attendees.

Those folks who, only a few months earlier, had been some of the loudest and most flamboyant voices in the city were now uncharacteristically reserved. Journalist requests, made through P.R. reps, were now being greeted with, "No comment."

It wasn't long before Ackerman heard the knock on his own door and took the *perp walk* to the waiting unmarked car, as the neighbors in his Old Westbury neighborhood looked on.

If the feds believed he would break, then they had made a terrible miscalculation. Ackerman may have polished his appearance from his Hell's Kitchen days, but he was still the same kid. The agents did their best to bully, threaten, promise and cajole, but Ackerman's response, much to the dismay of his attorney, remained a constant, "fuck off."

Despite the threats, the case against Ackerman was weak. He'd been smart enough to realize the jeopardy he was putting himself in, as his social circle began to expand, and he had started using *cut-outs* in his endeavors. He became the conduit for their requests, or as he liked to put it, "I might know a guy who can help."

The feds had a pool of witnesses ready to testify that Ackerman had provided them everything from cocaine to kids, but they were all tainted by their own glaring misdeeds and his attorneys were able to plant the seeds of doubt into the minds of jurors. During cross examination, the overwhelming majority of *witnesses* had to admit that Ackerman's involvement had been limited to merely arranging a meeting for *them*. Even then, some admitted that they had been heavily using drugs at the time and might not have had a *clear* recollection of the events.

Despite their valiant attempts, the feds could never identify any of the cut-outs beyond a street name, not that it would have mattered. Word hit the street quickly that New York City was no longer *safe*. The majority heeded the warning and left for parts and places unknown, some however ended up sharing a resting place with Jesse.

He had escaped the most egregious charges, but fell to the feds old standby: tax evasion. Ackerman was found guilty of five counts and was sentenced to five years at Federal Correctional Institution, Englewood, in Colorado. It was bad enough that he was being shipped across two-thirds of the United States, but he was told that he would at least be housed in the adjacent minimum-security *camp*. That promise lasted until he was processed into the system and then, in a last minute, *fuck you very much*, decision he was placed within the main prison. Apparently the inmate population at the camp was *overcrowded* for the entirety of his incarceration.

"So how exactly does Ackerman fit into this equation?" Maguire asked.

"They started snooping around in the financials of Home2Home and he's benignly listed as the company's chief marketing officer, yet when you look at the shareholders he has a majority stake in the company."

"I guess he figured out how to problem solve some of the logistical issues while he was locked up," Maguire said.

"I think it is safe to assume that this isn't the only city that he's marketing," Barnes replied. "You want me to reach out to our friends over at the FBI?"

"Not yet," Maguire said. "For the moment let's keep this compartmentalized and on a strict *need to know* basis. If the media even gets a sniff of this, they will turn it into a political circus. It will be page one for weeks. I've got to assume that if Ackerman is running an operation, he'll have shut it down already. He will probably wait to see how things look after the smoke clears. Have the squad run him down and have a chat. Chances are that he doesn't know what we have, so let's just handle this as a friendly inquiry and see what he gives up. He's got information and I want it. If they have to play 'let's make a deal' to get that info, so be it."

"Understood."

"If there is anything new, and I mean *anything*," Maguire said with added emphasis, "I want to know immediately. It doesn't matter if it is two in the afternoon or two in the morning."

"I will," Barnes replied, as she stood up to leave.

"One other thing, Sandy."

"Yes?"

"Close the circle on this. I want everything to be treated as *a need to know*. You can take information in, but it's as a one-way street."

"Even with the investigators?" she asked.

"Them, Billy, hell I'd prefer that you not even share it with your X.O.," Maguire replied. "One slip, however innocent, and you and I both know this will be headline news and that career ending express train will pull into *our* station."

Barnes gave him a bit of a quizzical look before responding, "Yes, sir."

"Thank you, Sandy."

When she had left the office, Maguire reached over, picked up the phone and pressed one of buttons.

"I need you to come into my office," Maguire said, when the man answered the phone.

A moment later Antonucci appeared in the doorway and Maguire waved him in.

"Shut the door, Ang," he said, "and grab a chair."

"Is there a problem?" Antonucci asked, as he took his seat.

"Potentially," Maguire replied and began giving Antonucci the *bumper-sticker* version of the information that Barnes had given him.

When Maguire was finished, Antonucci let out a low, slow whistle.

"You know that these kinds of things rarely end well, boss."

"That's an understatement, Ang," Maguire replied. "And now for the *pièce de résistance*, apparently Chief Acevedo knows."

"Fuck," Antonucci muttered under his breath. "Sorry."

"Don't be, it was my first thought when I heard the news as well."

"He'll call Flores, if he hasn't already."

"I know," Maguire replied. "That's why I want you to check and keep checking."

"I'll get right on it," Antonucci said, getting up from the chair.

"This investigation has a short political shelf life, Ang, and I will need to eke out every minute that I can."

"The moment he reaches out to her you'll be the next to know, boss."

"Thanks," Maguire said, as he again picked up the phone and pushed a button.

"Luke, find out where the mayor is."

CHAPTER TWELVE

Gracie Mansion, Manhattan, N.Y.
Monday, October 27th, 2014 – 6:21 p.m.

The Chevy Suburban made its way along East End Avenue until it reached the intersection of East 88 Street, where a marked NYPD RMP sat blocking the entrance to Carl Schurz Park. Peter May flicked the rocker panel, that activated the vehicles emergency lights, and watched as the RMP backed up. Beyond the vehicle, several large steel bollards began to retract into the ground.

As the Suburban pulled ahead, the uniformed police officer manning the entrance to the mayor's residence waved them through the wrought-iron gate and snapped a salute. Maguire returned it, as was customary, even though he knew the officer couldn't see through the vehicle's darkened windows. Old habits die hard.

The vehicle came to a stop, just inside the main gate, where Gemma Townes stood waiting for him, the collar of her jacket pulled up against the cool night's air that was blowing in off the East River.

In a city obsessed with titles, Townes held the unassuming, and unpaid, position of a senior advisor, but the reality was much different. Although Townes was relatively young, politically speaking, she'd just turned thirty-two in August, McMasters had originally offered Townes her choice of positions within the administration, but she had turned them all down, including that of first deputy mayor. Gemma was a self-made woman, and she had no intention of opening up her life, or her financials, to public scrutiny. Perhaps one day, and for the right job, but that day wasn't now. Still, her status within the administration was well known, and she was often referred to as McMasters' *whip*.

Luke Jackson exited the vehicle, surveying the immediate area for any threats, however unlikely in this controlled environment, before opening the rear passenger door.

"Good evening, Gemma," Maguire said, as he exited the vehicle. "Sorry to keep you working so late."

"Oh, it's no problem," the woman replied, "Are the details of this visit something I need to know about?"

"Probably," Maguire replied, "but that's a call the boss will have to make."

"Understood," she replied, as she led him toward the entrance to the Susan B. Wagner Wing of the mansion.

"Does the boss have something going on?"

"No," Gemma said. "Mrs. McMasters has banished the election war-room from the residence. We've been pulling some late-niters here, and she doesn't want the chaos impacting the children's schedules; so we just set-up shop in the ballroom."

"I guess you have to be prepared," he replied, quickly moving forward to open the door for the woman.

"Thank you," she said, as she stepped through the doorway. "Who says chivalry is dead?"

"Not me," Maguire said with a smile. "Although I sometimes get the feeling our ranks are shrinking."

"Not every change is for the better," Gemma replied, as she paused in the vestibule. "He's waiting for you."

Maguire made his way up the half-dozen steps and then walked through the open double-doors which led into the large ballroom.

It was one of Maguire's favorite rooms in the mansion, with its vaulted ceiling, Wedgewood blue walls, white Corinthian columns and pilasters, and polished hard wood floor. But now the room's elegant furnishings were gone, replaced by several large tables covered in binders and stacks of documents. McMasters stood in the far corner, behind a table which now acted as a makeshift desk.

"I guess it's getting serious?" Maguire asked, as he walked into the room.

"I'm not sure whether I should dig in for the fight or just run like hell and get as far away as I can," McMasters replied.

"That doesn't sound very Marine like."

"Well, if they just wanted me to run the Corps, perhaps it wouldn't seem as daunting," McMasters said, motioning Maguire to take one of the empty seats, "but now I have to babysit the Army, Navy and Air Force."

"To be fair, you only have to babysit the *flyboys* Monday to Friday during normal business hours."

McMasters laughed at the colorful nickname for the members of the Air Force.

Every branch of the military had its own, usually lesser, opinion of the others. It was all part of the *esprit de corp* they felt for their respective branches. Amongst themselves, they might refer to one another in jest as *squids, jarheads, grunts, flyboys,* or *puddle pirates,* but let someone from the outside attack one and they would all come to their aid.

"Do you have any idea what the operating budget is for the Department of Defense, James?"

"I was just a 1st Class Petty Officer," Maguire said. "I spent most my career being told by my chief that the Navy had run out of money for equipment and that I should just be happy I was getting a damn paycheck."

"Well, they lied to you."

"I'm shocked," Maguire replied, pressing his right hand against his chest in feigned surprise. "You mean we didn't have to do more with less?"

"You tell me," McMaster said, sliding a document across the table.

Maguire picked it up and began to read it.

"Holy shit, that buys a lot of left-handed monkey wrenches."

"Isn't that the truth?"

"Well, I'd like to give you a good reason to turn down the job, but when you hear why I'm here, it will sound a lot more appealing."

McMasters frowned, as he sat down behind the table. When he'd gotten the call that Maguire wanted a meeting right away, and in person, he knew that it would not be good. Now he steeled himself for the news.

"How bad?" he asked.

"I just got word that Jack Barone's step-daughter was murdered."

McMasters' body slumped back against the chair, his jaw fell open and his eyes went wide in shock. He looked as if he had just been sucker-punched by some unseen enemy.

"No,…. No," he stammered, "That can't be."

"I'm afraid it is," Maguire said, as he watched the man stand up and begin pacing the floor.

"When? How?"

"The Midtown South Squad got the call yesterday morning," Maguire said. "When they arrived, they found a young woman dead from an apparent self-inflicted hanging."

"Hanging? I thought you said she was murdered?" McMasters asked.

"According to the medical examiner, the hanging appears to have been staged to disguise the real cause of death."

As Maguire watched, McMasters walked over to the make shift bar, which had been setup near the fireplace, and poured himself a large whiskey.

Was politics worth all this? he thought, as he watched the man down the drink in one large gulp.

McMasters poured a second drink and walked back over to the desk and sat down. "Okay, tell me everything you know from the beginning."

Over the course of the next half hour Maguire filled him in on every known detail of the Amber Skye / Mikala Stevens investigation.

McMasters took it all in thoughtfully, as he nursed his drink.

"Does Jack know yet?"

"No, the squad was waiting for me to tell you before they made the notification."

"What am I supposed to say, James?" McMasters asked earnestly.

"I don't have an answer to that, sir," Maguire replied.

Over the course of his career, Maguire had to make several death notifications and they were never at an opportune time. In fact, most came at the most vulnerable of times; in the dark of the night. Even now the words, '*I'm sorry to have to tell you...*' came back to him like a cold chill. Losing any family member was a difficult thing, but the loss of a child, was beyond words.

"Who else knows?" McMasters asked.

"Just a small group of people," Maguire replied. "You, me, the Chief of Detectives, several members of the detective bureau, and the school administrator."

"We need to keep this under wraps," McMasters said, as he got up and began pacing again.

"Sir, the girl was murdered. We'll do our best, but we need to be prepared that word will eventually get out."

"You're the goddamn police commissioner, James," McMasters said, with a flash of uncharacteristic anger. "Are you telling me you can't handle *this*?"

Maguire's jaw clenched, as he stared hard at McMasters and composed his response.

The chilly silence was broken only by the monotonous *tick, tick, tick* of the second hand on a large ornate clock, which hung on the opposite wall.

"Is everything all right in here?"

Both men turned around to see Gemma Townes standing in the doorway.

"Yes, Gemma, my apologies," McMasters said sheepishly. "Everything is fine, a gentleman's disagreement on how to get the World Series back to New York."

The woman nodded before reaching out and closing both doors.

"I'm sorry, James," McMasters said, as he sat back down in his chair. "It's just that I can't imagine how this news will go over with Jack and Arianna."

"I'm not the enemy," Maguire replied, "and I'm not heartless. I can do my best to keep this as quiet as possible, but realistically we need to get ahead of this in case it leaks."

"You said Amber Skye was the victim. As cold as this may sound, the fact is that no one in this city is interested in Amber Skye. So let's keep that name on the paperwork and see if we can give Mikala some dignity in death."

"I'll do the best I can, sir," Maguire said, as he got up from his chair.

"Please let me know when they've made the notification and I will contact Jack," McMasters said. "I would like to arrange a meeting between the four of us so they can hear the details in private."

"Yes, sir," Maguire replied.

He turned and made his way toward the large wooden doors, his footfalls echoing off the floor, and left the mayor alone with his thoughts.

If this was the price of politics, he wanted nothing to do with it.

He opened the door just as Gemma Townes was coming through a side door.

"No one, who hasn't sat in the chair, can understand the pressures of running the city," she remarked, as he shut the door behind him.

"True," Maguire remarked, as they walked down the stairs together, "but that is something you should probably consider *before* you campaign for the right to sit there."

"You've always fascinated me, James," the woman said. "I'm curious; do you always see things in black and white?"

Maguire paused at the door and thought about the question for a moment.

"No, Gemma, I don't," he replied. "Truthfully, things would be simpler for me if I did."

"How so?" she asked, intrigued by his response.

"Because black and white is just another way of saying good and bad," he explained. "You're either helping me or hurting me. It's the shades of gray in a person which make you wonder where they stand."

Maguire reached out to open the door, but his hand reached it a second too late, as Townes hand grabbed the doorknob first.

"Remember, sometimes not knowing is half the fun," she said with a smile, before opening the door for him. "Goodnight, James."

"Goodnight, Gemma," Maguire said, before slipping out the door.

The weather had taken a turn for the worse while he had been inside. Maguire felt a blast of cold rain sting his face. A few less degrees and it would have been sleet.

"Just another fine Navy day," he mumbled to himself, as Luke Jackson held the door open.

"Sir?"

"Nothing, Luke," Maguire replied. "Just get me out of here."

As they drove back through the gate, Maguire turned around and looked up to see the shadowy images of two people standing in the Ballroom.

Add one more to the list of people who know, he thought.

This was the part of the job he hated.

Everyone looked at the front line guy as having the toughest job, but it was also the easiest. It was a world of black and white. It didn't matter whether you were chasing someone through the backyards of Brownsville or through the back-alleys of *Whogivesafuckistan*, as his old partner used to refer to it. Bad guys were bad guys. It wasn't until you began to get farther away from the action that the world became a whole lot more *gray*. Where someone sitting in a desk, thousands of miles away, came up with rules of engagement that said you had to politely ask: '*please, may I?*,' before you killed the *sonofabitch* who was shooting at you.

Not that there weren't good people working away from the action, but it was sometimes harder to differentiate between who was your friend, who was a *blue-falcon*, and who was just out to hurt you.

It was days like this when the loss of Rich weighed heaviest on him. Rich had been the political guy. It wasn't that he was himself a politician, but his years with the Secret Service had taught him how to handle those types of folks much better than Maguire ever could. Rich would take their shit, smile affably, and then do what he needed to do. Maguire always found himself having to control his desire to pummel some sense into them.

The immortal words of Senior Chief Petty Officer Roy K. Gentry, affectionately known as *Mother* to his misguided children, echoed in his head, "SEAL's do not play well with others."

"Where to, boss?" Peter May asked, as he pulled the Suburban out onto East End Avenue and headed south.

"Home," Maguire said, as he reached into his jacket pocket and retrieved the cell phone.

He scrolled through the numbers and selected one, listening as the call was answered and a woman's voice came on the line.

"Let them know, Sandy."

CHAPTER THIRTEEN

Turtle Bay, Manhattan, N.Y.
Tuesday, October 28th, 2014 – 7:11 a.m.

Devin Ackerman stared down at the digital clock on his desk.

Lucky my ass, he thought, as he watched the red LED display flashed: 7:11

Any other time and it might have been genuinely funny, but now it was more ludicrous than humorous. His luck had most likely run out on Sunday morning; when those two blithering idiots had found her body.

In the old days he would have gotten a call and the matter would have been discretely taken care of. But in the old days men were men and not a bunch of pussies that lost their lunch at the sight of a dead body.

What the fuck were you thinking, you dumb little bitch?

Amber had been one of his top earners; an energetic little piece of ass who kept the men coming back repeatedly.

He remembered the first time he had met her. One of the other girls had introduced her to him. At first she seemed *timid*, but something about the way her clothes hugged the curves of her body told him to give her a shot. It didn't take long to realize that it had all been an act. She might have played the part of a lamb during the day, but a lioness came out to prowl when the sun went down.

Amber had been one of those rare individuals who seemed to thrive in this line of work. Some women just went through the motions, but Amber seemed to flourish in the temptress's role.

She didn't just spread her legs, and take one for the team, but she actually played the entire game. Everyone who came to her had a story to tell. They all had their pet fetishes, even if they didn't admit to it. She listened and then she responded. Amber took the time to coax it out of them and then she gave them everything they wanted and more. The one thing that was certain, when they walked out the door, was that they would be back. They always came back.

It wasn't long before Amber Skye's social calendar was booked solid, but what was even more interesting was the fact that regular clients were more than willing to pay double for the opportunity to take her out on a *date*.

He scowled and slammed the palm of his hand down on the top of the desk angrily.

For Ackerman, losing her income hurt more than her death. He could always replace a body, but it would be a long time before he could find someone with her natural talent. He paid her to fuck, and he paid her damn well, so the idea that she offed herself, while chasing her own freaky orgasm, made him more angry than remorseful.

Even worse, the bad news had already begun to spread among his clients. Amazingly, it seemed as if everyone had a change of plans overnight. His cell phone had blown up late last night and continued into the morning.

"Devin baby, I know its short notice, but the director has me flying out to Toronto to do some re-takes. I'll call when I get back in a few weeks."

"Sorry, but I just remembered I have a shoot in Atlanta next weekend. I'll have my secretary reach out to reschedule. It probably won't be until after the New Year."

"Mr. Ackerman, this is Mr. DiNero's assistant. He asked me to call you and let you know that he's been asked to be a presenter at the Radiance Film Fest next month and won't be able to meet with you in New York. He said he'd reach out to you when his calendar frees up."

They were like seedy little rats abandoning the ship. They all liked to pretend they had the biggest balls on the playground, but the minute anything threatened their world they ran like little girls.

Actually, that was insulting to little girls, he thought.

Around three he had given up on the idea of getting any sleep and went into the office early; to try to do some damage control. He did his best, but he soon realized that it was all for naught. He had to accept that this year would end badly.

November and December were two of the hottest months for his *business*, as everyone headed to New York City for the holidays, but the way things looked right now, Home2Home would be lucky to end in the black. The Category A rentals were the legit ones and the ones that paid the bills. As far as the IRS was concerned, H2H flew under their radar, thanks to the skills of a former IRS employee, turned private sector accountant. The company made just enough of a profit to avoid setting off the bells and whistles. But it was the proceeds from the Category B rentals, the ones that never made it to paper, were they all enjoyed their lucrative lifestyles.

The Category B's were the sole territory of Ackerman. None of the other members were involved in it, nor did they want to be. *Plausible deniability* they called it. They provided the corporate cover and Ackerman handled the details, which included *very* healthy cash bonuses.

Now he had to figure out how he would explain to them that Christmas would not be very *merry* this year.

Is this what those dipshits on Wall Street go through? he thought, as he picked up the pen and began to tap it nervously against the desktop.

Ackerman swiveled around in his chair and stared out the large picture window. Out to the east, the sun was rising over the horizon. He got up from his chair and walked over to stand in front of the window. From his vantage point, up on the 48th floor, he could see the United Nations below; watching as a never-ending procession of cars and people made their way along the congested city streets.

He'd grown up just two miles west of here, but it could have been two thousand miles, when he considered the difference between his life then and now. In the old days he had to scrounge up enough change to buy a pack of cigarettes, now he enjoyed smoking King of Denmark cigars, while sipping on a vintage Macallan single malt whisky.

"Mr. Ackerman?"

He closed his eyes and let out an audible sigh at the sound of his secretaries intrusive voice coming over the phones intercom.

Ackerman turned around and picked up the phone, "Yes, Miranda?"

"Sorry to disturb you, sir, but there are detectives asking to speak with you."

And now it could all be gone because that stupid little bimbo couldn't just get her rocks off like everyone else.

"That's fine, Miranda, show them in."

Ackerman hung up the phone and sat back down behind his desk. He picked up some papers and began reviewing them.

Appearance was everything, and he wanted to make sure that their first observation of him reflected *normalcy*.

A moment later he heard the door open.

He glanced up from the papers as they walked in and then stood up.

"Can I help you?"

"Mr. Ackerman, my name is Detective Russo, this is Detective Martinez. We're from the Midtown South Squad."

"What's this about?" Ackerman asked, as he shook their hands.

"We'd like to ask you some questions about an apartment you lease over at 1411 B-way," Russo replied. "Apartment 23 to be specific."

"Please have a seat," Ackerman said. "This is about Amber, isn't it?"

He could have feigned ignorance, but that would have been an immediate red flag. That they were here meant that they had already pieced together a large part of the puzzle; now it was time for him to play along and attempt some damage control.

"It is," Martinez said.

"It's a terrible tragedy," Ackerman replied. "I was blown away when I got the call."

"What can you tell us about her?"

"She was a sweet kid; very outgoing, very personable," Ackerman said thoughtfully. "I was introduced to her at a party about two years ago."

"Do you mind telling us why she was staying in one of your apartments?" Russo asked.

"Amber was young; she enjoyed the mid-town party scene. I offered to let her use one of my vacant apartments when she was in town so she didn't have to worry about traveling back and forth."

"So do you always make it a habit of letting young women crash in your apartments or was this a *special* arrangement?" Martinez asked.

"I don't appreciate the tone of your question, detective," Ackerman said coolly, "nor the inference."

"Look Mr. Ackerman, we could beat around the bush all day or we could just cut to the chase," Russo said. "We're well aware of the fact that, besides supplying upscale apartments, Home2Home provides other *amenities* to their clients which aren't listed on the company's brochures."

"This is sounding a lot like a conversation my attorney might be interested in being a part of."

"Perhaps," Russo responded, "If we were interested in the specifics of that amenities program, but we're not. Plus, if you brought him into the conversation he would just tell you not to talk to us and then we would have to find someone else interested in what we had to say, you know, like the nice folks over at the Internal Revenue Service."

Ackerman stared at the woman stoically, as he processed what she had said. She met his gaze with one equally devoid of emotion. They were like the last two hands left in a high stakes poker match and the only thing he was holding was his dick. He could try to bluff his way out of *this* conversation, but it wasn't like it would go away. If they weren't talking to him, then the odds were good they would talk to *someone*, and that prospect didn't sit well with him.

He knew that once the feds started digging into his affairs, it was game over. His attorney might be able to thread the fine line between escort service and what constituted prostitution, at least with criminal charges, but money was money when it came to the IRS. He'd had an attorney for his last go round with the feds and he'd lost that battle. Prison sentences didn't become *more* appealing with old age.

Ackerman picked up his coffee cup and took a sip.

"So what *are* you interested in, detective?" he asked, as he set the mug back down on the desk.

"We want to know who was footing the bill to enjoy some quality alone time with Amber." Martinez asked.

"Look, I want to help you out here, but it's not that easy. It's one thing for you to come in here and tell me how you're not interested in the *big picture*, but you need to understand that our clients expect that we will aggressively protect and maintain their anonymity at all times."

"Even the ones that commit murder?" Martinez asked.

Ackerman's neck snapped audibly, as he turned to look at Martinez.

"Murder?" he asked. "Hold on, wait a minute. I was told that Amber had killed herself accidentally."

The shock that registered on Ackerman's face was genuine enough and it told the detectives they'd been dealt another card to play.

"That's one possibility," Russo replied, "but you need to remember that we are still in the preliminary stages of this investigation. We also have to consider the possibility that she might have had someone help her along on her journey into the afterlife."

"Look," Ackerman said defensively. "I run a legit escort service. The men and women who stay with us are looking for conversation and companionship in a very impersonal city. You know how it is. They want someone to go out to dinner with them, the theater, maybe even an art gallery. I will not say that some of the girls might *blur* the lines on a few of the more obscure laws, from time to time, but it is not something I would ever condone. That being said, we need to remember that everyone involved is a consenting adult and I find it hard to believe that any of the customers, who use the services of Home2Home, have any sinister intentions."

"You might be one hundred percent right about that," Martinez said. "All we need is the name of whoever Amber's companion was Saturday night into Sunday morning."

Ackerman folded his arms across his chest, as a scowl grew on his face.

"Look, just give us a name," Russo said. "No one has to know and we'll make sure that nothing ever comes back on you. We'll say we identified them through some surveillance video."

So this is what it means to be caught between a rock and a hard place? he thought.

"You make it sound easy," Ackerman scoffed.

"One name and we go away," Martinez replied. "How much easier can that be?"

"Why don't you let me reserve judgment on that, until I see the name," Ackerman said, as he turned in his chair and began tapping the keys on his laptop computer.

Martinez glanced over and shared a quick victory smile with his partner, while the man's attention was diverted. A moment later, their premature celebration came to an abrupt end.

"That can't be right," Ackerman said, as his fingers began tapping the keys aggressively.

"What's wrong?" Russo asked.

"Well, according to this, Amber wasn't seeing anyone this weekend?"

"Are you sure?" she asked.

"Yes, I'm positive," he replied. "The client she was supposed to be with had canceled out; he said he had a scheduling conflict."

"Are you absolutely sure about that?" Martinez asked.

"He's currently on a book tour in Australia," Ackerman replied. "I'd say that's absolute."

"Does he have a name?" Russo asked.

"Is that necessary? I told you he isn't even in the country."

"I'm sure you're a really nice person, Mr. Ackerman, but forgive me when I say that my boss will require me to provide him more, in terms of proof, than just your *word*."

"*Fine*," Ackerman said tersely, as he picked up a pen and wrote the name down on a piece of paper.

Russo picked up the paper and read the name.

"*Sonofabitch*," she said softly, before handing the paper to Martinez.

"I hope you're happy," Ackerman replied. "Are we through here?"

"If you're right, and it wasn't him, can you think of any other suitors who might have had an ax to grind with Amber?" she asked.

"Like I said, Amber was good-natured and very well thought of. I can't imagine anyone wanting to hurt her."

"The medical examiner would argue otherwise," Martinez said. "Just in case, how about you give us a list of anyone else she might have entertained over the last few months?"

"Look, detectives, I'm not trying to be an asshole here, but I've done all I can," Ackerman replied. "I run a business and I have to be mindful of privacy issues."

"Amber's dead, Mr. Ackerman," Russo said. "I don't think she will mind you helping us."

"It's not the dead I'm afraid of, Detective Russo, and as nice as they say the afterlife is, I'm really not in a rush to join her there. Look, I've already gone out on a limb. If you want more information, than you need to come back with a warrant."

CHAPTER FOURTEEN

Southampton, Suffolk County, N.Y.
Tuesday, October 28th, 2014 – 11:28 a.m.

"Welcome home, chicky," Melody said, as Genevieve Gordon, her executive assistant and best friend, walked into the home office and collapsed into one of the large, blackberry leather, wingback chairs.

"I'm getting too old for this crap," Gen said brusquely, as she opened up the portfolio in her lap.

"Yes, one's late *thirties* can be such an inherently difficult time," Melody replied, as she removed her reading glasses and laid them on the desktop.

"What I need is an assistant," she continued, ignoring her friend's sarcastic jab. "Someone who could operate efficiently in this fast-paced environment and whom I could trust to handle the critical, often time-sensitive, issues, but the only problem is they aren't available."

Melody was taken aback by Gen's comment. The two women's relationship was more akin to sisters, yet she had never once confided in her that she had been looking into finding an assistant; let alone identified someone for the position.

"Everyone's available for the right price," Mel replied. "We'll just offer them more money."

"Sadly, money isn't an option for them."

"Well, now you have me intrigued. Who is this mystery person?"

"Alas, she is me," Gen replied with a dramatic sigh at the end for good measure.

"And you are an idiot," Melody said dismissively, as she picked up her reading glasses and put them back on.

"Being this good is a curse that I must bear for the greater good."

"I'm the one who needs an assistant to put up with all your shenanigans."

"Can't we just clone me and make our lives easier?"

"How about I fire you and then re-hire you at half price?"

"You know, you can be so hurtful at times," Gen said with a feigned pouty expression on her face.

"Good thing I know you don't have any feelings left to hurt."

"*Whatevs'*," Gen replied, "So are you going to tell me how your meeting with the *Queen of Mean* went?"

Melody picked up her coffee cup and took a sip, as she leaned back in her chair, "It was *interesting*."

"Cut to the chase, Mel, she wants you to come and work for her, doesn't she?"

"Yes, she does."

"I knew it," Gen said, slapping her hand against her thigh. "I told you this meeting was more than just some talk on campaign fundraising. What does she want you to do? Treasury, Economic Council, OMB?"

"No," Melody replied. "She wants me to be her secretary of state."

Gen's eyes widened, and she leaned back in her chair, "Wow. I didn't see that coming."

"You and me both, chicky. I'm still trying to come to terms with it."

"What did you tell her?"

"Nothing yet," Melody replied. "I have until the end of business today to say no."

"You're not going to say no."

"I'm not? I'm glad you and James are so convinced."

"Why would you?" Gen asked.

Now it was Melody's turn to be sarcastic.

"Because it's the secretary of state, duh."

"And you don't think you can handle that? Please."

"Do you have any idea what the secretary of state does?" Melody asked.

"Fly around the world, get handed expensive gifts and attend lavish banquets," Gen replied, tongue-in-cheek.

If she heard the humor in Gen's comment, Melody ignored it. She got up and began pacing the small room.

"The secretary of state is the representative of the President to the rest of the world. Not only do they advise the President on matters relating to U.S. foreign policy, but they supervise that foreign policy. Have you seen the condition of the world lately? How the hell do you supervise that kind of chaos?"

Gen didn't respond; there was no need to.

Long ago she had grown accustomed to Melody's problem solving *routine*. When confronted with a difficult issue, she paced and talked out loud; not for anyone else's benefit, but for her own. She knew that Melody needed to *hear* the problems before she could address them.

"The world is a shithole, Gen," Melody continued. "The Middle East is spiraling out of control, thanks to the continued, unchecked interference by Russia and Iran, and South Africa is running a respectable second place. We're fighting two overt wars, that we don't seem to know how to win or walk away from, and a list of covert ones that would make your head spin. And on top of all that we have to deal with that ballistic-idiot in Asia."

"Don't forget the drug wars in Mexico, the Kurds in Turkey and the *end-of-the-world-as-we-know-it* threat of global warming or is that climate change now? I always get them confused. Which reminds me; I need to work on my tan before the apocalypse hits."

"You're not helping."

"Look, I get it," Gen said. "When you look at the world it all seems rather daunting, but perhaps you are looking at it from the wrong perspective."

"And what is the right perspective?"

"Most of these conflicts have been raging for decades, and they span many administrations," Gen replied. "I mean just look at the Israeli-Palestinian conflict; that has been going on since the forties and has outlasted dozens of secretaries of state. So the bar for you would be rather *low*."

"Your faith in me is breathtaking," Melody said, as she sat back down in her chair.

"No, what I mean is that the position of secretary of state has been held by a variety of people, from military generals to career politicians. Not taking anything away from them, but perhaps it is time for a new approach, new ideas. Maybe the world could use a little less *risk-management* and a little more *problem-solving*."

"And you think I'm that person?"

"Haven't you always been, Mel?" Gen asked. "I mean it is what we do."

"What we do is business," Melody replied. "There is a big difference between that and geopolitical matters."

"I guess you haven't looked at our corporate bottom line lately, but I have. If we were a country, our combined net worth would place us ahead of countries like Bolivia, Malta and the Ukraine. If you don't think buys us a seat at the table...."

"What we do doesn't impact the course of the free world," Melody interrupted.

"Doesn't it?" Gen asked. "The last time I looked, GDL doesn't manufacturer church pews or cooking books."

"You're right," Melody replied, as she turned her gaze away and looked out the windows.

Off in the distance white caps were breaking on the cresting waves of the Atlantic. She loved this view because it put things in perspective. Any time she began to take the accolades and praise to heart, all she had to do was look out her window at the power and majesty of the ocean for a reality check.

"I guess my fear is that I will fail."

"And do what?" Gen asked, leaning forward in her seat and resting her arms on her legs. "Cause conflict, cause a war? You're already too late. Face it Mel, you can only go upward in this game."

"So I have to give up everything I know, everything I am good at, and take a gamble that I can be just as effective in politics?

"Nothing ventured, nothing gained," Gen replied.

"So, hypothetically speaking, if I agreed to this, what would I have to do to leave the company, but still maintain some form of control? I mean, let's be honest, even if every star aligned, and I was hailed as *the* secretary or all secretaries, this would be a four year gig, eight at the most. What do I have to fall back on when I am done?"

"Well, you might be a media darling today, but that will change pretty quickly, once you are nominated. All those folks who loved you over at Forbes, Fortune and the business shows, will look for a scoop, good or bad, to report on."

"That doesn't bother me," Melody replied. "I've been called bad names before."

"It'll get *worse* once you get confirmed," Gen shot back. "All those folks who kissed your ass on the Hill, the same ones who came begging to for campaign contributions, will come after you with a vengeance because you work for *her*."

"I've given to both sides, for crying out loud," Melody protested. "I'm an independent."

"This isn't about party *affiliations*, this is about party *politics*. Right, wrong or indifferent, the moment you raise your hand, you will become a target. You could walk on water and they will accuse you of not being able to swim. Worse, the media will go along with it and half the people will despise you for being *aquaphobic*."

"And this is supposed to encourage me to accept the offer?"

"No, but when you do....."

"If I do," Melody replied.

"*When* you do," Gen corrected her, "and it is better if you go into it with clear glasses. Being proactive to expected threats is a lot better than trying to be reactive as the blows are raining down on you."

"Hence my reasons for wanting to have something to fall back on," Melody said.

"Well, the first thing they are likely to focus on is whether there are any potential conflicts that would allow for a *quid pro quo* arrangement. You will have a lot of liability regarding GDL."

"So I will need to **temporarily transfer** title, management and authority of all my holdings to a trust under someone else's care?"

"Yeah," Gen replied. "We will have to go over everything with counsel, but we will not be reinventing the wheel; this happens all the time. However, all that being said, you will still have to be careful. Every decision you make will be highly scrutinized. As secretary of state, you will need to take extra care, when it comes to looking over all the fine print, and recuse yourself from any decision makings if a conflict of interest arises."

"Like what?"

"Say, for example, that after you and the prime minster of the aforementioned country of Malta have an amazingly productive summit, that countries military suddenly decides that they want to purchase a new class of coastal patrol boats that GDL just happens to provide...... See where I'm going with this?"

"Gotcha," Melody said. "But I won't be able to disconnect myself entirely from my past, nor do I want to. It would be nice, after all of this is said and done, to have a place to go back home to."

"No, and I am sure that Eliza has already factored that in to her selection process. Speaking from a business perspective I also don't foresee you coming back into the corporate world, when the time is right, as being much of a problem. Having a former secretary of state on the board is something any company would kill to have. For now, you're just going to have to do your best and cede control over to someone you trust."

"And therein lies my problem," Melody replied. "Normally it would be an easy decision, and I would put everything into your hands, but nothing about this is easy."

"Why? What's wrong?" Gen asked.

"For starters, I can't imagine saying yes to this offer without having *you* by my side. I know it's rather selfish of me, but the only way *I* could accept this position is if *you* agreed to be my chief of staff."

Gen leaned back in her chair and stared at Melody.

Checkmate, she thought, as a smile appeared on her face.

Melody just smiled back.

Gen slowly began to clap her hands, accepting that she had willingly talked herself into her own corner.

"Oh God you're good," Gen said. "You truly missed your calling. You should have gone into acting, or maybe politics is in your blood."

"Hey, hey….. Don't be hateful."

"Oh no, no hate here, I'm just acknowledging your mad skills."

"Really? Seriously? You had to see this coming?"

"I think I just let myself get caught up in exploiting your, now obviously feigned, uneasiness."

"Well, in all seriousness, you have a choice," Melody said. "You have your own stake in GDL and I will not ask you to just walk away from that."

"I owe that stake to you."

"No, you earned that stake through your business acumen and tenacity," Melody replied, "but those are also the things I want to take with me."

"You know I would never say no to you, Mel," Gen replied. "Where we go one, we go all."

"So we're really going to do this?"

"I guess we are," Gen said, and then chuckled.

"What's so funny?"

"I was just thinking how down-right *karmic* all this is."

"How so?"

"Well, think about it for a moment. All these years, all the companies we bought up. How many times did we restructure them, in order to make them financially viable? Sometimes we had to cut people loose, downsize operations for the benefit of the company, and now here we are effectively firing ourselves."

"Now that you mention it, I guess we are, aren't we?"

"You know, it was kind of funny when it was just you on the hot seat, but the more I think about it, what happens if we do fuck things up?"

"Either we get permanently fired or we start World War III."

"Well *hell's bells*, I'm certainly glad there's no real pressure."

"Speaking of pressure, how do you think Gregor will be with all of this? I mean you have a family to consider now."

"You're my family too, Mel," Gen protested.

"You know what I mean. It's just not you and Gregor anymore; you also have a son to think about."

"To be honest, with the amount of traveling I have been doing, this might actually be more to his liking," Gen replied. "Not that I have any illusions that political life will be more *stable*, but the hours might be a tad more predictable, as long as we manage to keep the flames of global discontent at bay."

"Well then, I guess I have a call to make."

CHAPTER FIFTEEN

City Hall, Manhattan, N.Y.
Tuesday, October 28th, 2014 – 2:43 p.m.

"Let's just cut the crap, Tom," McMasters said with annoyance. "We both know why Davis is pushing this affordable housing bill, and it has nothing to do with those poor bastards in Brooklyn."

"I don't know what you're talking about, Mr. Mayor," Tom Ferguson, chief of staff for City Councilman Rod Davis, replied.

"Hmmmm, well let me see if I can enlighten you a bit. Your bosses brother is Elroy Davis who is a partner over at Kinnear, White and King; one of the leading contenders for the Bed-Stuy construction award."

"Councilman Davis' has recused himself from the bid process..."

"Really, Tom?" McMasters said, cutting the man off abruptly. "We're going to play that game? 'Oh look, it's all on the up and up, I recused myself and I can't help it if my asshole buddies on the council approved it.'"

"I don't think we need to refer to the duly elected council members as assholes."

"Then they shouldn't try to treat me like I'm a goddamn idiot," McMasters replied. "The construction area saddles right up to a large portion of neighborhoods that have already been gentrified. Have you seen the rental prices in that neighborhood?"

"Yes, but over fifty percent of these new apartments will be guaranteed to cost only fourteen hundred a month."

"Only fourteen hundred a month?" McMasters asked sarcastically. "Oh my God, that's fantastic news, whatever was I thinking? Oh wait, I know what I was thinking, the average income in those areas is about thirty grand a year!"

"Well, for some it might be a bit tough…"

"Might be? Well it might be a bit tough if they also want to eat and put clothes on their backs, but hey the views will be great, won't they, Tom?"

The man let out an exasperated sigh.

"Hey, let me ask you a hypothetical question here," McMasters said.

"Shoot," Ferguson replied, a weary look appearing on his face.

"Just for argument's sake, let us assume you can't rent out those apartments allocated for low income, what was the number again?" McMasters asked, sorting through some papers on his desk. "Oh yeah, here it is, eighteen hundred apartments, so let's say you can only rent half that number, are you planning on leaving them vacant?"

"You know we can't do that," the man replied. "It would make the whole project unsustainable."

"This whole project has never been sustainable and you know it. This was never about the poor, but about expansion and lining corporate pockets. I'm not sure whether to be pissed at your boss for thinking I was too stupid not to see it or to think I would just go along with it."

"Whatever you might believe, there is a need for these apartments," Ferguson said.

"Tom, I'm the mayor of all of New York City. I understand there is a need, but I have to deal in reality. Right now they want a green light to put up apartment buildings that will displace a large block of residents, many of whom cannot afford to move back there. Do you know what happens then?"

"No," the man replied.

"They get dumped into already overcrowded neighborhoods and have to fight for the resources there that are limited to begin with. Do you know how that will play out in July and August? Let me answer that for you, *not well*."

"So I take it you're a no?"

"Until I see a modification that brings down that number to a rate below one thousand a month you can count me as a *hell no*."

"The council will not be happy," Ferguson replied.

"The city council better work for their constituents or I'll be the least of their worries."

Their conversation was disturbed by a knock on the door.

McMasters looked up to see his secretary standing in the doorway.

"Sir, I'm sorry to interrupt, but Commissioner Maguire and Chief Barnes are here to see you."

"Thank you, Allison. Please show them in."

"I'll convey your concerns to the council," the man replied, as he got up from the chair.

"Thanks, Tom," McMasters said, shaking the man's hand, as Maguire and Sandy Barnes entered the room.

"Please, have a seat," he said, pointing toward the empty chairs across from his desk.

"I hope we didn't interrupt anything?" Maguire asked, as the two of them sat down.

"No, you saved me from doing or saying something politically stupid," McMasters said, taking his seat.

"Well then, I guess *you're welcome*," Maguire replied.

"Let's see if you can save the rest of my day. I got a phone call that they are on their way. Do we have any update?"

"Nothing good," Maguire said. "We confirmed she was working for an escort service run by a guy named Devin Ackerman."

"Jesus Christ," McMasters said, "and I am supposed to tell that to Arianna Barone?"

Most cops would tell you that this was the part of the job they hated the most; the feeling of utter helplessness. In a line of work where you were trained to respond to any crisis and handle it, being put in a position where there was nothing you could say or do to make it better was cruel.

Mikala Stevens might have been a high-priced call girl, but that didn't make it any less difficult to tell to a grieving parent. It also didn't matter whether that parent was the wife of the New York City Public Advocate or some single mother living paycheck to paycheck in the Bronx.

Barnes averted her gaze, choosing to stare at the brass plaque that adorned the front of the mayor's desk. Maguire didn't have that luxury.

"Yes," he replied. "There's no way to make it sound any better than it is."

McMasters stared at Maguire, processing what the man had said.

You know he's right.

Just then a knock interrupted his contemplation and McMasters looked up to see Allison in the doorway once more.

"Sir, Advocate Barone and his wife are here."

"Thank you, Allison, please show them in."

All three stood up, as the couple entered the room.

McMasters stepped out from behind his desk and made his way over toward them.

"Jack, Arianna, please accept my sincere condolences," he said, as he shook Barone's hand and then hugged his wife.

"Thank you, Alan," the man replied, his voice sounding almost brittle.

Maguire hadn't had too much interaction with Jack Barone, since taking over the helm of the Department, but the man who walked into the room differed greatly from the man he remembered. His face was pale and his eyes had a distant look to them, as if he couldn't focus on anything. They had a term for it in the military; they called it the *thousand-yard stare*. It was used to describe the unfocused look of soldiers who had become emotionally detached from what they had seen. The term had since carried over into the civilian world and described the look of dissociation among victims who'd suffered some severe trauma.

A trip to the morgue will do that to a person, he thought.

In contrast, Arianna Barone appeared as if she was barely holding on to her composure by the barest of threads. When she removed the oversized sunglasses, you could see the red tinge around her eyes; a visible testament to the hours she'd spent crying. Unlike her husband, she didn't have a vacant stare. Her eyes told the emotional story that no parent ever wanted to hear.

"Please have a seat," McMasters said, as he ushered the couple toward the couch against the back wall. Maguire and Barnes repositioned their seats, so they were now facing the couple, and McMasters sat down in another chair.

"If there is anything Jill or I can do, please do not hesitate to ask," McMasters said.

"Thank you," Barone replied.

"Before we begin, is there anything I can get for you, coffee, water,…?"

"No, thank you, Alan, we are okay."

"Well, you already know Commissioner Maguire," Alan continued. "This is Sandra Barnes, his chief of detectives."

"Commissioner, Chief," Barone said, as he wife sat beside him, her body trembling slightly.

"I've asked them to be here today, to give you a private briefing of what is going on with the investigation."

You little fucking chickenshit, Maguire thought, *so much for you telling her anything.*

Barone nodded his head, reaching over to take his wife's hand in his, as if to brace her for what was about to come.

"James, if you would," McMasters said.

Maguire glared at McMasters for just a moment, before turning his attention toward the couple.

"First, let me say how deeply sorry I am for your loss," Maguire said, "and I will try to be as delicate as I can."

"I appreciate that," Jack replied, "but my wife and I want to know what happened to Mikala."

"I understand, sir. What I can tell you is that Mikala's body was discovered early Sunday morning by maintenance workers responding to a work order. When they entered the apartment, they found her and immediately called the police. The initial investigation focused on an accidental death, but we now believe that she was murdered."

Arianna began gently sobbing.

"Why do you think she was killed?" Jack asked.

"Early in the investigation it appeared that her death was accidental, but the medical examiner feels that someone else was involved and that it was arranged to look that way."

"Do you know whose apartment it was?" Jack asked. "Have they been interviewed yet?"

"The apartment was being used by your daughter, sir. There were no other occupants."

"That's impossible," Jack replied, a look of confusion on his face. "Mikala attends Columbia, she lives on campus."

"Not all the time," Maguire replied. "According to her roommate she spent most of the week at school, but was gone a lot on weekends."

"How is that possible?" Barone asked. "Mikala had no job, no income, we paid for her tuition. She had a credit card which she used for personal expenses, but I saw the bill every month. There were no extravagant charges and there was no rent for an apartment."

Maguire paused for a moment, lining up the right words to tell them as delicately as possible.

"We believe that Mikala used an assumed named for the apartment," he explained.

"But what if it wasn't her? Perhaps it was a friend's apartment, and she was just there?"

Maguire took a deep breath. He didn't have to like it, but McMasters had pinned this one on him and he had to be upfront with them.

"Mr. and Mrs. Barone, there is no easy way for me to tell you this, but our investigation has revealed that Mikala was working as an escort using the name Amber Skye."

The man's eyes went wide in shock at the admission and his wife let out a loud gasp.

"What the commissioner is saying..." McMasters interrupted, trying his best to spin the conversation away from the accusation.

"*Stop*," Jack said sharply, holding his gaze on Maguire as he held his hand up toward the mayor. "Let *him* finish."

"As I said, your daughter was using an apartment which belonged to a company that leases several in that building. Our detectives identified the company and interviewed one of their board members. He confirmed that Amber Skye used that apartment."

"So you're telling me our daughter was a *prostitute*?"

"No, I am not," Maguire replied. "I'm telling you we know she worked as an escort. According to the company that she was employed by that involvement was benign; consisting mostly of dinner or social events with visiting celebrities, businessmen, and the like."

"Do you believe that," Arianna Barone asked in a raspy voice.

All eyes immediately turned to look at the woman.

"At this point in the investigation we have no information that would lead us to conclude that her work went beyond that."

"So you think she was killed by one of her *clients*?" Jack interjected.

"Right now we simply do not know," Maguire admitted. "We are still in the investigation stage, but we will do everything in our power to identify and bring whoever is responsible for her death to justice."

"And what will that do, Commissioner? Will that bring our daughter back?"

"No, sir," Maguire replied, "it won't."

"Commissioner, you said Mikala's death was meant to look like an accident, how did she die?" Arianna asked.

"Mrs. Barone, I don't think you want to know..."

"No, but I do, commissioner," she replied.

Maguire took a deep breath, steeling himself.

"Initially we believed that she had died as the result of a failed attempt at autoerotic asphyxiation," Maguire explained. "That is when a person ties a..."

The woman raised her hand to stop him, "I'm aware of what it is. Why don't you think that was the actual cause of death?"

"During the autopsy, Dr. Godwin, the medical examiner, found signs of strangulation. It was his determination that this was the actual cause of death and that the rope that was used in an attempt to cover it up."

"Were there any other indications? Any signs of force?"

"From what I am aware, and Chief Barnes can correct me if I am wrong, there were signs of sexual activity, but there was no other bruising that would have showed that it was not consensual."

"So can we *really* be sure it was murder?" Jack asked.

"I'm not sure what you are asking."

"What I am asking is whether it is possible that Mikala, and whoever she was with, engaged in consensual sexual intercourse, perhaps even rough sex, and that her death was probably accidental?"

"Mr. Barone, I'm an investigator, not a doctor, I can only go by what the medical examiner is saying."

"But it's not implausible, correct?" McMasters interjected, seizing the opening that had been presented to create some *spin*.

"This really is outside my purview," Maguire replied, directing his comment directly toward the Barone's, "and I have to rely on the information I get from the medical examiner. That being said, Dr. Godwin is very well respected within his profession."

"Well, to the rest of the world, an obscure, and otherwise unremarkable, woman named Amber Skye is dead. All I am asking you to do is exercise your discretion to keep *her* obscure and allow us to bury *our* daughter in peace."

"I am sure that Commissioner Maguire will do everything in his power to protect Mikala's name and to respect your family's desire to mourn her passing in private," McMasters said.

"Thank you, Alan, that's all we are asking for," Jack said, as he stood up and held his hand out to his wife.

Maguire looked over at Arianna and could see the muscles of her jaw ripple, as she clenched her teeth and stood up.

McMasters, Maguire and Barnes all stood up.

"Unfortunately, we have to make arrangements for our daughter now."

"Please let me know if there is anything I can do for you," McMasters said. "The resources of the city are at your disposal."

"Thank you, Alan," Jack said.

"And thank you, Commissioner Maguire," Arianna said, as she extended her hand to him, "for your honesty."

"I am truly sorry," Maguire replied.

"I know," she said. "It was nice meeting you too, Chief Barnes."

"Ma'am," Sandy said, nodding her head.

The three of them watched as the Barone's left the room and the door closed behind them.

"Christ I need a drink," McMasters said, as he walked back over to his desk.

"Sandy, would you mind giving the two of us a minute?" Maguire asked.

"Not at all," she replied.

"Thank you."

"Good seeing you again, Mr. Mayor," she said, before turning and making her way toward the door, a wave of relief washing over her that she didn't have to be a witness to what was coming next.

Maguire turned back toward McMasters, as the man removed a bottle of whiskey from his desk and placed two glass tumblers on the desk.

"Would you like a drink, James?"

"No, what I would like is an explanation."

"About?"

"About how the hell you expect me to keep a lid on a homicide investigation?"

"Do we actually know if it *is* a homicide, James?" McMasters asked, as he poured himself a drink. "I mean as well respected as

Dr. Godwin may be, he is still a human being after all, and it's not like doctors are infallible."

"I don't believe we're having this conversation," Maguire said in amazement.

"Wait; hear me out for a minute. Let's just say that, prior to her death, our victim was enjoying some consensual sex which was a little rough. Maybe she's satisfied, maybe she's not. When her lover departs, perhaps she decides to have her own fun and takes it too far. That could explain the different marks, right?"

"So you just want me to ignore the M.E.'s findings and pretend it wasn't a homicide?"

"Does that matter?" McMasters asked. "I mean, let's be honest. How many homicides are you up to now?

"Three hundred or so," Maguire replied.

"Have your detectives solved them all?"

"No," Maguire said tersely.

"So the unsolved murder, assuming we actually do know if it is a murder, of Amber Skye is going to be relevant how?" McMasters asked, taking a sip of his whiskey.

"We keep playing this damn name game, but the truth is our victim isn't Amber Skye, it's Mikala Stevens, and she's the public advocate's step-daughter."

"And who knows that particular truth, James? How many people?"

"This is a bad joke, right?" Maguire asked suspiciously. "You can't be serious."

"Look, all I am saying is that we owe it to the public advocate to do our best to keep this under wraps."

"And if we can't and the media gets hold of this?"

"Well, I would cross that bridge when *you* get to it."

Just then the phone on the desk buzzed.

McMasters reached over and pressed a button, "Yes Allison?"

"Sorry, Mr. Mayor, but I have the director of environmental remediation on the line."

"Okay, tell him I will be right with him," McMasters replied, and then pressed the *hold* button. "I have to take this, we're trying to reclaim vacant land up in the Bronx and turn it into a park."

"Far be it from me to stand in the way of such pressing matters," Maguire said sarcastically, as he turned and headed toward the door. "If you're successful, perhaps you can consider naming it after Amber Skye."

Sandy Barnes was waiting for him in the hallway.

"Well?" She asked. "How did everything go?"

"Fine," Maguire said curtly, as they made their way out of the building.

"Why do I get the feeling it is anything but fine?" she asked, when they walked out of city hall.

"They want this covered up," he replied, as they got into the waiting SUV.

"He can't be serious?" Barnes asked. "And if the media finds out?"

"Apparently the mayor feels *I* should cross that bridge when *I* get to it."

"What the hell is that supposed to mean?"

"Let's just say I have a funny feeling that it's the same damn bridge they use to lead the lambs to slaughter."

"God, I fucking despise politicians," Barnes said in disgust, as the vehicle pulled away from the building. "What are you going to do?"

"I don't know yet; it's still a work in progress."

CHAPTER SIXTEEN

Sheraton Times Square Hotel, Manhattan, N.Y.
Tuesday, October 28th, 2014 – 3:17 p.m.

Eliza Cook sat on the couch, her stocking feet resting on an ottoman, as she sifted through polling numbers on her tablet.

"Where are we at with the Times endorsement, Em?" Cook asked her assistant.

"I heard back from Daniel Ramirez this afternoon. He said that the editorial board plans to issue an endorsement on the second."

"Nothing like waiting till the last goddamn moment, huh?"

"He blamed the delay on the paper's owner being out of town this past weekend, so they had to wait for him to sign off on it."

"I know Leon Katz is older than dirt, but surely he's heard of text messaging or emails."

"I don't think Katz is your biggest supporter," the woman replied. "I had Anderson do some digging into the donor database, looks like he is hedging his bets. If I had to take a guess, I'd say he waited until the most recent poll numbers came out to make his decision."

"Doesn't surprise me," Cook replied. "Leon has always been a shifty little fucker."

"It's probably the wrong time to ask, but Daniel wanted to know if they could get a sit-down interview before Election Day."

Eliza lowered her head slightly, just enough so that she could see over the reading glasses she was wearing, and stared at Emersen.

"Are you fucking kidding me?"

"Please, don't kill the messenger, boss," the woman replied.

Cook lowered the tablet and leaned her head back against the couch, as she contemplated the request. Her relationship with the Times could best be described as adversarial, and that was on a good day. While they ultimately sided with her, on a majority of issues, they couldn't help but act like pretentious bitches while doing so.

"Who did he want to send?" Cook asked.

"Jen Rubin, I believe."

Eliza chuckled upon hearing the name, "Oh isn't that rich."

Jen Rubin was a prissy little shit who honestly believed that her journalism degree, which her parents paid handsomely for her, gave her the right to *knock over apple carts* in the pursuit of her brand of investigative reporting. Their paths had crossed once before when Rubin had written a particularly salacious piece questioning the need for new furniture at the State Department. While the article was grossly inaccurate, and lacked even a modicum of actual *investigative* journalism, Cook didn't entirely blame Rubin. Eliza had suspected that one of President Walter Berhe's *Kool-Aid* drinking minions had snitched on her, after she'd had a falling out with him over his decision to support a radical militant faction in Syria.

For all the platitudes the media put out about his supposed *statesmanship*, the truth was that Berhe was a thin-skinned narcissist who took political pettiness to staggering new levels. It had always been assumed that Cook was his heir-apparent, and that she would parlay a cabinet position into a sanctioned presidential run. But after their last *televised* blow-up, Berhe had abruptly pulled his support for her and instead backed Mario

Deluca, a dark-horse candidate from New York, who was more in line with his world views.

Despite being from the great state of New York, Cook trounced Deluca in one primary election after another. The final nail occurred in April when he failed to win his own state's primary. Everyone with a political pulse knew that it was over, especially considering Cook's strangle hold on California. So, with the handwriting on the wall, the party bosses had insisted that they bury the hatchet for the good of the organization and their base. It sounded good, but the party had no interest in the *base*, beyond the donations they received. To them, an unresolved split would have caused a decline in their bottom line and they would not allow that to happen.

For her part, Eliza put a charming, yet completely contrived, smile on her face, as the two of them played 'kiss and make up' for the cameras, but behind the scenes the pompous ass couldn't leave well enough alone. Berhe insisted that his election had been historic and, as a result, his legacy was more important, more significant, than the results of any *common* election. He sought promises, through the party, for continued funding for the political action committee that he was forming. Berhe said it was urgent that the right people were elected to continue the work that he had started. They were all too happy to acquiesce to his demands, providing that he agreed to attend regular fund-raising events during the year. For someone who loved the camera as much as he did, it was an easy agreement.

When it came to endorsing Eliza, he had a different set of demands. He went to great lengths to explain to her the time and effort he had put into ensuring that the right people were in critical staffing positions. These people, he explained, shared his long-range vision of quiet, but resolute, change. The average person, Berhe argued, could be *swayed* by political campaigns and their votes could not be taken for granted, but if the right people were kept in place, they could go about their work quietly and efficiently, unaffected by the days prevailing political winds.

Eliza had nodded diligently, as she pretended to listen to his rambling. There was no point in having earnest dialogue with someone who was politically deaf. He'd obviously never heard the old adage, *'the man on the top of the mountain didn't fall there.'* The mistake her former colleagues had made was in thinking they could control their monster once they had created it. When the time came, she accepted the document Berhe offered, listing all the names of the people he wanted kept in their *critical* positions, along with his endorsement. The endorsement she ran with, watching her poll numbers soar in the key inner-city districts, while the document went into a file marked: *Expendables*.

But that purge would take place later. For now she had more pressing matters, such as establishing her rules for the media.

"Okay," Eliza said, "go ahead and green light the interview."

"You want me to schedule it?" Emersen asked quizzically.

"Yes, I do. Don't we have a campaign stop in Michigan on Sunday?"

"Yeah, it's the first stop on a three-fer," Em replied. "We have a rally at one thirty in Flint and then we are heading to Cincinnati, Ohio for a four o'clock and we finish in Wilkes-Barre, Pennsylvania at seven thirty before heading back here."

"Good, call Daniel and tell him to have Ms. Rubin meet us at LaGuardia and she can have her interview while we are in route."

"I'll let him know," the woman replied.

"Then you can make sure she *misses* that flight."

"Ma'am?"

"I don't want to see her on my plane; do I make myself clear?"

"Yes, but how do I keep her off?"

"I don't care if you have to kick her scrawny little ass down the boarding ladder in your Jimmy Choo's, Em," Cook said matter-of-factly, "Just don't let her on the goddamn plane."

"Yes, ma'am," Emersen replied cautiously.

Lee had worked with Cook long enough to know that when she told you to do something, she didn't concern herself with how you did, just that you got it done. If need be, she'd utilize her kick-boxing skills, and take an assault charge, before she ever let the reporter get on the plane.

Failing Cook was not an option. She reasoned that, if all turned out as planned, she could always count on a presidential pardon in a few months.

"Where are we at with the networks?" Cook asked, changing subjects.

"The CBS / Journal show you up by six points and the ABC / Post have you leading by seven."

"What's the sample size?"

"Both are likely voters, but they are under one thousand each."

"A thousand; what kind of bullshit numbers are those? I couldn't get a consensus on Chinese takeout with those numbers," Cook replied. "What are the internal numbers telling us?"

"As of Wednesday, we are showing a four point lead, up from three," Emersen said. "That last ad that Whitmore ran cut into our numbers a little bit."

Cook frowned at that news.

Two weeks earlier their internal poll numbers were even higher than the networks, but her opponent, California Congressman Duncan Whitmore, had pulled out a last minute ace-in-the-hole card and ran with it. It was a hot-mic moment, from her first senate campaign, and she had made the novice mistake of thinking the twenty thousand dollar a plate dinner was a safe place to talk. It wasn't.

She was asked a question about her views on same-sex marriage and how she resolved that with her church upbringing. Cook had laughed it off and said, '*Sometimes you have to look them in the eye and tell them what they want to hear, but then you have to go out and vote your conscious.*' While Cook had forgotten about it, a few minutes after she had said it, she learned that technology never forgets, after Whitmore's camp got a hold of a copy and ran it in all the key battleground counties.

The ad opened with a view of the Oval Office, with all its trappings, and then the audio began to play. It was only a brief few seconds until the screen went to black and a disembodied voice asked, 'If Eliza Cook is willing to lie to your face, imagine what she will do when you're not watching her?' The screen then flashed a rather unflattering image of her.

Eliza grudgingly admitted that the ad was a nice piece of work.

Her camp had immediately wanted to refute the ad, by making the argument that it was a snippet which had been *taken out of context*, but she had nipped that in the bud. She had given thousands of speeches over the years and she couldn't remember if that, or anything else, had been taken out of context. The last thing she wanted to do was get caught up in a *terminal deluge* of never-ending little leaks, so she did what she had always done and went on the offensive.

Once the ads hit, she scheduled a trip to the theater, ensuring that the media would flock to the event. To be on the safe side, her campaign sent out an email to Shondra Barrett, a reporter who worked for the Post, who was openly gay. Barrett had always been viewed as sympathetic to Cook's positions and had worked on stories with her staff in the past. The aide informed Barrett that Cook, schedule permitting, might be available for a comment after the performance.

As Eliza exited the stage door, she was met by a scrum of reporters being held at bay by Secret Service and NYPD officers. Eliza acted surprised, but her eyes sought out Barrett and she headed over to the woman.

"Madam Secretary, what do you have to say about the ad being run by your opponent?" Barrett asked.

"Mea culpa," Cook replied. "I said it and just like any other person I have my regrets."

"Regrets that you said it or that it was caught on tape?"

"No, I don't care that it was caught on tape," Cook said dismissively. "In the age of the internet, every one of us has said something that hasn't *aged well*. I remember a time when Congressman Whitmore said, on the House floor, that our troops would be home by Christmas. That was seven Christmas' ago and we are still putting up fake pine trees for them in the desert. Situations change, opinions are revised, and you sometimes have to be honest and admit that you were once against something. What comes next, an ad that accuses me of using bad language when I sing along in the shower? I guess I must go home and scrub all my playlists."

"That might be a topic for another interview, Madam Secretary," Barrett said with a laugh. "So are you now saying you *evolved* on the issue of same-sex marriage?"

It was the precise opening Cook had wanted and Barrett teed it up perfectly.

"Shondra, I've been married to my dear husband, Harry, for thirty *blissful* years," Cook said facetiously. "So let me be perfectly clear, if Steve and Bob, or Laura and Joan, want to join me in the trenches of *happily-ever-after*, who am I to say no? More importantly, come January, I will make sure that no one else says they can't."

"Thank you, Madam Secretary," Barrett said, as Cook turned and made her way back toward the waiting Suburban.

And just like that, she had managed to get her presidential train back on its tracks. Not only had she taken all the steam out of the Whitmore ad, but she had thrown some red meat toward the media. The next day her opponent found himself on his heels having to explain why troops were still deployed after *promising* he would do everything to bring them home. With each passing day her polling numbers began to creep back up.

"Where are we still polling down?"

"Wisconsin hasn't bounced back and Colorado has been a little sluggish in its recovery," Emersen said.

"Get together with the traveling team and let's get a rally scheduled in Green Bay by Friday. I want to hit them hard. Where is Vernon?

"Senator Mays is in Los Angeles," Emersen said. "He's speaking at a fundraiser for the mayor."

"Okay, reach out to his advance team and have them ready to head out to Colorado by Saturday if we need to."

The conversation interrupted by a knock on the door.

Eliza looked up to see Dean Oliver enter the room.

"That will be all for now, Em," Eliza said.

"Yes, ma'am."

Oliver waited until the woman left the room.

"You wanted to see me?" he asked.

"No, I didn't," Cook said tersely, "but you made that necessary."

Oliver's face remained impassive.

"When I ask you to do something for me, I expect it to be done in such a manner that there are no loose threads."

"You wanted the problem gone, it's gone. What thread did I leave loose?"

"The thread where it changed from an *accident* to an *intentional*," Cook said dryly, as she got up from the couch. "Come with me."

She walked over and opened another door. Normally it would have led to another bedroom, but these weren't normal times and she wasn't a normal guest. She was the former Secretary of State and she not only held a top secret security clearance, but still had knowledge of sensitive compartmented information (SCI) and special access programs (SAP). As a result, additional protocols had been established to provide her with a means of secure communication, including a sensitive compartmented information facility, commonly referred to as a SCIF.

The SCIF was a secure room within a room and there were no external connections. It was a sterile facility where she could view or discuss sensitive information without having to worry about outside surveillance or spying. In this instance, it was about as sensitive a topic as one could get.

Cook waited, while Oliver removed his cell phone and sat it on the table outside the doorway, and the two of them entered the small room.

She shut the door behind them before she continued, "If I wanted this matter screwed-up I could have hired some half-assed, wannabe *Guinea* hit-man from Jersey to go and fuck it up for a whole lot less than I am paying you."

"I'm not sure what you mean."

"They know the little bitch didn't kill herself and now the local cops are putting the pieces together."

"How the hell did they find the body so soon?"

"Apparently her plumbing leaked," Cook said sarcastically. "When the medical examiner got a hold of her, he found evidence of your handiwork."

"You of all people should understand that there are no guarantees in anything, Madam Secretary," Oliver replied. "Just better odds."

Cook closed the gap between the two of them until she was almost chest to chest with the man. The ever present congenial face that Cook was publicly known for had vanished and in its place was something more *dangerous*. In any other environment,

Oliver might have been the more physically dominant one, but here in the small room he saw a side of Cook that sent a cold shiver down his spine.

"*Unfuck* this, Dean," Eliza hissed. "Do I make myself clear?"

The man swallowed hard, "Crystal, ma'am."

Cook took a step backward as the *darkness* faded from her face.

"I'll take care of the investigation," she said coolly. "You just make sure that there are no more loose strands for them to exploit. The last thing I need is for some burned-out, alcoholic detective, with two ex-wives and crippling child-support, working some overtime and unraveling this ball of shit."

"I'll take care of it."

"Good, because I would really hate for you to end up being one of those *loose strands* I have to cut free."

"Yes, ma'am."

CHAPTER SEVENTEEN

Penobscot, New Hampshire
Tuesday, October 28th, 2014 – 3:59 p.m.

Alex Taylor picked up the cigarette from the ashtray on her desk and took a long drag; relishing the sensation before slowly exhaling.

It was cigarette number seven, which left only three more for the day and those she would save for later.

Since her brush with death, several months earlier, she had made an earnest commitment to get her life back in order. She'd traded in her whiskey for one glass of *alcohol-free wine* in the evening, also known to the rest of the world as grape juice, and cut her daily cigarette habit in half.

At her current pace she was confident that she would be a first-ballot inductee into the *boring old cop's hall of fame*.

"Fuck my life," she muttered, as she crushed the ember out just before it burned into the filter.

Some days, like today, proved to be harder than others.

She closed her eyes and leaned back in her chair.

As a street-cop she'd always had a certain level of contempt for the bosses. Anyone above the rank of sergeant was fair game, because in her eyes they were the ones who pushed the agenda that the rest of them had to live with. So it was kind of *karmic* that she was now the chief of police and the one who had to deal with that agenda. Worse yet, she was the one having to deal with the politicians who drove that agenda.

It was just over two years into her small town law enforcement career and she was still butting heads with the powers to be, including her perennial nemesis, Sheldon Abbott, Penobscot's city manager.

She'd long ago figured out that Abbott had hired her for the chief's position because of her flaws, not despite them. He'd assumed that the *down-on-her-luck,* alcoholic ex-cop from New York City would be someone he could easily control and manipulate. He'd assumed wrong.

Despite her personal flaws, she was a professional pit-bull when it came to her cops and providing them with the tools they needed to do their job. Every year the budget committee tried to push their *do-more-with-less* agenda and every year she managed to *more or less* find a way to argue, threaten and cajole them into signing off on her budget requests, but this year was proving much harder.

Under the terms of the Penobscot city charter, all budgets had to be finalized before the members of the city board were sworn in on January 1st. Currently, two long-time sitting members were in an ugly re-election battle with two political upstarts and they were losing.

The problem for Alex was that she had a personal relationship to the two challengers in question. Dr. Peter Bates, who was Penobscot's favorite physician, as well as being Alex's boyfriend, and Mildred Parker, who was the wife of the late chief of police and Alex's surrogate mother figure. Because of this it put her in-direct odds with the board, whose members were now pushing back harder against her budget than ever before. Even Sheldon, who she could normally browbeat into submission, was making a stand.

To make matters even worse, one of the area's largest employers, Alpine Sport Outfitters, was closing up shop. Not only was Penobscot going to lose over two hundred retail sales and manufacturing jobs, but the city was about to take a major hit on tax revenue. Beyond the fiscal impact, Alex also knew that unemployment didn't make for tranquil personal lives and that was where the police entered the picture. The department was already down one officer and another was contemplating retirement next year.

There were several times over the summer that Alex considered pulling the plug, but each time her commitment to her officers kept her from doing it. Now all she had to do was figure out a way to keep their paychecks coming in.

You are a glutton for punishment, aren't you? she thought.

Her musing was interrupted by the sound of her cell phone buzzing.

Alex opened her eyes and glanced down at the display.

"*Ruh Roh*," she said, as she picked up the phone and answered it. "If you're calling me, you must really be in trouble."

"Is that anyway to talk to your old partner?" Maguire asked.

"Well that all depends," she replied.

"On what?" he asked.

"On whether this is a social call or you need bail money?" Alex replied. "Cause my time is free, but my pockets are empty."

"I'm good with the former," Maguire said with a laugh. "I just needed someone to vent to; someone who knows how to keep their trap shut."

"We just talked like four days ago, how bad can it be?"

"I have a suicide that turned into a homicide that just went political."

"Killer or the *killee*?"

"Victim is the step-daughter of Jack Barone, the public advocate," Maguire said. "By day she was a journalism student at Columbia, but it looks like she was moonlighting as an escort."

"Well it sucks to be you," Alex replied with a chuckle.

"Ain't that the truth? What makes it a problem is I feel like I'm being painted into a corner."

"How so?"

"The original report listed the victim by an alias and now they, meaning the mayor and family, want to keep it that way."

"I can understand that," Alex replied. "Nobody wants their kid id'd as a *pavement princess*."

"Yeah, but how the hell am I supposed to investigate a homicide if I can't name the victim?"

"Have you asked yourself why no one's interested?"

"I know why," Maguire replied. "McMasters is being groomed for a cabinet position by Eliza Cook and the public advocate will take over as mayor when McMasters resigns. I assume neither wants to have this kind of political black cloud hanging over them."

"That's some cold fucking shit," she said. "So what do they want you to do?"

"Apparently, they want me to make it go away."

"What about just dragging it out?"

"How so?" Maguire asked.

"Say the political stars align and Cook gets elected. McMasters steps down and follows her to D.C. to prepare for confirmation hearings. That means Barone gets sworn in right away, correct?"

"Yeah."

"So rein in the investigation for now. Keep everything close to the vest until after the post-election smoke settles and then have your people open it back up."

"Let me get this straight. You want me to wait until McMasters is safely tucked away in D.C. and Barone is named acting mayor to put the target on my back?" Maguire asked sarcastically. "That sounds like an awesome plan, partner. Why don't I just go up to the roof and commit *seppuku*?"

"I didn't say it was a good plan," she replied. "I was just giving you an option. I mean let's be honest. It sounds to me like you're stuck between the *Scylla* and *Charybdis*."

"If we're being honest, it sounds more like I am stuck between a firing squad and the electric chair."

"Weren't you the one reminding me recently that, and I quote, *'no good deed goes unpunished.'*"

Maguire sighed loudly.

"Look, you and I both know what you want to do here, rookie, but this isn't *Sector Adam* and you're not just some cop in Brooklyn North. Like it or not, we are white shirts now. You don't have to like the rules, but sometimes you just have to suck it up and play the damn game."

"My, how you have matured," he said.

"Kiss my ass," she replied. "Is that mature enough for you?"

"You know there are times when I hate you," he said.

"Yeah, that usually coincides around the same time that you know I'm right."

"I guess I'm lucky that those times don't happen very often."

"Listen to me for a moment, because I'm being serious," she said. "I know you better than anyone. I know what's going on in that head of yours. You called me to get me to agree with you, but I can't. Not because I don't think you should do it, but because I'm looking at the big picture here."

"And what's the *big picture*, Alex?"

"Say you investigate this now. How are you going to do it? You can't *quietly* investigate a homicide, especially when it involves the two oldest professions: *sex & politics*. It's New York City; word will leak faster than you can keep up with it. The media will have a field day and the ensuing scandal will be front page news through the election cycle. The result is you piss off McMasters and you're fired. But, if you wait till McMasters is gone, and you investigate it later, someone will out you as trying to cover it up for political gain. The media will still have a field day, but on top of it they will pin the cover-up on you. Again, the result is you piss off Barone and you're still fired."

"You missed your calling," Maguire said. "You should have skipped police work and just gone into motivational speaking."

"We all have our gifts," she said, choosing to ignore the barb from her old partner. "The truth is you're pretty much fucked either way, so, if I were you, I would just choose option 'C' and roll the dice."

"There is something inherently wrong about not doing your job, Alex."

"James, black and white is that academy bullshit; real life is just varying shades of gray."

"Damn, I never thought I'd live to see the day that Alex Taylor went *legit*."

"Eh, I consider myself as being more of a pragmatist these days."

"I guess that makes me an idealist?"

"No, it makes you a cop," she replied. "Your heart has always been in the right place, James. It was in the right place in the Seven-Three and it was in the right place whenever you did your *froggie* shit. The problem is sometimes doing the right thing isn't the right thing to do."

Maguire remained silent.

If anyone had asked him to name the closest people in his life, Alex was at the top of the list. She had been there with him at the high points and she had certainly been there at some of the lowest points, but she didn't know everything. There was a part of him that wasn't so *clean*; it was a part that he kept hidden away and one that he would take to the grave.

Everyone had secrets, some even had skeletons, but Maguire had also gained a few ghosts along the way. To be fair, there were no *innocents* in his closet, but that didn't negate the fact that some had been judged and dispatched to the afterlife; *sans* the formalities of due process.

For a moment he had a flashback of Patricia Ann Browning's brown eyes staring up at him; three .9mm rounds buried in her chest.

The shooting had been ruled a justifiable homicide by the district attorney up in New Hampshire. The woman was, after all, a murderous psychopath who had taken Alex hostage and was about to kill her when Maguire had fired the fatal shot. But that woman was *Tatiana*, Patricia's alter-ego, and how she had reached that dark, evil place in her life was complicated.

Patricia was just as much a victim as anyone. She had been physically and mentally abused, by the sadistic Keith Banning, until who she had once been simply ceased to exist. It would have been more humane for the man to have killed her outright, than to let her become a monster that needed to be destroyed.

As Maguire had stared into her eyes, he knew that what she had become was unredeemable, at least in this life. As long as she lived, she would be a threat to those Maguire loved, and it was a game he could no longer afford to play.

In the end, Patricia Ann Browning had taken her last breath long before the last drop of blood drained from her body.

"Hey, you there?"

"Yeah, yeah, I'm here," Maguire said, as he shook his head, chasing away the haunting image. "I know, you're right."

"Wow, I'll never get tired of hearing that," Alex said with a laugh. "Anyway, it doesn't matter what I, or anyone else, tells you, you need to do what *you* feel is right, James."

"Even if I get fired for it?" he asked.

"If they would fire you for doing your job, do you really want to work for them?"

"That's a valid point."

"Besides, if they fire you that opens up a spot for me," Alex quipped.

"That's my Alex," Maguire replied. "Always thinking ahead."

"Just be careful, rookie," Alex warned. "When you start messing around in sex and politics, sometimes getting fired isn't the worst thing that can happen to you."

"I'll tread cautiously."

"Just promise that you'll call me before you do anything stupid."

"So you can stop me?" he asked.

"No," she replied. "So I can join you."

CHAPTER EIGHTEEN

Southampton, Suffolk County, N.Y.
Tuesday, October 28th, 2014 – 4:42 p.m.

Melody's fingers tapped nervously on the desktop, as if playing a melodic tone on some phantom piano, while she waited for Eliza Cook to come on the line.

It was one thing to reach a decision in her mind, but it was something entirely different to make it a reality. As each second ticked by she found herself second-guessing her choice.

She chased the negative thoughts from her mind, as she leaned back in the office chair and glanced up at the large, framed photo on the wall across from the desk. It was the cover of Forbes magazine; when she had first been named to the list of the richest women in America. It featured her in a form-fitting red dress which, coupled with her long blonde hair, was in stark contrast to the all-black cover. When the issue had first hit the newsstands it had been panned by most business outlets as being overtly sexually, which it was, but it was also the magazine's all-time bestselling issue.

She hung the image on the wall not out of hubris, but of humility; a reminder to herself not to become *that* woman. The image itself was a stark and powerful portrait of someone whom she viewed as her *alter-ego*.

The rest of the world saw Melody Anderson, the confident, successful businesswoman who took on the corporate world and beat them at their own game. She had beauty, brains, and brawn and was skilled at using all of her attributes to achieve her goals. She, on the other hand, saw something much different. When Melody looked in the mirror, she saw a shy young girl who loved reading and was exceptionally good at math. That image was a far cry from the woman in the photo who stared back at her. She was much more at home in a pair of faded jeans and an oversized sweatshirt than she was in a designer dress.

"Please hold for Secretary Cook," a soft voice said on the other end.

Here we go, she thought.

"Melody, my dear, I was beginning to think you would stand me up," Cook's cheerful voice said, a moment later.

"No, not at all," she replied. "Like you said, I was just getting all my ducks in a row."

"That sounds promising. Does that mean you've made your decision?"

"I have," she said, swallowing hard. "I'm deeply touched that you've honored me with this opportunity and I accept your gracious offer to serve in your administration."

It took about five seconds to say, but the ramifications of those few simple words would be felt for decades to come.

"Oh, Melody, I can't even begin to tell you how happy I am to hear you say that," Cook replied. "Of course, you do know that the clock begins running immediately?"

"I assumed as much," she replied. "I've already sat down with my assistant and we've drawn up a framework for the attorneys to move control of my companies into a trust."

"I admire your commitment to my victory," Cook said warmly. "I wish the polls shared your resolve."

"Does anyone take these polls seriously anymore?"

"Unfortunately, yes," Cook replied. "Sadly, it's not the polls themselves, which are often problematic because of archaic methodology, but the message they convey. A flawed poll means nothing, unless it convinces potential voters that there is no reason to waste their time. A voter who looks out their window on a cold, rainy day is less likely to head out and cast their ballot when the latest polling suggests their candidate is up or down beyond the margin of error."

"That is a good point," Melody replied. "I never thought about it that way."

"I'm glad you agree, because I'm going to ask you to pack a bag and hit the campaign trail with me."

"Wow, you do move fast," Melody said with a laugh.

"A moving target is harder to hit. Besides, it has been my experience that playing offense is much more enjoyable than being on the defense."

"When and where?"

"Tomorrow," Cook said. "I have a private campaign dinner to attend in Richmond and I want you to join me. For obvious reasons we will keep your new position quiet, at least until after the results come in on Tuesday, but I want you with me to quell some fears."

"Quell them or cause them?"

"Well, perhaps a little of both," Cook replied. "It doesn't hurt to keep people guessing. We'll be staying overnight in D.C. I'll have my staff get you a room at the Hay-Adams. We'll be having a breakfast roundtable early Thursday morning and then a couple of afternoon chats before coming back to the city to regroup. Unless of course we're needed someplace else and in that case we'll be on the move again. By Monday morning you won't know whether you're in Washington, D.C. or Washington State."

"I guess it will be good practice."

"I know it's asking a lot, especially on such a short notice, but the next week is going to involve a lot early mornings and late nights. Are you up for it?"

"Sounds like finals week at Wharton," Melody replied.

"Well, with slightly better food. I just hope James won't be too lonely without you."

"He's a big boy," Melody said. "Besides, he's working on something big and I'm sure he wouldn't mind the excuse to stay late at work and focus on it."

"Oh, I do love police intrigue," Cook replied. "You must dish on the flight down to Virginia."

"I do have a few questions, if you don't mind."

"No, of course not, ask away."

"What is my latitude in bringing people in to work for me?"

"Well, I think it is only fair that you get the same autonomy that I did, at least when it comes to naming your chief of staff, counselor and executive secretary. Your inner circle should be compromised of people you trust. Do you have anyone particular in mind?"

"I will have to think about the executive secretary position, but I'd like to bring Genevieve Gordon in as my chief of staff."

"Oh, I think she would be a very good choice," Cook replied. "I rather like her. She's a little spit-fire; reminds me a bit of myself back in the early days."

"I am sure she will appreciate hearing that," Melody said.

"With some of the other positions, I think that is something you and I need to discuss at length," Cook replied. "I have some people I would like to place in key positions, some you may already know, but we can discuss that when the time is right. There are also some officers and career diplomats I identified, during my tenure at State, who are doing stellar work in some of the various bureaus. Mostly their work has been glossed over by the current administration. I'd like to see some of them get elevated up the organizational chart."

"I'm all for rewarding people who do quality work," Melody said.

"I believe you will benefit from their knowledge and experience, not to mention that it will make your job a lot easier. But, that being said, I have to be honest with you, Melody, there are some permanent residents in Foggy Bottom that you need to be very careful with."

"The fabled *deep state*?" she asked.

"Discount them at your peril," Cook said cautiously. "I went into it believing that as the secretary of state they would all do my bidding, but I learned that the organization always outlasts the individual."

"That sounds ominous," Melody replied.

"That's because it is," Cook countered. "There are tens of thousands of State employees around the globe and the vast majority of them are dedicated workers. But I can guarantee you that several them, especially among the Senior Executive Service, will remain loyal to Berhe and continue to promote his globalist agenda. They will stay behind and I can assure you that they will see what we are trying to accomplish as a direct threat to their *status quo*. I saw it first hand while I was there. You issue a directive that goes against their viewpoint and the foot-dragging begins. Either they will tell you it can't be done or, if you don't keep a steadfast watch, they will slow-walk it until you are gone. I don't imagine that there have been any real improvements under Behre's piss-boy, Lucian Ambrose."

Melody shuddered at the mere mention of the man's name.

Ambrose was a D.C. legend, but it was not for any grandiose political achievements. He liked to play the part of an American aristocrat, but he lacked even the basic charm of a snake-oil salesman. While Ambrose liked to act as if he came from old money, the reality was that he came from old *middle-class* money. He knew all the wealthiest and influential people growing up because his father had worked for them. His father had worked as hard as he did to so that he could afford to put young Lucian into a private school; along with the blessings of a few well connected benefactors. The boy was just on the fringe of their society, a hanger-on, but he had one thing going for him, his height. At 6'7" Ambrose became the pride of the Dorchester High School basketball team. He made the varsity team in his sophomore year and then led them to back-to-back state championships in his junior and senior years. It was at one of those games that his social luck had changed and he caught the eye of Annabelle Morgan.

Much to the dismay of her family, Annabelle, or Annie as she was called, became smitten with the lanky Ambrose. What started off as a spring fling soon became serious and they became a steady couple during his senior year at Dorchester. So serious that the two ended up getting married just about nine months, give or take a few weeks, before their daughter, Angelina, was born.

Feeling more of an obligation to Annie and their granddaughter, her family paved the way for Ambrose's successes by discretely placing one stepping stone in front of the other for him to follow. An Ivy League law school was first, followed by a posting at a prestigious legal firm in Providence. It didn't take the firm's partners very long to recognize that the degree conferred upon Ambrose was basically useless, so he was often relegated to conducting case law research and never actually saw the inside of a court room.

When he ran for congress, Annie's family again did most of the ground work, by identifying a district where an entrenched party representative was retiring, and buying the young couple a home there. A few favors later and the retiring member whole-heartedly endorsed the young man for his seat.

To call his political career lackluster would have been *kind*. Ambrose enjoyed all the trappings of his new position, but not any of the actual work. He signed onto bills as a *co-sponsor*, when it was expedient to do, so but never did any of the heavy lifting. In this way he didn't expend any real political capitol, yet built up an impressive amount of favors owed to him. He became a known quantity to the party bosses, who learned how to use his loyalty to press their agenda. His reward for being the good *foot-soldier* was better committee assignments.

When quiet whispers began to surface, about an illicit affair, with a married staffer, they moved to act quickly. The Morgan family was a *significant* donor to the Rhode Island party coffers, and they would not allow a sex scandal to destroy that.

The staffer was quickly *promoted* to a higher paying position, within Homeland Security, and Ambrose stepped down to graciously accept an appointment as Berhe's ambassador to Liechtenstein, a position created solely for him. Then, when Cook went rogue on him, Berhe brought Ambrose back into the fold knowing full well that the man would eagerly preserve his agenda, for a shot at political redemption.

Even now, in the waning days of the administration, he was making the rounds of any news show that would give him airtime, to make the case for staying the foreign policy course that Berhe had set.

"I would strongly advise you to go in knowing that Lucian will have set-up pitfalls designed to stifle any form of progress," Cook said to Melody. "We won't be able to remove all of them, at least not in a timely manner, so you will need to learn how to identify and circumvent the ones that remain."

"I don't dispute what you're saying, and I defer to your first-hand experience, but I have to admit that I find it deeply troubling to believe that representatives of this country's government would act against its best interests."

"If you're troubled now, wait until *you* experience it first-hand, my dear," Cook said. "As much exposure as you have had to the political system, you will find it pales in comparison when you become part of it. You will find that many within the system are not in it for the country's benefit, but for their own. Sometimes it is for obvious reasons, like fortune or power, but other times it is for ideological reasons and those are often the worst. Show me someone who is in it for the money and I can find common ground with them, but someone who is a true-believer in a cause cannot be reasoned with, they become a cancer that will spread until it destroys the host."

"What do you do then?"

"First you identify the problem and then you *kill* it," Cook replied coolly, before adding, "Metaphorically speaking, of course."

"Of course," Melody said with a laugh.

"But that's enough shop talk for now. Why don't you and Ms. Gordon join me for lunch here tomorrow? Shall we say about 11:30? We can discuss the vision I have going forward and then we can all fly down to Virginia together."

"That sounds wonderful," Melody replied.

"Give my love to James and tell him I said to take a break from police work and spend some quality time with you, before all this insanity begins in earnest."

"I will do that," Melody said, "and I look forward to seeing you tomorrow."

"I'm so glad to have you on board, Melody. See you tomorrow."

CHAPTER NINETEEN

Queens, N.Y.
Tuesday, October 28th, 2014 – 7:38 p.m.

Devin Ackerman pressed down hard on the brakes of his black Mercedes Benz S550, narrowly avoiding slamming into the back of the yellow taxi that had unexpectedly come to a stop in front of him.

"Are you fucking kidding me or what?" Ackerman screamed, as the car's wipers worked diligently to clear the rain from the windshield.

He'd been sitting in bumper-to-bumper traffic on the Queensboro Bridge for the last forty-five minutes. A sea of bright red brake lights of the cars in front of him fueled the anger building up inside him.

This is no fucking way to live, he thought, as he gripped the steering wheel tightly.

The lack of sleep, coupled with the visit from the cops, had kept him in a bad mood all day and now this traffic jam was like a rancid little cherry on top of it all.

"You should have just taken the tunnel you cheap bastard."

On any normal day he would have been far away from this nonsense, but he'd gotten a call earlier in the day from his buddy Tim, an adult film producer who had a studio in Long Island City. Ackerman had funneled girls, who didn't quite make the escort cut, to Tim in the past and now the man was reaching out to return the favor. Tim had said that he had a farm-fresh girl who was too over-qualified to just end up being some *mattress actress*. Despite the current heat that he was feeling, Ackerman knew that things would return to normal soon enough and that he would need a suitable replacement for Amber. So he had agreed to meet them over at some upscale yuppie bar off Vernon Boulevard in Queens. A decision he was now deeply regretting.

As the car made its way around the bend in the road, just past the Silvercup Studios' building, he saw the cause of his current nightmare. Up ahead, a large yellow NYC Department of Transportation construction vehicle sat parked in the left lane with its large directional arrow directing drivers to move right. They had completely shut down the exit for Queens Boulevard and all traffic was now being diverted to the Northern Boulevard exit.

"No, this can't be real," he roared. "There is no fucking way you are doing construction in a goddamn downpour."

Ackerman slammed the steering wheel repeatedly, physically venting his frustration, while adding emphasis to his commentary.

The cautionary tale of the horror of rush-hour traffic in New York City was a lie. If it had only been an hour long, there would be no way of measuring the sheer joy and bliss commuters would feel. The lie was that there was *always* traffic in New York City. It didn't matter if it was two in the afternoon or two in the morning. If it wasn't the weather, it was an accident, or the president, or a film production, and if all those failed, an ill-timed construction project.

As the car slowly inched forward, Ackerman could see a group of men, wearing hard-hats and hi-vis yellow construction vests, gathered under the protection of the west bound overpass with nary a tool in sight.

What the fuck do they care, he thought. *They're getting paid good money to screw-over the rest of us.*

As his car drew abreast of the group, he rolled down his window and yelled, "I hope you all catch pneumonia and die you cock-suckers."

None of the men even bothered to glance over in his direction; they had all grown immune to the customary epitaphs hurled at them, although one man in the middle extended his arm up high and offered Ackerman a one-fingered salute.

"Your mother," he said, as he rolled the window back up.

As the Mercedes reached the end of the off-ramp, he turned left onto 21st Street and began making his way through the rain soaked, traffic snarled side streets of Hunters Point.

Fifteen minutes later he arrived at his destination, but it still took him several more minutes until he found an available parking spot. As he put the car in park, the cell phone sitting in the cup holder began to buzz.

"Like I need this shit right now?" he asked rhetorically, as he stared at the familiar number on the display.

Ackerman took a deep breath and let it out slowly before answering the phone.

"Hello?" he said.

The anger in his voice was gone now, replaced by something that could only be described as *meek*.

"Yeah, I can talk," he replied.

Ackerman listened intently, as he stared out the window.

The streetlights were distorted by the raindrops on the windshield, making them appear like large colorful orbs, but the otherwise cheerful looking display could do nothing to brighten the *darkness* of the conversation he was listening to.

"I'm not sure what you want me to say," Ackerman interjected. "It's not like I killed the little slut. I'm just as much a victim in all of this."

Again he listened to the verbal harangue.

"What do you mean?" he said, trying to control the anger creeping into his voice. "I lost one of my best girls, I'm out a shitload of money, my phone has been blowing up with cancelations, many of whom I bent over backward to appease because of *you*, and now I have the cops breathing down my neck."

Ackerman leaned over and opened the glove box. He reached inside and grabbed the unopened pack of cigarettes. He'd quit smoking them months ago, but he kept the pack around in the event of an unforeseen emergency.

If anything was going to qualify as an *emergency*, this was it.

He tapped the pack several times against the dashboard, and then ripped the protective cellophane off, as he listened to the irate chatter.

Ackerman could count on one hand the number of people he'd ever let talk to him this way and still have fingers left to spare.

"You make this sound so easy," he replied, as he slipped a cigarette into his mouth and lit it. "I can control a lot of things, and I can keep a lot of people under control, but a cop with a subpoena isn't one of them."

Ackerman cracked the window, to allow the cigarette smoke to escape. He hated being put in this position. He understood the business he was in and had always taken extra precautions to keep himself as insulated from problems as he could. If something arose, he dealt with it or he made it go away. Most things could be remedied by money or a liberal application of force. Neither of those solutions was currently available to him under these circumstances.

"No, the impression I got was that they were focused solely on her. Right now all they think is that I'm trying to protect some rich assholes in Hollywood, but you and I both know the potential shit storm that is on the horizon. Some *A-lister* getting his rocks off, with a barely legal bimbo, will be the least of our problems if they start digging into shit."

Ackerman took a long drag on the cigarette, the rush of nicotine making him feel slightly light-headed for a moment.

"Look, I will do everything in my power to keep this quiet. If they show up with a subpoena, my lawyer is prepared to file a motion to quash, but realistically that will only buy us a brief respite. If they show up with a search warrant, we're fucked. Let's not forget, they're calling this a murder investigation."

The problem with being in this type of business *relationship* was that it was never equal. Ackerman, who was normally accustomed to being the one *giving* the orders, now found himself in the unenviable position of *taking* them. People like this didn't get bogged down with the details, they told you what they wanted done. Whether or not what they were asking you to do was even possible didn't concern them.

"Like I said, I will do my best," Ackerman replied, "but you also need to be realistic about this. There are things that I cannot guarantee."

A second later the phone went silent after the call was terminated on the other end.

"Well good fucking bye to you too," he muttered angrily, tossing the phone onto the passenger seat.

Ackerman wanted to be pissed, but he knew that this had been a self-inflicted wound.

When he had first been approached he had jumped at the opportunity. It had opened up a world for him that in the past he could only have dreamed about. There had been no need for any coercion; no *gun-to-the-head* moment. No, he had willingly gone along with the proposition, because he wanted the money and the access that came with it. He rationalized that everyone involved was an adult, or at least an *almost-adult* in a few instances, but there were no innocents. All he did was provide a service for a nominal fee. What they did *beyond that* was their choice. If some celeb or politician wanted to have a little extra fun on the side, with boys or girls, it wasn't his place to judge.

Ackerman wasn't the morality police. To him it was a business transaction; plain and simple.

In some ways this little business relationship was like a marriage. When things were going good, and the money was rolling in, people ignored the bumps in the road, but that only applied when times were good, and these weren't good times. Now the question was, what was he going to do about it?

It was clear from the conversation that this bag of shit was being laid at his doorstep. Ackerman was all for being loyal, but he'd already gone to prison once and wasn't looking to repeat that experience any time soon.

There was an old mafia saying, '*a fish with its mouth closed never gets caught.*' And while that was true, it wasn't reality. He'd made the mistake of getting into bed with celebrities and politicians, neither of whom was renowned for being tight-lipped. Eventually, someone would talk first and they would get the best deal. That's how it always worked. Everyone hated a snitch until they ended up in cuffs; then it became every man for himself.

Ackerman reached over and picked up the cell phone. He scrolled through the contacts until he found the number he wanted and hit the call icon. After several rings the call went to voice mail.

"Hey, it's Devin, something is brewing and I will need you to get out in front of it. Call me back as soon as you can."

CHAPTER TWENTY

1 Police Plaza, Manhattan, N.Y.
Tuesday, October 28th, 2014 – 7:51 p.m.

"Look at you burning the midnight oil."

Maguire looked up to see Sandy Barnes standing in the doorway and motioned her in.

"I was going to call you, but as I was leaving, I saw your Suburban in the garage."

"Melody is home getting ready for a trip," Maguire said, as Barnes sat down in one of the chairs. "I figured I would just end up being in the way."

"Smart man," Barnes replied.

"Why are you here so late?"

"Well, you see, it's like this..."

Maguire leaned back in his chair, crossing his arms over his chest. "That's never a good way to start a sentence, Sandy."

"Well, don't expect it to get any better," she said.

"I really need to keep a bottle of Jamison in my filing cabinet."

"After this case, I'd recommend that you keep two."

"Okay, just let me have it."

"I got a call from Billy Walsh. He said that his detectives had previously spoken to security at the apartment building and planned to pick up a copy of the surveillance video."

"Why did it take so long?"

"Supposedly the video system is all digital and only handled by their IT guy, who was out of town."

"So what is the problem?"

"Problem is that when they went to pick it up, they were told that there was an issue and that it wasn't available. When they pressed the IT guy, he told them that there had been some type of *technical glitch* and that the video was deleted instead of being downloaded."

"Well that sounds like some rather convenient bullshit," Maguire replied.

"That's exactly what they thought, but when they tried to push the issue, the head of security intervened. He told them that the video was gone and that there was nothing more to discuss; then he told them to leave."

"Do we know who the head of security is?" Maguire asked.

"I just got a name," Barnes replied, "Brian Reedman."

"Brian Reedman?"

"Yeah, you know him?"

"If it's the one I'm thinking of, yeah," Maguire replied. "We were detectives together in Intel."

"Makes you wonder why he was so brusque with our people."

"Well, his bread isn't being buttered by the city anymore, so I am sure he has adopted the corporate mindset."

"Even to the point of covering up a crime?"

"Well, to be fair, right now he doesn't know it is a crime."

"You have a point," Barnes replied.

"If it's him, I'd say he is just trying to protect his current paymaster."

"Well, considering the political feelings of *our* current paymaster, do you have any suggestions on how you want them to proceed?"

"Cautiously," Maguire replied.

"I think I made that pretty clear already to Billy."

"Have them stand down on the apartment building portion of the investigation; at least for the time being. The security director pool is a small fraternity. I'll make some calls and find out if it's the same Reedman I worked with. If it is, I'll go over there myself and have a chat with him."

"Hopefully you'll have better luck with him."

"*Hopefully*," Maguire replied.

There was a time when the *blue family* counted for something, but times had changed; even having worked with someone in the past guaranteed nothing. To make matters worse, he and Reedman hadn't been all that close to begin with. Reedman had been assigned to the Municipal Security Section, the part of Intel which protected the mayor and other local dignitaries. Maguire had worked in the Public Security Section which handled protection for high-profile dignitaries like the

President, the Pope and foreign heads of state. As a result, there was a certain amount of *sibling rivalry* which existed between the two and it bubbled up every so often.

One event in particular stood out in Maguire's mind. He'd been handling the security detail for a presidential fundraiser event when he fielded a call from Reedman looking to arrange a photo-op for the former city comptroller. He'd reached out to Rich, who was with the Secret Service and was able to set-up a quick meet and greet with POTUS, before he departed the venue. However, when the time came for Reedman to reciprocate, Maguire learned, that even within a supposed family, some streets were *one-way*.

"I'll see what I can do," Maguire added. "So where are we at with Devin Ackerman?"

"Not sure," Barnes replied. "The detectives went out and had a chat with him. Their takeaway was that he was basically clueless as to what actually happened to our victim. They convinced him they weren't interested in whatever extracurricular activities he was running, but that they needed to know who Amber met that night."

"Do I really want to know?" Maguire asked.

"Well, that's the problem. According to Ackerman's records, she wasn't meeting with anyone."

A scowl formed on Maguire's face, as he contemplated the news. If there was one thing he didn't need right now was another mystery to solve.

"No one?"

"Not according to Ackerman. When he looked it up, it turned out the guy who she was supposed to meet, this past weekend, had canceled because of a scheduling conflict."

"And we are sure of this how?"

"Does the name Stefan Bishop ring a bell?" Barnes asked.

"You're not serious?"

"I wouldn't joke about that."

Not only did Maguire know who Stefan Bishop was, so did just about every man, woman and most adolescent kids. He was a prolific sci-fi writer who was hailed as the *king of speculative fiction*. He'd amassed over sixty books in the genre; eight of which had been turned into major motion pictures. He also had an estimated worth of several hundred million dollars. Maguire could only imagine the shit storm that would erupt if word of his potential involvement leaked out to the press. You didn't even hint at people like that being involved in a sex scandal without iron-clad evidence to back it up.

"And we know beyond a doubt that he wasn't with her this weekend?" he asked.

"Yeah, they reached out to his publicist who confirmed that he has been on a book tour in Australia since October 4th. At the time of the murder he was doing a book-signing in front of several hundred adoring fans."

"Well, as long as he hasn't figured out how to time-travel, I guess that puts us back to square one."

"Pretty much," Barnes replied.

"What about any other *clients*?"

"They tried to get more information, but Ackerman balked. Prying out one name was hard enough, but he's not willing to give us *carte blanche* without paper."

"You think it's worth getting a subpoena?"

"I'm sure he won't be thrilled, but they said it appeared as if he was simply trying to cover his ass."

"I'll speak to Angela Washington in the morning and have her draw-up a *subpoena duces tecum*. If he's just looking to play CYA that should suffice, if not then we're shit out of luck."

"I need not remind you, but we're already treading in dangerous waters."

"Someone has to," Maguire replied.

Barnes stared quietly at Maguire, and he could almost hear the gears spinning in her head.

"Come on, Sandy, out with it."

"I get it," she replied hesitantly. "I do. We're cops at heart and we've been there before. Trying to deal with the aftermath of the tragedy, to make heads or tails out of what happened, all while meting out some form of justice for the victim and punishment for the perpetrator, but I have to ask will it be worth it in this case?"

Maguire stayed silent for a moment, as he considered the question.

The truth was his own thoughts had been consumed with it ever since he'd walked out of the meeting at city hall. Being police commissioner wasn't a job he'd ever wanted, or even imagined he'd ever be doing, but life was odd that way. In his heart he was still a cop, not a politician, and try as he might, he just couldn't switch sides as easily as some of his predecessors had done.

"Have you ever had a case that has haunted you?" Maguire asked softly.

"I don't know if *haunted* would be the right word, but I have had a few that have stayed in my head throughout the years."

"Then consider yourself lucky, Sandy," he said. "Back in December of 1999, I was in Street Crime. We were having a brutal cold snap. It was so bad that all the local shitheads had abandoned the streets to stay warm. My team was hitting all the usual spots in Brooklyn North, hoping to kick something up, but it was just dead. We'd grabbed some coffee at a Dunkin' Donuts on Myrtle, and were about to head back to our base over on Randall's Island, when my partner, Joey Faggione, says to head over to Wyckoff and Myrtle. When it came to collars he was the eternal optimist. We'd been sitting there for about fifteen or twenty, minutes when we see this old lady come out of the subway station. She's getting ready to cross the street when this little shit-bird comes be-bopping up from the hole, snatches her pocketbook, and pushes her to the ground. We bail out of the car and the race is on. Joey stopped for a minute to make sure our victim is okay, while I chased the perp up Wyckoff. It's cold as fuck. The wind is stinging my face and making my lungs burn with each breath of air I take."

"He makes a right on Gates and really opens it up. I mean he's hitting NFL wide-receiver speed. Next thing I know, I hear the squealing of tires behind me and then Joey goes flying past me in the unmarked. The kid looks back and immediately heads up the sidewalk, trying to keep the trees between him and the car. Joey speeds past him, to cut him off at the end of the street, and I see this kid take a sharp left turn, jump a gate, so he can head down the alleyway. It was obvious that he had done this before. Only problem was he misjudged his speed going over the gate and missed the alleyway. When I got there I hear screaming coming from the bottom of the stairway that led to a basement. At first I thought he was just hurt, but then I realized there was something weird about his screams. It was fear, not pain. Joey and I get down there, cuff him up, and we find out why he's screaming; he'd landed on a body."

"The Eight-Three shows up and everyone wants to know what happened. It turns out the body was of a young girl, around twelve or thirteen years of age. Squad does a canvas, but no one is missing from any of the area houses. They try to match it up with any missing person reports from the surrounding precincts, but they come up empty. M.E. determined death was caused by strangulation, but that was it. No other signs of any physical or sexual assault. I stayed in touch with the lead investigator and he told me they had taken to calling her Angel Blue, because of the blue blanket she'd been wrapped up in. To this day the identity of that little girl, and why she was killed, remains a mystery."

"I remember that case," Barnes said somberly. "I was in the One-Oh-Four back then."

"When I was in Intel," Maguire said. "I was working a protection detail during the U.N. General Assembly. I was partnered with a guy who'd been in Brooklyn South Homicide and we had a lot of time on our hands. I asked him the same question I asked you and, without missing a beat, he said that he had lost count. I asked why it bothered him so much and his answer was profound. He said that when they first heard of a person's death, the family and friends were usually devastated. They'd cry, scream, and collapse in each other's arms; desperate to find some comfort for the pain they were feeling. As the days turned into weeks, and then into months, the pain would gradually dissipate and life would return to normal. Maybe not the old normal, but a new normal; it had to be that way. They were alive, and they needed to live. No one could live in a perpetual state of agony. The family and friends would move on, but for the homicide detective, things were different. It wasn't personal, it was professional, and moving on was much more difficult. The unsolved ones gnawed at you, haunted your waking moments. It was like death itself was taunting you, reminding you that you were the last hope for the victim and you simply weren't good enough. When I came back here, after our little meeting, the first thing I did was to pull the crime scene photo of Amber Skye and remind myself this isn't personal, it's professional."

"Even if that means you might suffer professionally by pursuing this?" Barnes asked.

"Sandy, if I am more worried about keeping this chair, instead of doing the job that comes with the chair, then I don't deserve to be sitting in it."

"I think the last person to sit in that chair and have that same sentiment was Theodore Roosevelt."

"Yeah, and if memory serves me correct, they pulled the rug out from under old T.R. for being so diligent."

"He didn't land too hard," Barnes replied. "Governor, vice-president, and president."

"I think it's a safe bet that this flag," he said, hooking his thumb behind him at the ceremonial flag of the New York City police commissioner, "is the last one I'll ever have."

"Ah, never say never," she replied, with a wry smile. "So we will still continue to investigate this?"

"Yes," Maguire replied, "but *very* discretely."

CHAPTER TWENTY-ONE

Whitestone, Queens, N.Y.
Tuesday, October 28th, 2014 – 9:12 p.m.

Arianna Barone sat on the window seat, staring out into the darkness, as she cradled the crystal tumbler, half-filled with whiskey, in her hands.

Outside, an angry rain pelted the second-floor bedroom window, but even the raging storm was no match for the emotions swirling around inside her. Arianna looked down at the black, churning waters of the East River, as she took a sip of her drink. She'd already become numb to the burn of the amber liquid, as it went down her throat.

She glanced back over her shoulder and carefully examined the room she was in; it was *her* room, Mikala's room.

That isn't entirely true, she thought, *but it was supposed to be*.

They'd always had a rather strained relationship, no thanks to her parent's interference, but the two of them had been working on repairing it.

When Mikala first began attending Columbia, she had reached out to her and asked if they could have coffee together. At first Mikala had resisted, but eventually she'd agreed to it on the condition that they met on neutral territory; in this case a Starbuck's within walking distance of the school.

The first time was the hardest. It was obvious that Mikala had a very sizeable wall up, which was understandable. Arianna had to chip away at it carefully. On one hand she knew that her father, Preston Grant, was at the core of their family *issues*, but on the other hand, he also represented the only real parental figure Mikala had ever known.

Arianna knew all too well the intense pressure of growing up in the Grant household. Childhood was no excuse for falling short scholastically and failure was never an option. Unfortunately, sexism was very much alive and well. Her two brothers, being heirs to the Grant name, were held to a much different standard. If they went out, and got drunk, they were just *sowing their wild oats*. The one time she did, and ended up getting pregnant, she was forever labeled a *tramp*.

Looking to her mother, for any type of support, was useless. Annabelle Stevens just stood there demurely, listening while her father berated her. It had always angered her, but in retrospect it made perfect sense to her now. While her father had never physically abused them, he didn't have to be. The verbal abuse was just as effective and didn't leave any scars you'd have to explain. It took her years to come to terms with the fact that her mother had been just as much a victim as she had been.

Arianna had always feared that Mikala would be the next victim, but it didn't take long for her to learn that her daughter was different than she had been. Mikala had an inner strength, and a stubbornness, that must have driven her grandfather crazy.

At times, Mikala could be very hard to read. Sometimes it felt as if she was opening up, but Ariana always got the impression that there was a line that she would go up to, but would never allow herself to pass. Still, Arianna had hoped for reconciliation.

As Mikala had started to share more about herself, Arianna listened and learned. When her daughter had told her how much she loved the color purple, Arianna had the spare bedroom repainted. When their conversation had turned toward the generic furnishings at the dorm room, Mikala had said she wished she'd had more room so she could put in a real four-post bed. Arianna then replaced the previous one.

To anyone else it might have seemed foolish, but she had been given the chance to re-connect with her daughter and she would not waste it. They had even reached the point where they had been talking about Mikala coming out to spend the Christmas break with them and she wanted everything to be perfect.

But now that would never happen.

What other secrets did you have? she wondered, as she took another sip of her drink.

"Don't you think you've had enough?"

She turned to see her husband standing in the doorway.

"My daughter's dead, Jack," she replied, the words coming out slightly slurred. "I think I've earned the right to mourn her."

"I'm not saying you haven't, Arianna, but I'm worried about you; about the way you are dealing with this."

It was a typical Jack Barone reply.

She nodded her head and smiled dutifully, but it was a joyless smile.

He was always *concerned* about things, but it was rarely rooted in genuine concern. More often than not it revolved around how anything impacted him. So there was more at hand here than her being up in this room for hours, nursing a bottle of whiskey.

"And when you say you're worried, Jack, do you mean you're worried about me or are you just worried about the optics?"

"Look, I didn't come up here to argue with you," he replied, "but I need to know if you will be able to hold it together."

"Oh, I'm terribly sorry, do we have something equally pressing on our agenda, besides burying my daughter, that I need to address?" she asked sarcastically.

"We're supposed to be attending a rally tomorrow night for Congressman Waters," Jack replied, "but if you don't think you can make it, I'll...."

"You'll do what, Jack? Cancel?" she asked. "Are you going to tell them there is a family emergency you need to attend to?"

"I'll let them know you won't be attending."

"Of course," she replied, with a sardonic laugh. "Will it be the common flu or perhaps food poisoning? I know, how about I just die too? I'm sure you can parlay the whole widower thing into some political capital. It would surely garner you and the *good* congressman some sympathy votes."

"Arianna, I don't want to do *this* with you. I'm just saying that we have events already scheduled. If we have to alter them, we should do it sooner rather than later."

"How about you comfort me, Jack?" she asked.

It wasn't a sarcastic response, but one that could only be described as forlorn. If he heard it, he didn't show it.

"I'll just let them know you're not feeling up to it."

"So what you're saying is that you are still going?"

Jack starred at her with a baffled look.

"Carl is in a very tight race, dear, and the election is next week," he replied. "It's not like it can be rescheduled."

In a flash, Arianna's despondency disappeared, replaced by something more primal. Her face darkened and her jaw set firmly.

"Get out," she hissed, through tightly clenched teeth.

"Arianna, please...."

"*Get Out!*"

Her scream filled the small room, shocking Jack's senses.

In the nearly two decades that they had been married, he couldn't recall ever hearing her raise her voice, and if she had, it had never been directed at him. If the scream had caught him off-guard, it paled in comparison to the sound of the crystal tumbler whizzing through the air and smashing against the doorframe, mere inches from his head.

Barone turned away quickly; just in time to avoid taking the spray of glass shards and whiskey to his face. As he carefully turned back around, his wide-eyes revealed an equal mix of both shock and fear.

"I told you to get out," Arianna said, in a low, menacing voice.

Jack opened his mouth, as if to respond, but immediately thought better of it. He was in uncharted territory, with someone who was clearly beyond reason, so he did the only sensible thing he could and left the room.

Arianna stared at the vacant doorway for a few minutes longer and then turned her empty gaze back toward the window. Off in the distance she could see the long string of bright, white lights that framed the suspension cables of the Throgs Neck

Bridge, rising up from the roadway until they reached the tops of each tower, some three hundred feet above the water, where they changed into red warning lights.

Arianna reached down toward the floor, grabbing the long neck of the now half-empty whiskey bottle with her fingers, and raised it to her lips.

I wonder how much it would hurt to hit the water from that height? she thought.

CHAPTER TWENTY-TWO

1 Police Plaza, Manhattan, N.Y.
Wednesday, October 29th, 2014 – 8:06 a.m.

"Deputy Commissioner Washington" a woman's voice said on the other end of the phone.

"Angela, its Commissioner Maguire."

"Good morning, sir, how are things up on the 14th floor?"

"Crazy enough to make me wish I was still in the navy," he replied.

"Well, I could think of worse things than to be sailing around the world on the government's dime."

"That's the lie they tell you to get you to enlist," Maguire replied. "Then you end up on an aircraft carrier in the North Atlantic watching as four and five story waves come crashing over the bow."

"Oh hell no," she replied. "I think I'll just stick to my Caribbean cruises, thank you very much."

"Smart lady."

"I know you didn't call down here to get free travel advice," she said. "So how can I help you?"

"I need you to draw up a *subpoena duces tecum* for electronic records," he replied. "And I need it done right away."

"What is this regarding?"

"It's a homicide investigation that the Manhattan South Squad is looking into."

"Why don't you just ask Elliot Nader over at the Manhattan D.A.'s office?"

"Because this one is a bit *sensitive*," Maguire replied. "That's why I called you direct. I would like to avoid any unnecessary entanglements for the time being."

"You're the boss," Washington replied. "So whose day are we ruining?"

"It's a company called Home2Home, and the principal is a guy named Devin Ackerman."

"*The* Devin Ackerman," Washington asked.

"You know him?"

"I worked on his federal case," Washington replied.

"For or against?"

"For," she replied. "But he wouldn't even know me. I was a research clerk, while I was going through law school, at the office that represented him. You know that boy's into some really shady shit."

"Hence the reason I would like to keep it off the front page for now," Maguire replied. "Let's just say that he hasn't become any less shady in his old age and I'm sure that the *players* involved are just as formidable."

"You know the odds are good that he'll reject this."

"I know, but I'll cross that bridge when I get to it."

Just then there was a knock on the door. Maguire looked up to see Antonucci standing there and waved him in, motioning him to take a seat.

"So what are we asking for?" Washington asked.

"Any and all records, written or electronic, pertaining to the clients of a woman named Amber Skye," he replied. "Have it go back to the first of the year."

"Sounds to me like Devin didn't learn his lesson. I imagine these records will have the potential to be a nightmare."

"I'm not even sure it's limited to just the political sphere," Maguire replied. "This could be one of those scorched Earth situations."

"All I can say is better you than me," Washington replied. "I'll get this drawn up right away. Have the detectives ask for me and I'll hand deliver it to them."

"Thank you, Angela," Maguire said.

"Give me one sec, Ang," he said, as he pressed the button to end the call, then dialed the extension for Barnes.

"Sandy, I just got off the phone with Angela. She's going to draw up the subpoena right away," he said. "Have your detectives stop by her office and ask for her personally."

"Will do," Barnes replied. "And just for the sake of argument, what do you want them to do if he complies?"

"If he gives them the records, you tell them to get their asses back here lights and sirens. Then the four of us are going to sit in a locked room and see just how bad this situation really is."

"So we're going to go ahead with interviews?"

"I don't have the answer to that yet, Sandy," Maguire replied. "Odds are that the vast majority didn't even know who they were tapping, but we will not know until we look. Right now I'm trying to formulate a plan which, if the political bullets start flying, does its best to keep our people from becoming collateral damage in the crossfire."

"Okay, I'll get them on it," she replied.

"Thanks," Maguire said and hung up the phone.

"You might be too late on that last one, boss," Antonucci said.

"Sounds like you're about to ruin my morning."

"Our little friend on the 13th floor made another phone call."

"Son of a bitch," Maguire said, raising his hands to his face and rubbing his eyes. "Can't I catch just one goddamn break?"

Antonucci sat there quietly, he knew it wasn't his question to answer.

"When?" Maguire asked.

"Yesterday," the man replied. "Around 1645 hours. He was probably on his way home."

"So we have to assume she already knows something is up," Maguire said.

"Maybe, maybe not," Ang replied. "I checked, and the speaker flew down to Puerto Rico yesterday morning. It looks like she went down there with a bunch of congressional reps to push for statehood. Judging from the brevity of Acevedo's call, I think he got her voicemail. Anyway, he sent a text a few moments later asking her to call him."

"Did she?"

"Not yet, but that just means the clock is ticking."

"This whole thing is ticking, like a goddamn time bomb, Ang."

"If you don't mind me saying, why not just let it go?"

"I've been battling that question myself, but the reality is we can't. I'd like to be virtuous and say that I am like some proverbially *knight on a white horse* here, championing the victim, but the truth is I'm basically just fucked no matter what I do."

"How so?"

"If I simply give-in, and sweep this bag of shit under the rug, then I've failed the victim, let a murderer walk free and don't belong in this chair. However, if I investigate it to its rightful conclusion, then I am committing career suicide and I end up getting bounced out of the chair anyway."

Antonucci frowned, "I don't envy your decision, boss."

"If that was just the two choices I would be okay with it. I'd rather get bounced for doing the right thing than the politically expedient thing. That being said, there's a third possibility in play. Even if I play the part of the good soldier, and sweep it under the rug, it may still leak. In that case not only do I get bounced, but there's a very strong likelihood that the D.A. launches an investigation."

"A case where the cover-up is worse than the crime," Antonucci replied.

"Exactly," Maguire replied. "So stay on top of things, but do it quietly."

"Aye aye, sir."

CHAPTER TWENTY-THREE

DUMBO, Brooklyn, N.Y.
Wednesday, October 29th, 2014 – 11:53 a.m.

Dean Oliver sat at the dining room table, staring out the apartment's large, panoramic window, a half-eaten western omelet growing cold on the plate in front of him, as Eliza Cook's words echoed in his head.

"Good, because I would really hate for you to end up being one of those loose strands that I have to cut free."

There were very few people that Oliver was afraid of, but she was at the top of the list.

They'd first met years ago when he was assigned as a State Department, Bureau of Diplomatic Security liaison to the senate intelligence subcommittee that was investigating the discovery of a U.S. military arms cache that had gone missing in Nairobi, Kenya and then ended up in southern Sudan. Unfortunately, the regional security officer had been *tragically* killed in a hotel suicide bombing before he could testify, so Oliver had been sent in his place. At the time he had been the assistant regional security officer at the embassy.

Cook was formidable, and at times her questioning of him bordered on a hostile interrogation, but he held his own; begrudgingly garnering her respect. It wasn't till much later, after Cook had done some checking, that she learned that Oliver had been a special forces' intelligence sergeant and realized that he would never have folded. It was that prior *experience* that ultimately landed him his current position.

What the senate committee never learned, thanks to a creative blurring of the lines between truth and fiction, was that the cache had been part of a covert CIA operation, code-named *Safe Neighborhood*, which was intended to arm a local warlord who was allied with the Sudan People's Liberation Army, in his fight against the Sudanese Armed Forces. At the time the SPLA were fighting a civil war against the Sudanese government to establish an autonomous South Sudan. While the United States overtly maintained their distance from the conflict, behind the scenes they had taken on a more covert assistance role against the Sudanese government that had allowed Osama bin Laden to operate terror training camps in the Sudan desert.

The arms were delivered, but, much to the chagrin of the CIA, the warlord had accepted a more lucrative offer from the Sudanese government and the weapons ended up in the hands of the Sudanese military. To mitigate any potential political fallout, the *theft* of the weapons was attributed to Barasa Mwangi, a private security contractor working for the State Department, who had been responsible for checking vehicles entering and exiting the diplomatic compound. When the Kenyan Police Service went to arrest him, they discovered Mwangi dead from a self-inflicted gunshot wound to his right temple. The investigation was closed long before anyone realized that the man was left-handed.

After impressing her with his poise at the hearing, it wasn't long before Cook used her network of political contacts to pull some strings and had him assigned, at least on paper, to a non-existent desk at the D.C. field office. For all intents and purposes he was still a member of DSS, but in practicality he was all hers.

Cook recognized that Oliver had a particular set of skills which might come in handy someday. For his part, having a powerful senator as a benefactor was an offer that was too good to turn down.

At first, she used his services for rather mundane things, such as pre-employment background checks of potential staffers. These weren't the *usual* security inquiries; these focused more on finding the potentially exploitable bad habits in a person's life. If a staffer had a messy family problem, which came to the attention of the authorities, Oliver made sure the case disappear. It wasn't long before he was her full-time driver and bodyguard. When Cook ascended to the post of secretary of state, things took a different path.

Within days he was summoned from his cubicle in Dunn Loring, Virginia to *Foggy Bottom*. It was the first time he and Cook met in a SCIF. While he had been able to hide his previous role, in operation safe neighborhood, from the senate intel committee, he couldn't hide it from his new boss.

He'd sat there stone-faced, as Cook read off the transcript of his testimony. While he maintained a stoic façade, charges of perjury swirled around inside his head. When she got to the CIA after-action report, which detailed Oliver's participation in the neutralization of *subject one*, also known as Barasa Mwangi, he could almost feel the walls closing in on him. While it was unlikely that she would have him shipped off to Kenya anytime soon, there were other charges which could find him occupying a cell in a federal prison for a very long time.

When Cook was finished, she closed the folder over and asked if he had anything to say in his defense, to which he just replied, "No, ma'am."

"Well, in that case, you had better make sure this never sees the light of day," she said, sliding the folder across the desk to him. "Make arrangements to have any personal effects sent over from Virginia. You work out of my office now."

"Yes, ma'am."

"And for the record, Dean, if I ever send you on an errand to handle something as delicate as that, you'd better damn well make sure there is no paper trail left behind. Understood?"

"Crystal clear."

"Good."

And just like that he'd sold his soul to her.

Not that he had any *pangs of guilt*; he'd long ago resolved that issue for himself. He had spent enough time in shithole countries to learn firsthand that it was a *dog-eat-dog* world. There were no innocents in this line of work. The Army had trained him to be what he was, a cold and ruthless taker of souls, and there was no reason at this stage of the game to get contemplative about what his *purpose in life* was. Introspection was for people who'd lost their edge and were looking for a way out.

That didn't mean his recent miscalculation didn't weigh heavily on him. In fact, his current mood was about as dark and foreboding as the clouds that hung low in the distance over the lower Manhattan skyline obscuring the upper floors of many of the skyscrapers, including the new Freedom Tower.

What a stupid fucking name, he thought. *What the hell did it have to do with freedom?*

He'd watched with interest as the skeletal structure first cleared the tops of the neighboring buildings and then grew higher with each new floor. He'd thought they would have come up with some impressive new architectural design, but by the time they'd added the massive spire on top he'd concluded that this wasn't a monument to freedom; it was just another commercial office building.

For one thing, it was smaller than either of the original towers and they had to kiss someone's ass to get the building's spire included, as part of the *essential design* of the architecture, to claim the top spot. If they had really wanted to make a strong statement, they would have rebuilt the original two towers, added a few more floors for good measure, and hung a big, neon 'Fuck You Very Much' sign from the top of it. That was how you sent a real message to your enemies.

"I swear this country is being run into the fucking ground by pussies," he muttered in disgust, as he picked up the plate and headed off to the kitchen.

It was one reason he was so loyal to Cook. She might have had her moral *shortcomings*, but she wasn't naïve. She was decisive and put the needs of the country first. Too many in D.C. thought they could play nice-nice with the bullies of the world, who would realize the errors of their ways, and would throw away their weapons before breaking out into a chorus of *kumbaya*.

Oliver knew first-hand that the world was a tough place and our enemies only understood one thing, strength. If you wanted them to stop their bullshit, you hit them so hard it made them never want to get hit again.

He finished washing his plate, setting it down on the drying rack, then turned and made his way toward the bedroom, his footsteps bouncing off the unadorned, stark white walls.

The casual visitor to the apartment would have assumed that he liked the minimalist style, but Oliver embraced nothing beyond the bare essentials; at least for household furnishings. There was the dining room table, four chairs, a black leather couch, a twin bed, and nothing else.

Oliver maintained a zero electronic footprint. No television, no radio, no computer, nothing. Not that he was opposed to those things, he used them almost every day, in connection with his job, he just didn't want them intruding on his sanctuary. The only exception was his cell phone and that was because she made him keep it available at all times.

No, when he was here he preferred to be productive. The floor across from the couch was lined with stacks of books. There were a few novels, but most them were non-fiction works. They included biographies of famous and infamous influential leaders, history, military, theology, and science. Oliver's belief was that television and computers were the tools they used to dumb you down, but books educated you. The irony that his apartment was at the center of a neighborhood anchored in technology start-up companies was not lost on him.

He walked into the bedroom and opened the closet door. He fished a key fob out of his pocket and ran it along a seam of the back wall until he heard an audible *click*. Then he pushed on the wall, watching as it opened to reveal a small, but well stocked secret room.

Affixed to the right wall were a series of carbon fiber pegboard sheets that held an array of weapons; everything from a .50 caliber Barrett M82 *anti-material* sniper rifle to the Heckler and Koch G3 battle rifle. There were also several other pieces, from the venerable M-4 carbine to the MP-5 submachine gun. Directly underneath was a shelf that contained a variety of handguns ranging in caliber from .22 up to the venerable Colt .45.

Oliver reached down and picked up his Sig Sauer model P226. He slid the gun into a shoulder holster and then put the rig on. When he was done, he turned to the left and removed one of the numerous plastic shoe boxes that lined one of the shelves. He set it down on a small table and began rummaging through it; selecting a wallet, which he put into his pocket, along with several other items. When he finished, he walked back out, listening as the door closed behind him with a reassuring *click*.

Once outside, he grabbed a leather jacket and his car keys, from the coat rack next to the door, then made his way out into the hallway.

One of the primary reasons he had selected this apartment building was that it came with access to an underground parking garage, a blessing when it came to living in this area. Parking was not only rare, but if you found a space, there was no guarantee you'd find your car there the next day. Considering the variety of *tools* he kept locked up in the back of his blacked out Suburban, it was best to have it stored safely.

A few moments later the garage's steel gate opened and the big Chevy pulled forward, much to the annoyance of a hipster, sporting a bushy beard and man bun, who ignored the garage's warning alarm and attempted to cross in front of him. The man angrily yelled out something unintelligible, not that Oliver cared. He just sped up, forcing the man to jump backward, and flipped him off, as he drove away.

"Fucking pussies."

CHAPTER TWENTY-FOUR

Manhattan, N.Y.
Wednesday, October 29th, 2014 – 1:41 p.m.

"Good afternoon, Mr. Big-Shot Security Director."

Brian Reedman looked up from the screen of his laptop computer to see Maguire standing in the doorway.

"Holy shit," the man exclaimed, as he got up and came around the desk. "Talk about big shot! How the hell are you, Mr. Police Commissioner?"

"I'm doing pretty well, Brian," Maguire said, shaking the man's hand, "How about yourself?"

"I have a room with a view," he said, pointing toward the large window that overlooked the city. "Things could always be worse."

Reedman ushered him over toward one of the leather chairs, in the office's corner.

"Yeah, I have a view too," Maguire replied, as he took a seat, "but it just reminds me of how much I never get to go outside."

"Do you want some coffee?" Reedman asked, as he sat down across from Maguire.

"Nah, I'm good."

"It's a far cry from our days in Intel isn't it?"

"It certainly is," Maguire replied. "Who would have imagined back then where we would one day end up?"

"Well, you are a little bit higher up on the food chain than I am," Reedman said.

"It's not all it's cracked up to be. They give you a big title, but they chain you to a desk and only let you out when they need a piñata to beat up on."

"Sounds like the private industry, but at least your punishment comes with a nice retirement package."

Reedman frowned, after the words had come out. For a moment he'd forgotten how Maguire had come to his current position.

"I'm sorry, James."

"Don't be. It is what it is, Brian."

"I was shocked to hear about Rich."

"Thank you."

"You know, there were a lot of great people in the New York office, but he was one of the best."

"That he was," Maguire replied.

"I'm sorry I missed the funeral," the man replied, "but I was out of the country for a while. I sent a condolence card to his wife. How is she doing?"

"Mary is doing about as well as can be expected," Maguire replied. "She has her girls to take care of, and I think that helps to keep her mind focused a bit. They spend a lot of time on the weekends out at our place."

"It's nice to hear that she hasn't been forgotten," Reedman said. "It seems like the minute you're gone from the job, they forget you were ever there."

"That's the motto of the job," Maguire said. "When you're here you're the best, when you're gone you're a pest."

"Isn't that the truth?"

"So how long have you been here?"

"About six months now," Reedman replied. "After I retired, I got hooked up with the Bahrainis. I ended up running the protection gig for Prince Rashid bin Ali. He's a minor player on the *royal family farm league*, but the man has deep pockets."

"Tough life," Maguire replied.

"Yeah, it's a helluva lot better than putting in overtime slips for *time* that you can never take off. Still, after about a year I just couldn't keep up with the travel. My body, and my liver, needed a break. The kid's old man purchased a bunch of coastal real estate, both here and in California. He asked me if I wouldn't mind running a couple of them and getting security up to his liking."

"Not too shabby."

"Nope, when the weather gets nasty here I hop on the private jet he keeps over at Teterboro and by five I'm enjoying dinner with a view of the Pacific."

"It beats the hell out of *dirty water dogs* on the plaza."

"Yeah, from what I hear you ain't eating too many of them," Reedman replied. "Word is you're getting hitched soon."

"Bad news travels fast," Maguire said with a laugh.

"I've seen photos of your betrothed on the covers of several magazines. If that's *bad news* sign me up for two scoops."

"You're right; I'm definitely dating outside my league."

"So what brings you around to my little corner of the world?" Reedman asked.

"I heard through the grapevine that you had a little mishap with your video system."

"Yeah, *technology*," Reedman said dismissively. "It's not all they make it out to be. It always seems to break down when you need it most."

"What happened?"

"Supposedly a catastrophic hard drive crash, at least according to what the IT guy tells me."

"Catastrophic, huh? You check to see if any hammers have come up missing from your maintenance shop?"

"Not sure where you're going with this, but it happens more frequently than you think."

"Well, maybe I can help with that."

"How so?" Reedman asked.

"I happen to have a bunch of bored computer crime detectives sitting around with nothing to do. How about I send a few of them over to try to recover your missing data?"

"Nah, our guy is top of the line. If he says it's missing I'm okay with that. I wish I could help you, James, I really do, but I can't."

"You can't or you won't?" Maguire asked.

"I don't know what you want me to say."

"Let's cut the shit, shall we, Brian? You and I both know there's more going on than it seems. We both did the same goddamn work a lifetime ago. I know you're not an idiot. If this thing is as radioactive as it appears, you did the smart thing and got yourself a backup insurance policy."

"You know, as well as I do, that we all have to answer to *somebody*."

"Bullshit, Brian, this isn't about someone's *indiscretions*. I don't care who she was fucking or how she was doing it, but this is a goddamn homicide investigation and I'm getting a little bit sick and tired of people worrying about the fucker instead of the dead *fuckee*."

"Whoa, wait a minute, who said anything about murder?"

"Don't play naïve," Maguire said. "If there was nothing to hide, you would have gladly given the video to my detectives when they first asked for it, instead of playing this stupid little game."

Reedman's jaw set firmly in place, as he clenched his teeth. Maguire could see that he was in the throes of a moral dilemma. He had a professional responsibility to protect the company, and its clientele, but he'd also been a cop at one time. He might have been a one-way prick, back in the day, but he still bled blue.

"I'm not asking you to give anyone up," Maguire said, seizing the momentum of the conversation. "Just let me *see* the video and give me an idea of what I am up against. In exchange I'll give you my word that I will pursue this completely independent of your help. Neither you nor the company will ever be mentioned."

"Do you have any idea what you're asking me to do?" Reedman asked.

"No, Brian, I don't, and I won't unless you show me the damn video."

Reedman swallowed hard, as he wrestled with his choices. Without saying a word he got up and walked over to a large mahogany service table that sat against the far wall. On one end sat a large bronze statue of a cowboy on a broncing horse. Reedman laid the statue on its side and twisted the granite base, revealing a hidden compartment. He reached in and removed a USB thumb drive and set it on the table.

"I'm going to go out and get some fresh coffee," he said, with his back turned to Maguire. "I'll be gone for about an hour. Leave the drive and don't be here when I get back."

Maguire watched as the man turned around and headed out of the office, closing the door behind him when he left.

He got up and grabbed the drive, then sat down behind the desk. He slipped the device into the USB port and watched as a folder appeared on the screen. Maguire opened it up to discover there was only one video file shown, so he clicked it and watched as the surveillance camera monitoring program appeared on the screen. The view was divided into six separate windows and covered a variety of different camera locations including the garage, front entrance, elevator banks and a long hallway.

Maguire's eyes darted back and forth between the various screens. In a way it was nerve-wracking, like waiting for the train wreck you knew would happen, but didn't know exactly when. After about ten minutes he saw a glint of light flash at the far end of the hallway; from where the apartment door had opened. The dark figure of a man stepped out into the hallway and then the light faded away, as the door shut behind him.

So you were still alive, he thought, as he watched the man make his way down the hallway toward the camera.

The tension built with each second as the man drew closer. Then, as if on cue, the man glanced up for a brief moment and Maguire saw the face of Alan McMasters staring up at him.

"Jesus Fucking Christ."

CHAPTER TWENTY-FIVE

Windsor Farms, Richmond, Va.
Wednesday, October 29ᵗʰ, 2014 – 6:23 p.m.

"Coffee, ma'am?"

Melody looked up at the waiter standing next to her chair holding an ornate silver coffee pot.

"Yes, please," she replied.

Melody wasn't one for these types of events, but she knew that saying yes to Eliza's offer would bring about some necessitated changes in her life. By accepting the offer she became a politician and, like them or not, campaign events were a staple of political life. They came in a variety of different sizes and styles; the most common one being the big venue events. That's where the campaign got the most exposure, from media coverage to potential voter participation. Those were the bread and butter ones, where you could gin up the base and also raise some cash.

Beyond those were the private events and that is where the real money began adding up. On the low end you could get into an event for several hundred to a few thousand dollars, but the reality was that you were only getting *in* to that event. Most of the attendees had been *comped* by someone attached to the campaign. You could say you were there, but that was about the extent of it.

As you moved up the fundraising ladder you started to get into some serious money. You could fork over twenty-five or thirty thousand for a plate, but there are still no guarantees. What that got you was access. Beyond the politician, you were in a room with other connected people. Many used these events to secure admission to other things such as the business world, Hollywood, and more. At this price tag it also bought you favor from the folks on the host committee.

For the movers and shakers, those who wanted direct access to the politician themselves, and then you had better be willing to fork down some serious money. In this day and age it was not unheard of to see smaller, more intimate, events go for over one hundred thousand dollars a plate. That was where the real influence was and that was where Melody currently found herself.

Tonight's event was being hosted by Tomas and Alexandria Montoya. Tomas Montoya had come to America from Cuba, with his parents and sister, in July 1980 as part of the *Mariel Boat lift*. The young Montoya soon developed an affinity for video games, but it soon grew beyond gameplay. Over time, his interests began to expand into programing. After graduating college in 1993 he'd gotten a job working for Praxis Entertainment as a lead developer working on a new line of Sci-Fi shooter games. But by the 3rd installment, Montoya was disappointed in the company's overall lack of investment in improving the franchise, so he quit. He approached his father, Roberto, who owned a string of fast-food restaurants in the Miami area, and got a loan of ten thousand dollars to start his own company, Blue Waters Entertainment. When Montoya sold it in 2008, he walked away with just over thirty-two million dollars.

This evening he was playing host to a small, but very influential, group of people in his two acre hilltop estate along the James River. This group included a former speaker of the house, an ambassador to the United Nations, the CEO of a major social media company, two Fortune 500 CFO's, a Hollywood A-list director, and one of the preeminent lobbyists for the defense industry. They had all paid for the opportunity to not only listen, to Cook's vision of the future, but to provide her with some input on which direction *they* would like to see the country go in.

Cook sat at the head of the table, listening politely, as the conversation droned on. They tried their best to be *conversational* with her, but you could still hear the petitioning in their voices.

The ambassador was looking to make a move back into government service, and preferably something with a national security portfolio. The social media wonk was trying to convince her that silicone valley was poised to be an ally for years to come, as long as the government wasn't aggressive in pursuing their *bending* of some of the rules concerning data collection. The COO's were more interested in removing burdensome regulations, while the lobbyist spoke of the need to maintain our forward presence in the Middle East. Melody still hadn't figured out what the Hollywood director's angle was yet, beyond eating, drinking and smiling at her. Fortunately, things were winding down and, if she was lucky, they would be out of here before she had to talk to him.

"I have to admit that I was shocked to hear that you'd joined Eliza's camp."

Melody turned to her left to meet the gaze of Francis Shirer, the former speaker of the house. At first introduction he came across as a rather affable man. He had the disarming look of a stately grandfather, a bit on the portly side, with a soft, southern drawl and a mischievous twinkle in his eye, but it was all a rather deceptive ruse.

Shirer possessed a sharp wit and keen political intellect that made him a formidable person to deal with. He picked up on the subtle things that even the most politically astute persons missed.

"Oh?" she asked. "And why is that?"

"I never took you for the political type," he replied.

"I like to try my hand at new things, on occasion," Melody said with a smile.

That elicited a hearty laugh from Shirer.

"My dear, that's like saying you want to go swimming with the sharks because you've lived in Nebraska all your life."

"Well, I've sat on the sidelines and watched long enough. So when Eliza asked if I would give her my input on the financial sector I figured I could either bitch or help."

"How altruistic of you," Shirer replied. "I wish I had thought to ask for your help back when I was in the speaker's chair."

"Oh, I don't think you needed any help. As I recall, you were the last speaker who passed a balanced budget."

"That wasn't an overly impressive trick. I just forced people to be responsible."

"I would argue that getting the folks in D.C. to be responsible is pretty damn impressive," Melody replied.

"Regrettably, it didn't last very long."

"Maybe you should run again," Melody replied, giving the man a wink.

"That's very kind of you to say, my dear, but my days on the hill are long over. I'm very much happy to sit on the sidelines and prognosticate."

"Oh, does this qualify as sitting on the sidelines?"

"No, I'm just here for the food and the enchanting company."

"I guess that makes this a very expensive conversation for you," Melody said.

"Not for me," Shirer replied. "I'm here to listen for others."

"Oh really? Now you have me intrigued."

"Corporations pay lobbyists to advocate for them to candidates," he said. "I'm here to listen to what the candidates are proposing and then offer my recommendations on who to back, based on those proposals."

"And now that you have heard some of the proposals, who are you inclined to recommend?"

"Between Cook and Whitmore it's an easy decision," the man said. "Don't get me wrong, I like Duncan, as a person, but he's a California congressional clown. How he got the party nod baffles me to this day. Obviously our standards are waning."

Melody did her best to stifle the laugh.

"His pockets have been lined by everyone from the tree huggers to the wind farmers," Shirer continued. "He might be likeable, but his policies are erratic and he can be easily bought off."

"So you will throw your support behind Eliza?"

"Me? No," Shirer scoffed. "I am, after all, from that *other* party, but I will recommend that the money back her. She may play fast and loose with the rules, from time to time, but she's a known commodity and has the backbone to stand up to those nitwits in Brussels."

"I guess any endorsement is better than none," Melody replied.

"Well, to be honest, she became even more appealing when I realized you were on the *Cook Cruise.*"

"Me? Why?"

"Because I always got the impression that you supported *my* side of the aisle."

"I'll be honest with you, Mr. Speaker," Melody said. "I got signed up for a party back when I was in school and just never changed. If I had to say what my affiliation was it would be independent, which is a kind way of saying that both sides have failed me."

"Fair enough," he replied. "I'd have to agree that things haven't been improving very much in recent years. There was a time where we put the rhetoric aside to accomplish meaningful things, but now it just seems as if gridlock is the norm."

"So how do we fix it?" Melody asked.

"Unless you can issue 535 pink slips, I don't think you can."

"That doesn't sound very promising."

"That's just a Washington reality my dear. Remember, the people may elect them, but the party protects them. It's one reason why I think this election is so crucial. I wish it weren't so, but I see it as a tipping point. If we don't reign in the stupidity, I don't know if we will recognize this country by the next decade."

"And you think Eliza can do that?"

"She might have been part of the problem, but she also knows where all the bodies are hidden. More importantly, the parties know that she knows. If they give her any pushback, it will be for show, but I think they will be more inclined to play ball."

"I hope so," Melody said. "It would be a nice change of pace to have a government that was doing their job for a change."

"I'm hoping that your presence in Eliza's inner circle is a sign that the war on American prosperity is finally over. I'm all for government helping folks in their time of need, but I draw the line at the government causing their need in the first place. There are a lot of folks up on the Hill that failed basic economics and I don't want to be around when the money that funds their social welfare programs runs out."

Melody raised her coffee cup up in a toast, "Then let's hope that she can reverse the damage that has already been done, before it's too late."

"Here, here," Shirer replied, touching the edge of his glass to hers.

She took a sip of coffee and out of the corner of her eye she caught Gen peeking into the room. She held up her hand showing that Melody had a call.

"Please excuse me for a moment," she said, as she stood up and made her way out of the dining room.

"What's up?" Melody asked, as she stepped out into the hallway.

"James called," Gen said, handing her the cellphone. "I told him you were still in the dinner."

"And?"

"I don't know," Gen replied. "He just sounded *off*. I asked if he was okay, and he said he was, but I don't know. Like I said, he just sounded a bit off."

"Okay, I'll call him."

She walked outside, making her way down the cobblestone driveway, till she was away from the gathering of vehicles and Secret Service agents. When she felt she was out of earshot range, she called him.

"Hey, cowboy, what's going on?"

"Hi," Maguire replied.

From the tone of his voice she understood what Gen meant. Something didn't sound right and it scared her.

"Are you okay?" she asked, trying not to sound too alarmed.

"Yeah, I'm fine," he replied.

"Liar."

"No, it's just that I have a lot of stuff on my plate right now."

"You need to talk about it?"

"I wish I could, but I can't."

"That sounds pretty dire," Melody replied. "Are there problems with the job?"

"In a manner of speaking," he said. "It's one of those things I wish Rich was here to handle."

"But he's not, babe," she replied. "I get the feeling that it has less to do with the actual job than it does with the politics of the job."

"Damn you're observant."

"I was trained by the best."

"Thanks," he replied.

"I was referring to Gen," she said with a laugh.

"*Ouch.*"

"Just kidding, but in all seriousness I worry about you."

"You worry about me? Why?" Maguire asked.

"Because you're trying to be Rich," she replied, "but that's not who *you* are."

"Some days I don't even know who I am anymore."

"It sounds like you're trying to find an answer to a problem that just needs a big hammer applied to it."

"Did Gen give you that sage advice too?"

"No, that little pearl of wisdom came from a sexy SEAL who taught me that it's not always about being liked, but about being respected."

"I didn't think you listened to me."

"I try not to make it a habit," Melody said sarcastically. "But seriously, do you remember when I was having all those issues with Wilson Pope and the investigation into GDL?"

"Yeah?"

"You told me I had two choices. I could either try to mitigate the damage or I could just open the doors and say 'have at it.' It sounds like whatever issue you are dealing with centers on you trying to mitigate the damage."

"You're right, I am."

"Is it worth it?"

"I guess that depends on what side of the field you're on," Maguire replied.

"Over the years I've had to make a lot of really tough calls," she replied. "Despite what the media likes to think of me, I'm not a cold-ruthless bitch. When we had to cut jobs from a business we acquired, I *felt* those losses. I looked at every personnel record; I saw the *names* of the people. But while I felt it personally, I didn't allow it to affect me professionally."

"The needs of the many outweigh the needs of the few."

"Or the *one*," she replied.

"You're a smart woman, you know that?"

"Flattery will get you everywhere."

"I'll keep that in mind," he said. "So when are you coming home?"

"Hopefully tomorrow, but it just might be a quick turnaround. Eliza is talking about doing a rally in Green Bay on Friday. There's less than a week to go and I'm betting that we will be making a lot of pit stops between now and Election Day."

"Well, I guess I should get used to these new *hours*."

"Do you want me to walk away from it?"

For a moment there was silence on the line, as he thought about it. It was easy to be flippant about something, while it was in the theoretical phase, but once it became real, so did the *issues* that came along with it.

"No," Maguire finally said.

"Be honest with me, James," Melody said. "This train will only pick up steam in the coming days. If you don't want me to do this, tell me now."

"No, this politics *thing* is my issue to deal with. I'm not cut out for it, but I think you are the right person for the job. We can keep blaming the system for being broken, or we can put the right people in and get it fixed. I know you're that person."

"Thanks for the vote of confidence," she replied. "Remember what I told you, like it or not this is *your* department now. Your name is on the door and you have to run it *your* way. If Rich were here, he would tell you the same thing."

"Hey, what's the worst they can do, fire me?"

"I could think of worse things than to have you by my side," Melody replied. "I can always make you my deputy assistant for special projects."

"Oh really?" he said. "And what sort of special projects would that job entail?"

"Me," she said with a chuckle.

"Melody!"

She turned to see Gen walking toward her. Behind her there was a flurry of activity, as the special agents began taking up their positions in anticipation of a departure.

"Hey, cowboy, I have to run," she said into the phone. "Not sure when I'll be able to call you back, but you know what to do, so just do it."

"Yes, ma'am."

"Okay, I'll call you when I can," she said. "Love ya."

"Love you too, angel."

CHAPTER TWENTY-SIX

1 Police Plaza, Manhattan, N.Y.
Wednesday, October 29th, 2014 – 6:37 p.m.

"Commissioner?"

Maguire ended the call with Melody and looked up to see Peter May standing in the doorway.

"Yes, Peter?"

"Sir, I have Council Speaker Flores on the line," the detective said. "She's asking to speak with you."

"Not now, say I'm in a meeting," Maguire instructed the man. "Get a callback number and tell her I will call as soon as I can."

"Yes, sir."

Maguire got up and closed the door. Then he walked over to a filing cabinet and unlocked it. From the top cabinet drawer, behind the rows of stuffed manila folders, he removed a pre-paid cellphone. He powered the phone up, then dialed the number from memory and listened as it rang. A moment later he heard a familiar female voice on the other.

"Hello?"

"Hi, can I speak to Blaine?" Maguire asked.

"Sorry, I think you dialed the wrong number," the woman replied.

"My bad," Maguire said. "Have a good night."

Maguire ended the call, powered down the phone and slipped it into his jacket pocket for disposal, before returning to his desk.

It was part of an elaborate ruse they'd arranged; should they ever need to talk. There were four code names: Chloe, Blaine, Shani and Raven, each of which signified a different level of urgency.

Chloe was Greek and referred to young, *green* foliage. It was used when they just needed to talk. Blaine was an anglicized version of the Gaelic nickname *blá* given to a blonde or *yellow*-haired fellow. This name was cautionary and meant there was something critical for them to discuss. Shani was Hebrew for *red*. If this was used, it was a warning that there was an imminent danger present for the receiver. The final, and most dire, name was Raven. This referred to the *black* bird and literally meant that there was *danger-close*. Just like the bird, the receiver of the message would immediately take flight. Precautions would then be implemented to identify any surveillance and lose them by *any means necessary*. Once they were assured they were clear, they would make their way to a dead-drop where a chalk number would tell them which pre-arranged location they should go to.

The precaution wasn't as much for him these days, as it was for her; although they had both made their enemies over the years. Unfortunately, most of the people she had to protect herself from were her own. The spy game could be decidedly dangerous at times, especially when it was your father that was running the operation. He'd already interjected himself once, with disastrous results, and Maguire wasn't interested in a potential sequel.

A moment later he was drawn from his thoughts by the buzzing of his cell phone.

"Hello?"

"Are you okay?" Tzviya Harel asked.

He could almost hear the panic in her voice.

"I need to have a chat with you."

"What's wrong?"

"I need your help," Maguire replied. "Well, more like your advice."

"What kind of help?"

"Levitzki type help."

"You're joking."

"I wish I was, but I'm serious, Zee, and this has to be off the record."

When a nugget of intel came up in a discussion, it was usually considered fair game within the spy community. Something to be analyzed, evaluated, and stored away for future reference or use. You just accepted it as being part of the cost of doing business and it didn't matter what agency was involved, but she was more than just a Mossad agent. Maguire knew that, if she agreed, everything he said would never be repeated, but he respected her enough to give her at least some information to make that choice.

Meir Levitzki had been a Tel-Aviv politician and a member of the Israeli Knesset. He belonged to the Meretz Party and was a staunch support of the Palestinian state. While outspoken on many social justice issues, he considered by most as being *harmless*. However, that all changed during a routine accounting audit.

Levitzki and his chief of staff, Michal Haskel, routinely visited areas of Israeli and Palestinian conflict, hoping to draw support for a peace solution. One day, while processing invoices for payment, a secretary came upon a bill submitted by Michal Haskel, for a hotel stay in Nablus, a city in the northern West Bank. The only problem was that the secretary was a childhood friend of Ms. Haskel and on the date in question the two of them were having dinner in Jerusalem, some fifty miles away. The ensuing audit of claims filed by Levitzki uncovered several irregularities that led to a referral to the *Lahav 433*, the Israeli police anti-corruption unit. However, it didn't stay with them for long, after a copy of the hotels surveillance video showed that the room, believed to be that of Michal Haskel, was actually occupied by a woman named A'isha Jacir, whose brother was a member of *Da'wah,* the social service wing of the Palestinian terror group, Hamas.

Once Lahav 433 identified the Palestinian connection, they referred the case to the *Shin Bet*, Israel's internal security agency, which was responsible for Arab-related counter-terrorism activities in the West Bank. While Levitzki enjoyed playing the part of a tough guy for the television cameras, that façade was quickly stripped away when he was *interviewed* by members of Shin Bet. As smart as he thought he was, he actually had no idea who he was shacking up with. He'd been led to believe that Jacir, who he knew as Leila Farsoun, was just a community activist trying to shed light on the destruction of Palestinian crops in Nablus by Israeli farmers.

It didn't take them too long to realize that the only thing he was guilty of was trying to make the government pay for the piece of ass he was getting. Unfortunately for him, a forensic examination of his laptop computer discovered a key-logger program had been surreptitiously installed, effectively giving the Palestinians real-time access to it. The IT folks returned the favor by embedding their own program, code-named *olive branch*, into a tantalizing email file, sent by the Foreign Affairs and Defense Committee, outlining proposed Israeli Defense Force operations in the area of the Golan Heights.

While Levitzki's extracurricular activities might have proven to be a blessing in disguise, as the file containing olive branch was forwarded from one Hamas account to another, unlocking them all as it made its rounds, Levitzki himself proved to be another story. As the time approached for his next trip to Nablus, he began panicking. Fearing that he would give the plan away, and Jacir would figure out that he'd been caught, the Shin Bet decided to cancel it, *permanently*. While appearing at a news conference, to outline his latest proposal for a two-state solution, he suffered a chemically induced massive heart attack and died a short time later at a Jerusalem hospital.

Understandably, that *option* was not available to Maguire.

"When and where?" Tzviya asked.

"Your call," Maguire replied, "but the sooner the better."

"Tonight, after eight," she replied. "Now pay attention and don't write this down."

Maguire listened as she gave him the address.

"Find the back door," she said. "It'll be open, just make sure you don't bring any company with you."

"This isn't my first rodeo, Zee."

"Sitting behind a desk for too long makes people complacent," Tzviya said coolly, "and complacency kills."

He was about to reply when he heard the electronic beep alerting him that the call had ended.

"Same old, Zee," Maguire said, as he put the phone into his jacket pocket and stood up.

CHAPTER TWENTY-SEVEN

Turtle Bay, Manhattan, N.Y.
Wednesday, October 29th, 2014 – 7:14 p.m.

"Aruba?" Devin Ackerman fumed, as he read the email from his attorney, Mitchell Avanti. "You've got to be fucking kidding me."

He had spent most of the last forty-eight hours blowing up the man's phone with messages to call him, only to get some curt email about being in Aruba and having piss-poor cell service.

If this had been any other *issue*, it would have been the last, but Avanti wasn't just any run-of-the-mill attorney; he was a *fixer*. Ackerman had been introduced to the man through a friendly politician, whom Avanti had helped make a questionable consent case go away. So Ackerman had put the man on a hefty retainer, not for any particular problem, but should one ever arise, like now and the one time he needed him the man was unavailable till Friday evening.

"You useless fucking cock-sucker," Ackerman swore angrily, as he got up from his desk and walked over to the serving table.

He poured himself a double shot of whiskey and took a sip, as he tried to reign in his anger. There was no issue *yet*, but that didn't mean it wasn't coming. Ackerman was in bed with some heavy-hitters. He wasn't worried about the celebrities, or even the low level folks in Congress, but there were a select few that scared the hell out of him. Ackerman knew that if this case went sideways, he would find himself *persona non grata*. It wasn't the idea of being confined to a six by eight prison cell that worried him; it was the seven by two casket he wanted to avoid.

He downed the remaining whiskey, and refilled the tumbler, before returning to his desk. He wrote a terse email back to Avanti telling him to call him, the moment he got a cell signal, or he had seen his last paycheck from Home2Home.

"Asshole," Ackerman said, as he slammed the laptop screen down.

"Problems?"

Ackerman swiveled around his chair to see a man standing in the doorway.

"Who the fuck are you?" he asked suspiciously.

His secretary normally kept a watchful eye, screening all of his potential visitors, but she had left at six o'clock and must not have locked the front door.

"Oh, I'm sorry," the man said, reaching into his front pants pocket and removing a small black leather wallet. "I'm Detective Callaghan."

Ackerman scowled, as the man opened it to display a gold shield.

"Don't you guys have anything better to do than harass me?"

"I just wanted to ask you a few questions about Amber Skye," the man said, as he entered the office and casually adjusted one of the empty chairs before sitting down.

"Look, I don't want to seem like an uncooperative *prick*, but I told the other detectives that I had given them everything I could. If you guys want more information, you're going to have to come back here with a warrant."

"Well, to be honest with you, I don't work with those other detectives," the man replied. "I'm from the mayor's office."

He watched as the man reached inside his jacket to remove a business card and then slid it across the desk.

Ackerman picked up the card and examined it.

On one side was a gold-embossed detective shield and on the other was the official Seal of New York City. Beneath that was the man's title: *Detective Brian Callaghan – Office of the Mayor*

"That's awesome," Ackerman said, as he nervously tapped the edge of the card against the desk.

It was one thing when this was just being investigated quietly, but the fact that word had leaked out to the mayor meant the cat was out of the bag and things had taken a turn for the worse. Now he had to find out just how much they knew before he hired someone to go to Aruba and drag Avanti's ass back to New York.

"So what do I owe the pleasure?"

"The mayor just wanted me to stop by and make sure that there were no issues and to give you his assurances that he was *monitoring* things."

"Well, I'm sure that *he* thinks that is reassuring, but if he wanted to reassure me, I would stop getting visits from detectives in *his* police department."

The man smiled politely, ignoring the thinly veiled dig.

"Given the fact that Ms. Skye's body was found by civilians, it is hard to completely suppress the matter, but we are working to keep it as confidential as possible," he explained.

"I'm surprised he didn't just call me directly," Ackerman replied.

"Under the circumstances, I am sure you can understand why it would be best if there were no electronic records linking City Hall with Home2Home."

Ackerman grudgingly nodded.

He didn't like it, but he knew that it made sense. Cops didn't like unsolved cases. So if this matter didn't die off quickly and quietly, they would keep poking their noses in places it didn't belong and they would eventually find something. The last thing anyone wanted was a paper trail that might link them to some rather questionable behavior.

"So what do you want from me?" Ackerman asked.

"The mayor is getting updates on the case, but those only tell him part of the story. How much leverage are they using on you?"

Ackerman took a deep breath, "So far, not much, but I expect that to change."

"Why is that?" Callaghan asked.

"They were pushing for me to disclose the identities of Amber's *friends*," Ackerman replied. "I thought I would take the pressure off things, by giving up the name of who she was meeting on Saturday night, but it turns out that she wasn't seeing anyone."

"Really?" the man asked. "She was free on a Saturday night?"

"Well, she had something previously scheduled, but it got canceled."

"Did you give the other detectives that person's name?"

"Yeah, but it's a dead-end and they know it," Ackerman said. "The person she was supposed to meet with is out of the country."

"And they were satisfied with that?" Callaghan asked.

"No, they tried to go out on a fishing expedition," Ackerman replied. "They wanted me to give them a list of the people she had been with going back several months."

"What did you tell them?"

"I told them that if they wanted that kind of information they would have to do a lot more than ask nicely."

"That's reassuring to hear."

"Look, I'm not an idiot," Ackerman replied. "I've already written Amber off as a loss, I'm not going to lose any more revenue unless I'm forced too."

"Meaning?"

"I told them that if they wanted more information, they needed to bring back a warrant."

Callaghan frowned at the news, "What was their response?"

"If I was a betting man, I would say they are probably drawing it up as we speak."

"I don't think the mayor knew they were pushing the investigation this hard."

"Maybe he should remind his people who their boss is?"

"Getting into a dick-measuring contest with detectives isn't exactly a smart move. You might win the immediate battle, but all it takes is for one *Dudley Do-Right* to get his feelings bruised and turn a smoldering ember into a raging forest fire."

"Well, I've done all I can do, but you might want to take the message back to him that the clock is ticking."

"If the warrant gets quashed can they access the information through any other means?"

"No," Ackerman said, shaking his head, as he turned in his chair and pointed toward a small, black rectangular box next to his computer. "All the files are contained on this back-up drive and I'm the only one who has access. When I leave the office it gets locked away in the safe."

Ackerman never saw the gun that fired the fatal round into his right temple.

"I'm sure my boss will be very pleased to hear that," the man replied, as he unscrewed the suppressor from the gun's threaded barrel.

Over the course of the next several minutes he methodically went about getting Ackerman's fingerprints on every facet of the gun, including the spent shell casing and magazine, before running his gloved hand over the dead man's hand in order to transfer gunshot residue particles.

He wasn't overly concerned about the discharge alerting someone nearby. The suppressor did an acceptable job of dampening the noise to where it was unlikely to be recognized. Even if someone attempted to investigate, it was very unlikely they could pinpoint exactly where in the office building that the noise had originated from.

When he was done, he tossed the gun to the ground, in the approximate direction where the recoil would have carried it. He hated the thought of disposing of any gun, but it was a necessary evil. The pistol in question was a *ghost*, an untraceable firearm frame that had come off the assembly line sans serial number. It wasn't one of the crude 3-D printer versions, which often looked more at home in a sci-fi flick, but a fully functional piece that had been produced at a government black-site facility in Azerbaijan. They even went so far as to *obliterate* where the serial number would have been, just to keep any investigators guessing.

In Ackerman's case it would make perfect sense. A convicted felon would not have been able to possess a legal firearm, so having a defaced one would not seem out of the ordinary.

After he had finished staging the scene, he picked up the business card from the desk top before making his way over to the open wall safe, where he examined its contents. He removed several *questionable* items, but left the stack of money. After he was sure there was nothing else of intelligence value, he slipped an envelope inside and locked the door.

It would take them awhile to open the safe, but when they did, they would find a letter from the late Amber Skye, taking issue with her current financial arrangement, and a thinly veiled threat to out the sexual proclivities of a certain state politician. It would be enough of red-herring to cause investigators to consider that it was Ackerman who'd been behind her death and killed himself when the walls started to close in.

Once he had policed the scene, making sure to reposition the chair he had been sitting in, he reached over and disconnected the back-up drive from the laptop.

He paused in the doorway, one last time, and surveyed the scene with a practiced eye.

The man's lifeless body lay slumped over the left edge of the desk; blood pooling on the floor beneath him and the gun on the floor just a few feet away.

There was no need to disguise the cause of death. In this situation, he would give them exactly what they wanted to see.

Dean Oliver smiled one last time at his handiwork before turning around and leaving the office.

CHAPTER TWENTY-EIGHT

1 Police Plaza, Manhattan, N.Y.
Wednesday, October 29th, 2014 – 8:11 p.m.

Luke Jackson glanced up from the newspaper he'd been reading to see Maguire walk out of his office.

"You need something, boss?" he asked.

"No, Luke, I'm just heading down to the gym for a bit," he replied, holding up the athletic bag he was carrying.

"I'll come with you," Jackson said, as he began to get up from his chair.

Maguire waived him off.

"No need," he said. "I might be awhile. I have a lot of steam to blow off."

"Are you sure?" Jackson asked.

"Positive," Maguire replied. "In fact, why don't you and Peter just call it a day? I'm a bachelor tonight, so I think I'm just going to pull an all-nighter here. There's no need for you guys to hang around and baby-sit me."

"It's not a problem," the man said.

"It's an order, Luke," Maguire replied light-heartedly, as he continued toward the private elevator. "Now go home."

"Yes, sir," Jackson said grudgingly.

Maguire stepped inside and hit one of the buttons.

"I'll see you tomorrow," he said, just as the doors closed.

Maguire watched as the floor indicator light ticked off his decent, watching as it by-passed the floor for the headquarters fitness center and stopped in the basement garage. He exited the elevator and made his way toward the office, where he found a bored looking cop reading a book.

"I need a car," he said nonchalantly.

The cop glanced up from the book he had been reading, an annoyed expression on his face, until he realized who the request was coming.

Maguire managed to stifle his laugh, as the man nearly fell out of the old, rickety office chair as he came to attention.

"Sir," the man said, as he saluted Maguire.

"At ease, son," Maguire replied. "I just need a car for a few hours."

"But,....." the man stammered, "you already have a car."

"I need a *different* car," he said.

The cop turned around, looking up at a board where a series of keys hung.

"I have an unmarked Explorer."

"I'll take it," Maguire replied, holding out his hand.

"Yes, sir," the cop said, as he handed him the keys. "Spot thirty-four"

"I'll have it back in a couple of hours."

Maguire was making his way toward the parking spot when he felt the vibration of the cell phone in his jacket pocket. He removed it and looked down at the number.

"Fuck me," he exclaimed softly, as he saw Nydia Flores' name appear on the screen.

He ignored the call, slipping the phone back in his pocket, as he opened the door to the beige colored SUV. A moment later he pulled out of the garage and headed toward the Brooklyn Bridge. Traffic was particularly light this evening, and it only took a few minutes till he was exiting the bridge at Cadman Plaza.

Brooklyn Heights was not only convenient, but it made perfect sense. There were no tolls, nor any traffic cams to record your passage, and just two blocks away you found yourself in a predominantly residential area. More importantly, the streets were narrow and parking came at a premium. If someone wanted to do surveillance, they would have to expend a tremendous amount of resources and hope the stars aligned.

At this time of night, most of the residents were safely tucked away inside their homes, and the streets were tightly lined with cars; like sardines in a tin can. Maguire made use of the congestion, spending about twenty minutes circling around blocks. To anyone observing, he would have appeared like any other hapless resident trying to steal a *warm* parking spot from one of their neighbors. In a way it reminded him of hot-racking on a submarine.

Once he was sure that he had seen no surveillance *tells*, coming from the parked vehicles, he grabbed the first available spot that he could find. In this case, it was about four blocks from the location she had given him. He reached inside the bag and removed a jacket along with a knit watch cap. He slipped them on and got out of the SUV.

Now that he had determined there was no active *vehicle* surveillance, he had to rule out the possibility of pedestrian observation. He made his way along Pineapple Street, walking against traffic until he reached Columbia Heights. Then he ducked down the ramp at Fort Stirling Park and headed toward the promenade. He found an empty park bench and sat down.

To the casual observer he was just another sightseer, one of the countless numbers that came to stare out across the East River, taking in the countless lights that emanated from the office buildings that dotted the lower Manhattan skyline, or to look out to the south where the Statue of Liberty stood in the harbor, her torch burning brightly. But his choice to sit here was purposeful and he didn't move until he was sure that the rhythm of movement was *natural*.

Maguire exited the park and headed north toward Cranberry Street. He had spent time in this neighborhood, so he understood the general layout. It was a fairly affluent neighborhood that consisted of two and three story brownstone row-houses, most of which had been built prior to the Civil War. It didn't take long to locate the black, wrought iron door, which led to the rear yard of the house he was looking for. He glanced around before opening it and then quickly slipped inside.

Maguire took a moment to orient himself to his surroundings. It was an enclosed, but rather unassuming patio. Two Adirondack deck chairs flanked a cast iron *chiminea*, but there was little else to be seen. On his left was a set of concrete steps, which led to the back door of the house, whose interior appeared to be unlit. He knew that she was here and he also knew she was probably watching him with a little smirk on her face.

He made his way up to the door, opened it, and stepped inside.

"Hello?" he called out.

"Down here," a familiar voice called out. "And close the door behind you."

Maguire located the interior door that led to the basement and made his way down the confined staircase.

"It took you long enough," she said, as she stepped out from the shadows.

"I was just doing as I was told," Maguire replied, as his eyes adjusted to the light.

"You're losing your edge," Tzviya said sarcastically. "You used to be much faster."

"Only at certain things," he said dismissively, as he took the seat across from her and his eyes examined the sparsely furnished room. "I love what you've done with the place. Is it yours or theirs?"

Tzviya cocked her head slightly, as she curiously raised an eyebrow.

"Mine," she replied. "For when I need some time away, but is that what you really wanted to see me for, to critique my *decorating* skills?"

"No," he replied.

Even under these poorly lit conditions, he was still struck with just how beautiful she was. Zee's long black hair was draped playfully over her shoulders and he could almost *feel* her green eyes boring into his soul.

Maguire swallowed hard.

It was never easy to see her, yet he couldn't deny the fact that deep down inside he still longed for her. To anyone else she could appear almost fragile, but it was all a ruse. It wasn't a question of whether she was carrying a weapon; the reality was that she *was* a weapon. But in a way, that aspect of danger made her even more intoxicating.

"You're staring," she said.

"Do you want me to stop?"

"I'm not the one with the *fiancée*," she replied.

"That's not fair, Zee."

"Life's not fair, James," she shot back. "You'd better learn to deal with it."

"I did," he said tersely, "years ago."

"I'm glad that *you* were able to move on," she replied. "It must be nice."

The words stung just as much as any punch he'd ever taken.

Perhaps if they'd had a more traditional break-up, complete with all the requisite anger and screaming, they could have each moved on with their lives, but they'd never made it to that point. They were still very much in love when the fate of their relationship had been determined by her father, Major General Shay Harel, the Mossad's chief spymaster. But there was no way for them to take it out on *him*, so their anger simmered, almost as much as their desire for one another did.

Maguire raised his hands up in a show of mock surrender.

"So what did you want to talk about?" she asked, grudgingly letting go of the past.

"Look, Zee, I need your help," he said. "I'm out of my league on this one. You know politics and I don't mix well."

"You mentioned Levitzki."

Maguire looked around the room; she knew exactly what he was thinking.

"It's just us, James," she said.

"Sunday morning the body of an escort turned up dead in Midtown," he said.

"The sex trade can be a tough business," Zee replied.

"This one wasn't," he replied. "In fact, I'd say it was probably a cushy one."

"So what's the problem?"

"The last *suitor* to see her alive was the mayor."

"McMasters?"

Maguire nodded his head.

"You think he killed her?" she asked.

"No, I don't. I was able to watch some security video and I'm confident that when he left, she was still alive."

"Well, if he isn't your suspect, then it's just another sex scandal," Zee replied. "What's the big deal? He's not the first and he certainly won't be the last."

"The big deal is he is being vetted for higher office and the victim is the Public Advocate's step-daughter. I'm getting pressure to just make the investigation go away."

Zee leaned back in her chair and whistled softly.

"Now do you understand my predicament?" he asked.

Tzviya stared at him, her face impassive, as she processed what he had just told her.

It was a look he was very familiar with and it wasn't a good omen.

"No," she replied after a few moments. "What's the problem?"

"You're kidding me, right?" he asked incredulously. "I have a politically connected dead woman who was shacking up with the mayor and they want me to sweep this under the rug."

"And what do you hope to accomplish by pursuing this?"

"Justice," he replied.

Tzviya threw her head back and laughed, but it wasn't meant to be humorous.

Almost immediately, Maguire felt his face begin to redden.

"You're such a goddamn Boy Scout, James," she replied.

"You've called me a lot of things, Zee, but Boy Scout is a new one."

"Justice for who?" she asked.

"You can't be serious."

The humor left her face now and she stared at him intently, "Exactly who are the innocent, James?"

"She didn't deserve to die," he argued.

"Didn't she? She knew the choices she was making. We all make choices and there are always consequences to them."

Maguire shook his head in disagreement, "Screwing wayward old politicians and celebrities shouldn't carry a death sentence, Zee."

"And yet it did and nothing you do will change that. The real question that you need to ask yourself is how will airing this dirty laundry make it better? What will it accomplish?"

Maguire got up from the chair and began pacing.

He was angry.

Angry at the situation he had been put in by McMasters, angry that Barone wasn't pushing for answers, angry at Zee for not seeing the big picture, but mostly angry at himself for *feeling* she was right. He was the only one looking for answers, but even if he found them Mikala Stevens would still be dead.

"A woman died," Maguire said dejectedly, as he stared aimlessly at one of the dated wooden panels that lined the basement walls.

"People die every day, James," she said, her voice calm and even. "Did McMasters kill her?"

"No," he replied, his back turned away from her.

"Then my advice to you is let it go."

Maguire spun around quickly, "Let it go? Is that the new *guideline* I should establish for investigations? *'Does anyone really care if the person is dead? No? Well fuck it then.'"*

Tzviya leaped up out of her chair.

"God, you can be so fucking dumb sometimes," she uttered in exasperation. "Get your head out of that policeman mind-set."

The two of them now stood in the center of the room, squared off like two combatants in an area.

"Is McMasters the first piece of shit politician to stick his dick where it didn't belong?" Zee asked. "No, think about it. Does the name Mary Jo Kopechne ring a bell?"

Maguire nodded.

The story itself was synonymous with politics.

In July 1969, the woman was on Chappaquiddick Island attending a reunion for political staffers of the late Bobby Kennedy. Around midnight, the woman left the party with Massachusetts senator, Ted Kennedy, who had offered her a ride back to the ferry. Along the way, the car driven by Kennedy plunged off a small, unlit bridge into the Poucha Pond. He was able to extricate himself from the vehicle, but the young woman was not as lucky and she died in the submerged vehicle. Kennedy made his way back to the residence, but did not notify the authorities until the next day.

Kennedy, who at the time was considered a top contender for President of the United States, subsequently pled guilty to leaving the scene of an accident after causing injury and received a two month suspended sentence. He might have avoided serious legal jeopardy, but he could not escape the political fallout. While he held onto his senate seat, his reputation had been severely damaged and his aspirations for higher office never came to fruition.

"The Kennedy name was the closest thing to American royalty and he could have waltzed his way into the White House," Tzviya continued, "but that all ended that July night and do you know why?"

"Because he left her there to die," Maguire said.

"No," she corrected him, "because she had a *name*. Something your victim doesn't. This wasn't just some senseless murder, James; she was killed to cover something up."

"And that makes it better how?"

"No, it doesn't, it just makes it a reality that you need to accept. She wasn't killed by gang-bangers, nor was it a burglary gone bad; so you need to stop thinking like a cop. This was a hit. Someone made the decision that she had become a liability."

"And you have heard no chatter?" he asked.

"No," she replied. "No chatter at all. If you ask me my opinion, I would say that once the decision was made that it was most likely a one or two-person team. Considering the political implications, it was more likely one person. In and out, no fuss no muss."

"Three can keep a secret if two are dead," he said scornfully.

"Just understand that, if you continue to chase this, you will be pursuing a ghost."

"And you don't think I should?"

"I'm afraid that if you chase this ghost long enough, you will find it or, even worse, it will find you."

"Aw, you're worried about me," Maguire said with a grin.

"I've never *stopped* worrying about you, James," she replied, in an unmistakably serious tone. "Why are you doing this?"

"What do you mean?" he asked. "I'm the police commissioner, this is my job."

"No, this was Rich's job," Tzviya replied. "You inherited it, but is it worth it? If you choose to pursue this you'll sacrifice your career or maybe even your life and for what? These people don't even care about you. The value of your life is summed up in a flag they don't even respect."

"And what would you have me do, Zee? Just walk away from it all? Would you?"

Tzviya closed the gap between them, till she was standing directly in front of Maguire.

"Yes, James," she said softly. "If you asked me to, I would walk away from it all, for you."

The mood had changed and there was something different in her eyes now, something very familiar.

"This isn't *then*," he replied. "This is *now*. Things have changed."

"Walk away," she pleaded. "I'll come with you, just the two of us."

"And what about Melody?"

"I had you *first*," she replied, before wrapping her arms around his shoulders and passionately kissed him.

CHAPTER TWENTY-NINE

The Hay-Adams, Washington, D.C.
Thursday, October 30th, 2014 – 12:17 p.m.

Melody leaned back in her chair and rubbed at her weary eyes.

It had been after midnight when she had finally crawled into bed, only to be jarred awake by the ringing of her phone at just after five a.m. The quick dip into the cold shower had done an adequate job of *waking* her up, but she still felt lethargic; like the feeling she had when coming back from international trips.

She glanced over at the small bedside clock and groaned.

The breakfast roundtable session with the American Realtor's Association, to discuss plans to jumpstart housing sales, had gone longer than anyone had expected, which meant that there was little time to get caught up on all the new talking points for the afternoon sessions.

They had a one o'clock meeting with the National Federation of Cattleman's Organization to discuss the long-term effects that regulations had on the industry and how to overcome them going forward. Then at three they had to switch gears and meet with the Association of North American Pharmaceutical Manufacturers to address the issue of intellectual rights on patented drugs and the proliferation of counterfeit drugs being brought in from Asia.

Someone should really group these meetings by category, she thought, as she lazily turned in her chair to glance out the French doors.

The trees in Lafayette Square were replete in vibrant fall hues. Patches of yellow, red and orange leaves filled the park, providing a stark contrast to the gleaming walls of the White House; that sat just beyond the park.

In that moment it all became so very real for her.

How many people longed for the opportunity to get that eighteen acre piece of real estate in the heart of the Nation's capital? How many had died for it? How many had killed for it?

In the game of politics it was the equivalent of winning the Super Bowl. The world was full of kings, queens, and numerous other leaders, but there was only one President of the United States. Too many it was the culmination of a lifelong dream, but Melody couldn't help but wonder if it might not just be a well-veiled nightmare.

Her musing was suddenly interrupted by the sound of her door opening, followed a moment later by the loud *plop* of Gen's body collapsing onto the bed beside her.

"God, I need a drink," Gen said.

"Alcohol isn't the answer, chicky," Melody said, as she swiveled around in her chair.

"I know that," Gen replied, "but it's always my first choice."

"Well, since we're discussing delinquent behavior, give me a cigarette."

Gen sat up and stared at Melody with a bewildered look, "I..... I don't think I know what you're talking about."

"Oh cut the crap and pony-up."

A moment later Gen began fishing through her purse and tossed the pack to Melody.

"How did you know?"

"You're a stress smoker," Mel replied, as she removed a cigarette. "Besides, when you got me out of the dinner last night I got the distinct floral scent of recently applied *Chanel*, so unless you were chatting up one of the Secret Service agents, I knew you were trying to hide something."

"Do not tell Gregor," Gen said sternly. "I get enough shit about my *unhealthy* habits."

"Scout's honor," Mel replied, as she lit the cigarette and inhaled.

"So what are you stressed about?"

The combination of exhaling and trying to stifle a laugh brought on a coughing fit that lasted several seconds.

"You can't be serious," Melody said. "Maybe *that* has something to do with it?"

Melody gestured toward the White House, only to have Gen wave her off dismissively.

"Piece of cake."

"I'm glad you're so confident."

"Look at it this way," Gen replied. "We get to do cool stuff and spend other people's money for a change."

"And maybe start a war or two along the way."

"Well, then GDL gets to make some money outfitting the belligerents. I'd call that a win-win."

"You need to talk to a professional," retorted Melody.

"Speaking of talking," Gen said, shifting topics. "Have you heard from James?"

Melody frowned at the question.

"No," she replied, taking a drag. "I sent a text to him last night, but didn't get an answer. I tried calling his cell this morning, but there was no answer, and the office said he took the day off. To be honest, I'm getting a bit concerned."

A quizzical look came over Gen's face, "I'm sure it's nothing. Didn't you tell me last night that he was working on something *sensitive*?"

"Yeah," Melody replied, "but it's so not like him. I mean for his security people not to know where he is."

"C'mon, Mel, there is a big difference between James taking the day off and them not knowing where he is. Maybe whatever he is dealing with needs to be addressed outside the box."

"I'm sure you're right," Melody replied. "I think I'm just overly stressed."

"Look, God willing, we will be back home in time for happy hour. We can rest up before the next trip and we can reconnect with the boys."

Melody nodded in agreement.

"Hey, while we are on the topic of *reconnecting*, I wanted to run something by you."

"Shoot," Gen said.

"If everything comes to fruition, what are your thoughts about bringing Mary on board as Counselor?"

Gen thought about the question for a moment.

Beyond their friendship with Mary Stargold, she was considered a respected attorney and accomplished lobbyist, but it was that latter endeavor that might raise some issues.

"Her former ties to the gun industry could present some *issues*," Gen said, "but I don't think they are a non-starter. I think some of the more anti-gun folks up on the hill will try to stir some shit up, through their surrogates in the media, but I don't think they'll do much beyond that. Besides, it's not a position that requires Senate confirmation, so all it will be is blustering."

"Do you think she would accept the offer?" Melody asked.

"I think so," Gen replied.

They were approaching the one-year anniversary of Rich's murder; a milestone that was weighing heavily on everyone's mind. The chance to get involved in something as historic as this might be a welcome opportunity for their friend.

"I don't want to jinx anything, but if we're popping the corks on Tuesday night, then I'd like to make the offer to her on Wednesday."

"I agree, the sooner the better," Gen said. "If she accepts, then she will have a lot more to juggle. Imagine trying to figure out new schools for Sophie and Emily?"

"Dear Lord, no," Melody replied. "I'd rather tackle world peace."

"And I'm sure that Mary will feel the same way.

Melody glanced down at the silent cell phone sitting on the desk, "In fact, rather than upsetting *their* schedule, I think *Uncle James* should move into the Battery Park apartment and take care of them until the school year is up."

"God, you're evil," Gen said with a laugh. "You're going to make a helluva secretary of state."

Just then there was a knock on the door.

"Come in," Melody called out.

The door opened and Emersen Lee popped her head in, "Sorry to interrupt, Ms. Anderson, but Secretary Cook would like to go over a few things with you and Ms. Gordon before the meeting."

"Okay, Em, tell her we'll be right there."

Melody got up and walked over to the bathroom where she took one last drag on the cigarette before flushing it down the toilet. Then she reached over and picked up the perfume bottle from the vanity and spritzed some on her neck.

"Show time," Gen said, with feigned exuberance, as she got up from the bed.

"We'd better get used to it," Melody replied, as she began to retrieve her things from the desk.

Just then the cell phone began to buzz.

Melody picked it up and looked at the display, before slipping it into her purse.

"Who was that?" Gen asked curiously.

"James," Melody replied.

"Don't you want to read what he had to say?"

"Nope," Melody replied, as she headed toward the door, "All I needed to know was that he was alive, for now."

"Poor James," Gen said gleefully, as she followed Melody out of the room. "He does not understand just how royally screwed he is."

CHAPTER THIRTY

City Hall, Manhattan, N.Y.
Thursday, October 30th, 2014 – 1:32 p.m.

"Did I miss anything while I was at lunch, Allison?" McMasters asked, as he made his way toward his office door.

"Chancellor Meyerhof called," she said.

McMasters stopped in his tracks and turned toward his secretary, "Did Bob say what it was about?"

"No," she replied, "but he didn't sound happy. He just asked that you call him back as soon as you returned."

McMasters visibly frowned.

The city was at an impasse with the local union that represented the city's kindergarten teachers. The program had seen a rapid expansion under the waning days of the prior administration and now the educators were seeking pay parity with their counterparts in the public school system. Recent talks had broken down between the two sides and the union was threatening a strike.

"That's just wonderful," McMasters said sullenly. "God forbid the city experienced just *one* day without a problem."

"Oh, and Commissioner Maguire is waiting for you in your office."

McMasters took a deep breath, as he reached for the door knob.

"Hold my calls, Allison," he said, as he opened the door.

"Yes sir," she replied, returning her attention back to the computer screen.

McMasters walked into the office and shut the door behind him. He could see Maguire sitting in one of the chairs with his back toward him. He made no attempt to get up.

"James," he said with forced cheerfulness, as he made his way to his desk, "to what do I owe the pleasure?"

"Do you mind telling me what the fuck you were thinking?" Maguire replied.

"Excuse me?" McMasters said, clearly taken aback by the brusqueness of the question. "Would you like to rephrase that question?"

"Do you mind telling me what the fuck you were thinking, *sir*?"

"Just what the hell are you talking about, *commissioner*," McMasters asked angrily.

"You were *there* that night," Maguire replied. "You were with Mikala before she died."

Any anger McMasters might have felt, at the perceived insolence of his subordinate, immediately drained away, as his body slumped in the chair. For Maguire, it was all the confirmation that he needed.

"*Goddamnit*, Alan, what the hell were you thinking?" Maguire asked accusatorily, as he got up from the chair and walked over toward the window.

"I...... I......" McMasters stammered, "I didn't...."

"Didn't what?" Maguire asked angrily. "Didn't think this was a terrible fucking idea? Because I hate to break the news to you, but it was."

"I'm sorry I didn't live up to your lofty expectations, James."

Maguire spun around, "*My* lofty expectations? For Christ's sake, you were fucking Barone's step-daughter."

"I didn't know that at the time," McMasters said defensively, "At least not in the beginning."

"And that somehow makes this better how?"

"No,... I don't know," he replied dejectedly. "Things just happened too fast. Before I knew it I had feelings for her and she had them for me."

"Oh, so you were just going to throw everything away?"

"No, it wasn't like that, Mikala knew the limitations and she was okay with them."

Maguire closed his eyes, pinching the bridge of his nose with his fingers, as he contemplated the shit storm that threatened to engulf the political landscape.

"Does Barone know?" Maguire asked.

"No."

"When did you find out who she was?"

"I ran into Mikala and Arianna at a fundraising event on the Upper West Side. By that time I was already in too deep. She didn't seem at all fazed. I tried to tell Mikala that we needed to end it, but she swore that it wasn't a problem and that she could keep things discrete."

"Wow," Maguire said in astonishment, as he sat back down in the chair. "I mean as long as she could keep a secret, right?"

"Look, I know I fucked up," McMasters said defiantly, "but let's be reasonable, we were both adults, we weren't committing any crime."

"Uhm, excuse me, but did you miss the part about the dead body in the apartment?"

"I didn't kill her, James."

"You didn't have to," Maguire fumed. "Do you have any idea how this will play out if the media gets ahold of this? The district attorney will have a field day."

"That *can't* happen," McMasters replied.

"There's a world of difference between can't and won't," Maguire corrected him. "You need to figure out what you are going to do, because if this leaks I *won't* be able to contain it."

"For Christ's sake, James," McMasters said angrily. "I'm in line to be the next secretary of defense. This *cannot* leak, do I make myself clear?"

"How the hell do you think I can make this just go away?" Maguire asked. "A woman was murdered; a woman that you were having an affair with. I came here to warn you. If I were you I would figure out a plan to get ahead of this."

"If this leaks, we will all find our heads on the chopping block, my friend," McMasters warned.

"*We?*" Maguire asked. "That sounds like a threat, Mr. Mayor. If I were you I would tread very carefully."

McMasters held up his hands defensively, "Easy there, James, it's not a threat. All I am saying is that when the press gets ahold of matters like this, it's like blood in the water to sharks and sometimes innocent people get bitten in the frenzy. This is bigger than just one person. If I fall, the public advocate falls, if he falls you fall, do you see where I am going with this? I mean let's take a step back and look at this from an objective position."

"Say I take the hit," McMasters continued. "The minute they make the connection to Barone his political career is toast. That means that socialist cunt will stroll unchallenged into this office. Who do you think is first on the unemployment line?"

"You honestly think that possibility bothers me?" Maguire asked.

McMasters paused, his mind working overtime, as he tried to figure out the right button to push, to bring Maguire over to his side of the argument.

"Maybe it doesn't bother you, but have you thought about the ramifications to the city?" McMasters asked. "Think what you will about me, and perhaps you're right. I might not be an angel, but does the city deserve to bear the consequences for my actions? And while we are on it, what are my actions, James? What crime did I commit? I had an affair. Are we going to start castigating people for lapses in moral judgment? What's next, the firing squad at dawn?"

"Maybe that is something you should have thought about beforehand."

"You know very well the repercussions of Flores sitting in this chair," McMasters said. "The city will pay the price for decades to come when she is done leaving her mark, but there is also something else to consider."

"Oh yeah?" Maguire asked. "And what is that?"

"Your fiancée," McMasters replied.

"What the hell does Melody have to do with all this?"

"Do you really think she will survive the fallout from this *scandal*? I'd venture to guess that Eliza will jettison her long before she ever makes it to the Senate confirmation process. I mean, all is fair in politics, right?"

"You're some piece of work," Maguire said in disgust, as he got up from the chair and headed out of the office.

"I'm just putting it all out there so you can make an informed decision as to what you do next."

Maguire paused, as he reached the door, and turned to face McMasters.

"It all might be a moot point anyway," he said.

"And why is that?" McMasters asked.

"Because I think Flores may already know."

"Why do you think that?"

"Because I've already dodged several calls from her in the last twenty-four hours," he explained.

"Jesus Christ," McMasters said, leaning back in his chair.

"If you're a praying man, you might want to appeal to Him directly," Maguire said. "I know I could use the help."

"Rich always said you were a resourceful person, James," McMasters replied. "So go be resourceful, for *all* our sakes."

CHAPTER THIRTY-ONE

Turtle Bay, Manhattan, N.Y.
Friday, October 31st, 2014 – 7:16 a.m.

"Well this doesn't look good," Olivia Russo said, as her partner pulled their car in behind a marked RMP.

"No it doesn't, partner," he said.

The two detectives exited their vehicle and began walking toward the front door. As they approached it they met a uniformed officer walking out of an office building.

"Excuse me," Martinez said, flashing his shield to the cop. "South Squad, what do you guys have going on?"

"Guy blew his brains out upstairs," the cop replied.

"You got a name?" Russo asked.

"I don't," the cop replied, "but it's up on the 48th floor."

"*Sonofabitch*," Martinez said.

"You don't think,....."

"Let's go find out."

Martinez's suspicions were confirmed when the elevator doors opened and he saw a cop standing outside the front door of the Home2Home suite.

The cop looked up as they approached, noting the gold detective shields they had displayed on their outer coats.

"South Squad, Russo and Martinez," Olivia said.

"Damn, you guys got here faster than our own squad."

"We have a name on the vic?" Martinez asked.

The cop glanced down at his memo book, "Yeah, the vic's name is Ackerman, Devin Ackerman."

"Fuck," Martinez said angrily.

"Are you positive?" Russo asked.

"His secretary was the one that found him, so I'd say yeah," the cop replied.

Martinez and Russo stepped into the office when they met a uniformed sergeant.

"Hey, sarge," Martinez said. "We're from the South Squad."

"Are you guys looking for work?" the sergeant asked quizzically.

"Actually, your vic was helping us in another case," Russo said. "We were stopping by to do a follow-up interview."

"Hate to break the news to you, but that train left the station," he replied.

"So we've been told," Martinez said. "Do you mind if we take a look?"

"You give your names to the guy at the door?"

"Yep," Martinez said.

"I don't have a problem," the sergeant replied, "but you know the rules, *don't touch, just look.*"

"We won't," Russo replied.

The two detectives walked into the office and took in the scene.

Ackerman was slumped over the desk, a pistol lying on the floor a few feet away.

"Well happy fucking Halloween," Martinez said.

"Yeah, but is this the trick or the treat?"

"I guess it all depends on whether or not your name was in his computer."

"Well, at least we'll have time to take a look," she said, pointing to the laptop on the desk.

"Yeah, at least he didn't smash it to pieces before he boarded the last train for *eternity.*"

"Maybe it was his way of giving the world one last *fuck you.*"

Martinez made his way over to the desk to take a closer look.

"Uh oh," he said forlornly, as he stared down at the desk. "Don't count those chickens too quickly."

"What do you mean?" Russo asked, approaching him carefully.

"Look," Martinez said, pointing to an area on the desk.

"What am I looking at?" she asked.

"Take a look at that blood splatter."

Russo put on her glasses and leaned in closer, examining the spot next to the laptop that Martinez was pointing toward. It wasn't clear at first, but she soon realized what her partner was pointing too. As she scrutinized the dark blood stain on the desk, she could make out a very faint right angle.

A moment later she stood up, a scowl appearing on her face

"Are you fucking kidding me?" she asked, as she removed her glasses.

"Something is definitely *missing* partner," Martinez said.

"I think it's safe to assume they don't let you bring *things* past the Pearly Gates."

"Well if Ackerman didn't take it with him, who did?" Martinez asked.

"I think we need to make a phone call."

CHAPTER THIRTY-TWO

Southampton, Suffolk County, N.Y.
Friday, October 31ˢᵗ, 2014 – 7:23 a.m.

"Good morning, *mausi*. It's time to rise *und* shine."

Genevieve groaned audibly, as she buried her head under the pillow.

At any other time, Gregor's thick German accent was like music to her ears, but her recent case of sleep deprivation made it sound more like a nightmare. She forced one eye to open, ever so slightly, and immediately regretted it upon the realization that the sky outside was still dark.

"No, just five more minutes."

"*Nein*," Gregor said tersely, as he sat a coffee mug on the nightstand.

"Okay, okay," she replied. "Nine more minutes."

Genevieve let out a shrill squeal, as she felt Gregor's hands pawing at her waist.

"I'm up, I'm up," she said grumpily.

"I'm sorry, *mausi*," he said, as he sat down on the edge of the bed, "but Peter Bart is going out of town and I need to go over some personnel changes with Ernst."

"Where's Wolfie," Gen asked, as she twisted around until she was sitting up in bed.

"He's downstairs," the man replied, handing her the coffee mug, "with Melody."

"Thank you, *liebchen*," Gen said, as she accepted the steaming mug and took a sip. "Wait a minute, Melody is up already?"

"She was in the salon reading when I got up."

"Where's James?"

"I don't know," he replied.

"When was the last time you saw him?"

Gregor looked at her quizzically, as he thought about the question. "Monday, maybe Tuesday, why?"

"Because it's Friday," she said.

"Why are you so worried?" he asked. "He is a very busy man."

"No, you're right, it's nothing," she said dismissively, as she swung her legs over the side of the bed.

"*Mein Gott*," Gregor said somberly.

"What's wrong?"

"When a woman tells a man that he is *right* and *it's nothing* in the same sentence it is cause for alarm."

"Didn't you say that you had a meeting to go to, *dear*?"

"*Ich liebe dich*," Gregor said, as he got up and slowly backed away.

"I love you too, goofy man," she replied.

"What time are you leaving today?" he asked.

"Around noon," she said, as she slipped on a pair of sweatpants. "We're heading over to Pennsylvania for a rally, but I should be home before bedtime."

"It's okay," he said. "This work is very important and I am proud of you, *mausi*. Wolfgang will be too."

"Thank you," Gen said, as she wrapped her arms around him and hugged him. "You don't know how much that means to me."

"I'll be back soon," he said and kissed the top of her head gently.

Gen watched as Gregor walked out of the bedroom and then finished getting dressed.

Despite what she had said to him, she had the feeling that things were decidedly not okay and she needed to get to the bottom of it.

When she arrived in the salon, she found Melody and Wolfgang sitting on the couch playing a game of peek-a-boo. The scene caught her completely by surprise and she paused in the shadows watching them for a moment.

For as long as she could remember, the room, with its vaulted ceiling and opulent décor, had been used to entertain the wealthy and well-connected. It was beautiful, but it was also sterile. Now, Wolfgang's shrill laughter filled the cavernous room with *life* and the harder he laughed the more animated Melody became. Something about the moment was so pure, so innocent, that she didn't want it to end, but she knew all too well that innocence was *fleeting* and the harder you tried to hold on to it the faster it slipped through your fingertips.

Gen swallowed hard, chasing those thoughts away, as she stepped out into the light.

"If only your enemies could see you now," she said, walking into the room.

Melody looked up and smiled, "You don't think this conveys the image of a future kick-ass secretary of state?"

"At least you're not wearing some god-awful pant suit," Gen chided her friend, as she walked over and picked up her son.

"How's mommy's little man?" she cooed softly, before covering him with kisses.

Wolfie squirmed in her arms and began laughing loudly; the kind of innocent laughter that causes any adult in the vicinity to immediately smile.

"Mommy missed you so much," Gen said, as she cradled him in her arms.

"It's a shame they can't stay this way forever," Melody said.

"I don't know," Gen replied. "A part of me agrees with that sentiment, but another part imagines all the possibilities that are in front of him and I want to experience it all."

"You're going to be a great mother."

"Thank you, Mel," Gen said. "But he's also going to need his aunt and right now mommy *desperately* needs more coffee."

"You don't need to ask me twice," Melody said, as she reached up and accepted Wolfie back into her arms.

"You want some?"

"No, thanks," Melody said, "I'm about ready to float away."

"Did you have a rough night?" Gen asked inquisitively, as she refilled her mug from the carafe and took a seat on the couch.

"I certainly had a restless one," Melody replied. "I just think all these meetings have finally caught up with my subconscious."

"I'm sure poor James isn't happy about that."

"*Poor James* came home late and passed out the moment he hit the bed. I don't think he was conscious enough to enjoy my tossing and turning. He left bright and early this morning."

"Oh," Gen said coyly, as she took a sip of her coffee. "Is there something going on?"

"I'm not sure," Melody replied. "He just seems distant right now. Whatever case he is dealing with seems to be getting the better of him."

"Has he said what it is?"

"No," she replied, "which is unusual for him."

"Are things *okay* between the two of you?" Gen asked without trying to sound too intrusive.

"Yeah," Melody replied curiously. "Why?"

"Well, you couldn't reach him the other day, he wasn't here last night. I mean that's not exactly *reassuring*."

"He was in a meeting the other night," Melody explained. "Something to do with what he is working on and couldn't have his cell phone with him."

Gen raised her eyebrow.

"Stop it," Melody said. "Not everything is nefarious. I don't know what he is working on, but I trust him."

"I just wanted to make sure," Gen said. "I mean we are in a period of upheaval around here. Stress and chaos can cause people to disconnect."

"Is that what you think is happening to me and James?" Melody asked, slightly bemused. "That we have *disconnected*?"

"It happens," Gen replied.

"Oh, chicky, that is so sweet, but no, we are not disconnecting from each other."

"Okay, if you say so, but just remember, as much as I love James, you will always come first with me."

"I know that, but you will not have to choose sides. We are fine."

"That makes me very happy to hear," Gen replied, as she picked up Wolfgang and began bouncing him on her knee.

Melody smiled, as she watched the two of them, but deep down inside she couldn't help wonder whether she had said all that to assuage her friends concerns or her own.

CHAPTER THIRTY-THREE

1 Police Plaza, Manhattan, N.Y.
Friday, October 31st, 2014 – 8:22 a.m.

"So where do we stand with our coverage for Election Day?" Maguire asked.

"It's all hands on deck," said Deputy Commissioner Thomas Delaney, the head of the Department's Intelligence and Counterterrorism Bureaus. "We're working with our counterparts in the Secret Service and we will implement a full lockdown of both the Waldorf and Sheraton beginning this evening."

It was tough enough to handle the logistics of one presidential campaign headquarters, but at the last moment the Whitmore campaign had notified them that they were selecting the Waldorf to host their victory party. The campaign believed that the optics of the Waldorf were more presidential, so they had packed up everything in their Los Angeles office and made the move; which also allowed him faster access to several eastern seaboard states that he was trailing in.

"How much advance time are we going to have on potential moves?" Maguire asked. "It won't be too much trouble going into the weekend, but traffic's bad enough on the Grand Central without having *two* motorcades jockeying for a position at the same time in LaGuardia."

"It appears that the Whitmore campaign will be using Teterboro if the need arises," Secret Service Special Agent Brandon Whitehead said.

"That's a helluva ride," Maguire replied.

"Actually, Adam Richstein is loaning Whitmore his personal helicopter for the duration of the campaign," Whitehead said. "It's a Bell 525 that he keeps parked on the Westside."

"It's good to have rich friends," Maguire replied. "I wonder which cabinet position he's vying for?"

"Ain't politics grand?" Delaney said.

"You don't know the half of it, Tom," Maguire said with a knowing laugh. "With that being said, come Wednesday morning someone will be on the losing end. I hate to be the wet blanket of the party, but what arrangements do we have to get things back to normal?"

"Once we have a clear winner, we will begin to break down our protection elements on one campaign and reallocate them to the President-*Elect's* campaign," Whitehead said. "Secretary Cook already has stated that she plans to stay in the city for the foreseeable future. She has additional assets in place, because of her prior role as secretary of state, so we are ahead of the game in that respect. We would expect a seamless transition with the folks from the Presidential Protection Division. Of course we will be requesting that the NYPD not only continue to provide coverage, but to take adequate measure to harden the immediate area around the Sheraton and provide dedicated counter-assault teams."

"Of course," Maguire said. "And if Whitmore wins?"

"Should Congressman Whitmore win he has said that he plans on moving to D.C. within a day or two. The Washington Field Office will coordinate with P.P.D. to get that site up and running."

"Sounds like we have a solid plan in place, gentlemen," Maguire replied. "Now let's just hope that the political god's smile upon that plan."

The meeting was cut short by a knock at the door. Maguire glanced over to see Sandy Barnes standing in the doorway. Her expression told him it was not only urgent, but that it wasn't good news.

"You must excuse me," he said, as he stood up. "Tom, keep me apprised of any changes or needs."

"Yes, sir," Delaney said.

Maguire walked out of the conference room with Barnes in tow. Neither said a word till they entered his office and she closed the door behind them.

"Well, Sandy, what have you got?" he asked, as he sat down at his desk.

"Do you want the bad news or the even *badder* news?"

"You know, this is becoming an unpleasant little habit with you," he said with exasperation. "Give me the *badder* news and let's just get it out of the way."

"Ackerman is dead."

Whatever he might have expected, it was clear from the look on his face that this wasn't it.

"What?...... How?....... Where?" he stammered, hoping that it was all some cruel Halloween joke.

"Apparently sometime after six o'clock last night," Barnes replied. "When our boys went to serve him with the subpoena, they were too late."

"Wait, why did it take them so long? Didn't they get that subpoena on Wednesday?"

"Yes, they did," Barnes said, "They were heading out to serve it yesterday morning, but they got a notification to appear forthwith at the Manhattan D.A.'s office for an emergency Mapp hearing on a robbery case."

"You've got to be kidding me."

"I wish I was," she replied. "Some snot-nosed A.D.A kept them warming a bench over at Centre Street till late last night. Then he popped his head out and told them the guy copped a plea and they could go."

"Jesus Christ," Maguire said, slamming the desktop angrily.

"Billy didn't think you'd want to expand the pool of folks with access to this case, so he just had them head over there first thing this morning."

"So what happened when they got there?"

"Uniforms from the Seventeenth Precinct were already on the scene when they arrived. They'd responded to a 911 call and found him with an apparent self-inflicted gunshot wound to the head. They called the Squad C.O., who called Billy Walsh, who directed them to take the case from the Seventeenth Squad."

"Anyone complain?" Maguire asked.

"You mean like complaining about *not* getting a homicide case? No, I'm pretty sure the Seventeenth Squad looked at it as an early Christmas present."

"So what's the bad news?" Maguire asked.

"According to Billy, our detectives aren't convinced that everything is what it seems."

"Why is that?"

"One of the guys did a stint in a precinct evidence collection unit before getting his gold shield. He seems to think there's blood splatter on the desk which might indicate something was removed post-mortem."

"Have they seized anything from the location?"

"They have Ackerman's laptop," Barnes replied. "I sent one of my people up to bring it back to our computer crimes folks after the Crime Scene Unit is finished."

"Anything else?"

"Not yet," she replied. "Once CSU is done, they'll start combing the office to see what they come up with."

"I guess it would be too much to ask if we had any potential witnesses."

"Security said they got a report of a loud noise from someone on the forty-second floor, sometime around eight last night, but it's a *big* building. They took a look, but didn't see smoke or anything out of the ordinary."

"Any video?"

"Yeah, there is," she replied.

For a moment Maguire felt a sudden rush of excitement, as if they were about to catch a break, but it didn't last.

"And the quality is about as good as when it was first installed back in 70s."

"I'm almost afraid to ask if this day can get any better," he said sarcastically.

As if on cue, their conversation was interrupted by a knock on the door.

"Come in," Maguire called.

He watched as the door opened and Amanda Massi poked her head in, "Sorry to bother you sir, but I have Arianna Barone on the line for you. She says it's important."

CHAPTER THIRTY-FOUR

Whitestone, Queens, N.Y.
Friday, October 31st, 2014 – 11:41 a.m.

Maguire watched as the large wrought-iron gate slid effortlessly along the recessed track, allowing the Suburban to proceed up the cobblestone driveway. Just ahead of them, stood a two-story beige home, with terra-cotta roof and ornate black metal railings that lined the porch and the second floor Juliet balconies. The home had a decidedly Mediterranean feel which seemed at odds with the harsh fall winds.

When the vehicle came to a stop, Amanda Massi jumped out and opened the rear door.

"Do you want me to come with you?" she asked, as Maguire exited.

"No, Amanda," he said, "I've got this."

As he made his way toward the front door, he couldn't help but notice the festive Halloween decorations, which lined either side of the stone staircase, and just how strangely out of place they now seemed.

As he reached the top step, the front door opened and Arianna Barone stepped out to greet him.

"Thank you for coming on such short notice, Commissioner Maguire."

She was wearing a dark blue colored blouse and skirt, which contrasted starkly with her auburn hair, and her voice seemed just as fragile as it did when he'd first met her at City Hall.

"Not at all," he said. "And please call me James."

"Please, come in, James," she said, as she moved off to the side.

The house was eerily quiet, save for the repetitive *tick-tock* of the mantel clock that sat above the fireplace.

"You have a lovely home, Mrs. Barone," he said, as he removed his overcoat.

"It's Jack's home," she said somberly, motioning him over to the couch. "He designed it after his family's home in Otranto, Italy. I'm just the *caretaker.*"

"Well, then let me compliment you on your stewardship skills," he said with a smile.

"You're too kind," she said, as she sat down across from him. "Coffee?"

"Please," he said. "Black is fine."

Arianna poured two cups and gently slid one across the marble coffee table to him.

"On the phone earlier it sounded as if you wanted to discuss something important with me."

"Yes," she replied. "Mikala's funeral is tomorrow, just a small family affair in upstate New York."

"Do you need any assistance?" he asked.

"No," she said. "It has all been taken care of, but thank you. What I wanted to talk to you about was something *personal.* Tell me, James, where are you at with my daughter's murder? Honestly."

Maguire thought about it for a moment. Under normal circumstances he wouldn't discuss an active investigation, but this investigation had been anything but normal and, he reasoned to himself, they had already crossed that line in the last meeting.

"We've just learned that the man Mikala worked for might have committed suicide last night."

"Might?" she asked.

"Well, we're still investigating, so there has been no official determination as to the cause of death."

Arianna was silent for a moment.

"I wish I could say that I was sorry."

"I don't think anyone would find fault with that," Maguire replied.

"Yes, but it isn't very *Christian* of me, is it?"

"Being Christian doesn't make us perfect, Mrs. Barone."

"I guess that's a good thing," she replied. "Because if being perfect was the prerequisite to get into heaven, I don't think many of us would get there; certainly not Mikala."

"Ma'am?"

"Commissioner, I want you to know that I appreciate everything you have done, truly I do, and as a mother I want you get justice for my daughter."

"It sounds like there's a *but* hidden away in there."

"There is," she replied. "The truth is that Mikala was my daughter, but she wasn't an angel. I can't say I am too surprised, considering the upbringing she had, but that's also no excuse. In a way, I always thought of Mikala as being two different people. On the one hand she was intelligent, kind, and loving, but on the other she could be argumentative, combative, and even vindictive."

"I think an argument could be made that you have just described most young girls," Maguire replied.

"Yes, but thankfully most young girls don't possess the Grant DNA or its family money. Mikala it seems had an ample supply of both. If she felt strongly about something, she would have no qualms about marching headlong down the wrong path just to prove her point. I think it was her way of getting even with me for abandoning her."

"You knew what she was doing, didn't you?"

Arianna took a deep breath and exhaled slowly, as she stared down at the coffee cup; her trembling hand causing ripples to appear in the dark liquid.

"No," she replied, after careful consideration. "I didn't *know*, but I suspected. The more time I spent with her the more I knew something was amiss. Mikala happily fueled my suspicions by allowing me to overhear conversations or comments she intentionally let slip. It didn't take long to surmise she was engaging in some form of questionable behavior. I just felt that if I pushed the issue, if I tried to act like her mother, she would shut the door on our budding relationship and I would lose her forever."

"But even *questionable* behavior shouldn't end the way it did" Maguire said. "So why don't you want me to find justice for her?"

"Do you mind?" Arianna asked politely, as she held up a cigarette case.

"Not at all," he replied. "My old partner broke me years ago."

"I'd given them up," she said, as she picked up a lighter from the table and lit the tip, "but under the circumstances...."

"It's completely understandable."

"Please don't judge me harshly, or think me weak, Commissioner," she continued.

"I don't judge you, Mrs. Barone. In fact, I think you're incredibly resilient."

"Sadly, losing Mikala has caused me to take a long hard look at a great many things; life in general, my family, and even my marriage. My daughter chose her path, and the people she was with chose theirs as well. But what about the ones like me who are left to pick up the pieces; is it selfish to want to protect myself from any more fallout?"

"No, I don't think it is."

"I guess my greatest fear now is that if you continue to dig deeper, you will uncover other *revelations* and I am just not sure how much more I can afford to lose."

"You think your husband is involved in this?"

An uneasy silence filled the room, like the proverbial calm before the storm. Arianna fought to maintain the tranquil look on her face, but her eyes belied the anger and pain she felt inside.

"I'm sorry, please forgive me," Maguire said apologetically. "You don't have to answer that."

"No, it's fine," she replied softly. "When I first met Jack, I thought I had won the prize. He was handsome, a military man, and he lit up the room wherever we went. But I was young and I was naïve when it came to a lot of things. When he told me he wanted to get into politics, I was happy to put my career on hold and support him. I'd be lying if I said that I didn't like being in the spotlight and all the attention that came with it. I even used that as an excuse for the way people treated him, especially the women. It wasn't real, it was just politics. Deep down, I believed in Jack. I saw the way he was with people, the compassion, the empathy, and I truly felt he would use his position to help them."

"What changed?" Maguire asked.

"He got elected," she replied. "Like I said, I was naïve. I didn't want to see the seedier side of the *game*, so I simply chose to ignore it. When he asked me to help out on some of his pet side-projects, I did. I knew they were inconsequential, but I put everything into it and I kept busy. Sadly, all I did was free him up to attend his *boring* campaign meetings. By the time I knew something was going on, I didn't want to know."

"You're a lot more reasonable than most spouses would be, Mrs. Barone."

"No, I'm not," she said. "I'm just more honest. I've come to the realization that my life is all one big grand illusion, held together by the most tenuous of strands. Perhaps if Jack had stayed a pilot, we would be living in some godforsaken, mosquito infested air station in Louisiana, worrying about how to pay the bills or take a vacation. Maybe I would have come into Mikala's life early enough to have changed things for the better."

"Don't beat yourself up, Mrs. Barone."

"Oh, but that's what I do, James," she replied. "I sit here and I beat myself up. If I had only been a better daughter, a better mother, a better wife. Mikala did what she did for her kicks, my husband for his, and I am just left her alone wondering how the dream went so horribly wrong. The *dirty little secret,* that isn't a very good secret, is that sex and politics go hand in hand. For better or worse, I am married to a politician and the idea of destroying careers, just because they were screwing some college kid on the side, is not something I can get behind."

"I understand," Maguire replied.

"I hope you do," she replied. "We both know that if Cook wins, and takes McMasters with her, my husband is poised to be the next mayor. A scandal will destroy his career and most likely my marriage. It has been my experience that people who have lost everything are free to walk away from anything. I will turn fifty-one next month. I've already lost my daughter and I would prefer to not lose whatever is left of my life. I certainly hope you can see your way to allowing me to hold on to those last strands of my illusion."

"I think if anyone has earned that right it is you."

"Thank you," she replied, crushing out the cigarette in the ashtray. "Perhaps one day I will be able to repay your kindness."

"You won't have to," he said, rising to his feet. "You've already paid enough."

Arianna got up and she walked him to the door.

"If Jack should find himself in Alan's seat, I will make sure to remind him that you are a very honorable man. It's a rare commodity in this day and age."

She opened the door, as Maguire slipped on his overcoat and walked outside.

"Take care of yourself, Mrs. Barone and please call me if there is anything you ever need."

"I will," she replied.

Maguire began making his way down the steps, when he heard her call out to him.

"James."

Maguire turned to look back at her.

"Politics changes people; it corrupts them from the inside. Always make sure you are prepared to walk away from it, before it's too late."

Maguire nodded, then turned and headed toward the waiting SUV.

CHAPTER THIRTY-FIVE

1 Police Plaza, Manhattan, N.Y.
Friday, October 31st, 2014 – 5:11 p.m.

Maguire stared blankly out his 14th floor office window.

Fourteen stories below him, the outbound lanes of the Brooklyn Bridge were filled to capacity, as a bumper-to-bumper procession of cars tried to flee the city, but his thoughts were a million miles away.

His entire adult life had been formed around the principals of justice; the triumph of good over evil, but it was times like this that truly tested that belief.

Maguire raised the coffee mug, which had long since been refilled with a different type of *beverage*, to his lips and took a sip.

So far two lives had been lost to protect a secret and the killer, or killers, remained free.

"Don't kid yourself, Paddy, in this game there are no innocents."

The words of Senior Chief Roy Gentry reached out from the deep, dark recesses of his memories.

Maguire recalled the specific night those words were said, when he was sitting in a bar called *Froggies*, located just outside Naval Amphibious Base, Little Creek, Virginia. While Little Creek was the official home of SEAL Team Four, Froggies was the more popular *unofficial* one and it was where the teams went to unwind when they came back stateside.

His platoon had been taking part in Operation: *Noble Endeavor*, a South American based training initiative that was designed to increase the Colombian military response to combatting narcotics trafficking into North America. At least that was the plan in theory.

Once on the ground, they realized that the narcotics problem far exceeded any actual plan to eradicate it. Most of what passed for a plan consisted of hyperbole. Politicians were more than happy to speak eloquently about the brave war to end the violence that grew out of cocaine production, but it rarely evolved beyond empty platitudes.

The drug lords, from the various cartels, effectively owned the country. Like a corrupt octopus, their tentacles reached into every office from the executive to the judiciary. Long ago they had learned that they didn't need to fear the government if they owned it. In the grand scheme of things, a million dollar bribe was inconsequential to a billionaire. Still, there were certain individuals within the government and military who refused to bend a knee and vowed to fight.

The SEAL's had been sent to train and instruct the *Agrupación de Fuerzas Especiales Antiterroristas Urbanas,* the Columbian Army's top secret Counter-Terrorism Special Forces Group, also known as *AFEUR*. This group had been actively involved in counter-insurgency operations targeting both left and right guerilla groups.

One evening they were running two, nine-man patrols, which combined elements of SEAL's with their AFEUR counterparts, in the Chocó region, along the Panama border. Just after midnight, they received word that military intelligence had intercepted *real-time* intel of a large drug shipment being transported to a mountainous airstrip four clicks from their location. The combined units responded and setup a static ambush line.

Just before dawn, a four vehicle convoy came into range and they sprung their trap. It was fast and violent, but as soon as the smoke cleared it became clear to all involved that it was a cluster fuck. Rather than encountering a ragtag group of narco-traffickers, they had engaged an element of a counterinsurgency unit from the Columbian Army's 7th Division in Medellin, who were acting as protection for the drug shipment. The operation had gone from a simple *hit and run* to a panicked finger-pointing shit-storm at the general staff level. No one wanted to take the blame for the incident, nor did they have an *explanation* for why the counterinsurgency unit was operating there.

Immediately upon returning to their base, the two units were segregated, and the once friendly relationship had chilled. Realizing the rapidly deteriorating situation, and fearing that they might find their housing accommodations changed to jail cells, the SEAL officer in charge of the program, Lieutenant Robert 'Buster' Keaton, at the explicit urging of Senior Chief Gentry, got a satellite phone call to Naval Special Warfare Command which led to an *ad hoc* exfiltration courtesy of a CH-53E Super Stallion helicopter from the aircraft carrier, USS Harry S. Truman (CVN-75), which was conducting drills in the Atlantic. In the end, both sides agreed that it was beneficial to come to a gentlemen's agreement that the incident had never occurred.

That did little to assuage the anger that Maguire and his fellow SEAL's felt after being treated like criminals during their debrief aboard the Truman. Apparently the concept of *shooting back at people shooting at you* was lost on the rear-echelon folks.

Upon their return stateside, Gentry had called for his own team debrief at the local watering-hole. It was important for the integrity of the team that they be allowed to decompress and vent, especially after a compromised op.

Maguire had been sitting at one of the tables, bitching to two of his teammates, Thomas 'Saint' Moore and Charles 'Bubbles'

Baxter, about the hell they had endured, at the hands of their own people, over what the Navy was referring to as a *friendly-fire* incident.

"Those friggin' rounds didn't seem very friendly, as they were zipping by my head," Maguire said angrily.

"At least you managed to miss them all," Bubbles said, as he held up his bandaged forearm. "I got shot and I ain't even gonna get a Purple Heart for my troubles."

"Well, if we ever find our asses back in Columbia you can petition the military to award you their *Herido en Accion* medal," Saint replied.

"Fuck that shit," Bubbles said. "I've seen all I need to of that country. I ain't going back there."

"You'll go wherever the Navy tells you to go, Bubbles," Roy Gentry said, as he pulled up a chair and sat down. "Remember, it's not just a job, it's an *adventure*."

"Hooyah," the men replied in unison.

"Look, I've been in a couple more of these cluster-fuck situations than you boys have, and believe me, they don't get any easier with time. Don't kid yourself, Paddy, in this game there are no innocents."

"Still doesn't it make it right, Mother," Maguire grumbled. "It's not their asses on the line."

"You think they care?" Gentry asked. "We are just tools in a toolbox, Paddy. Someone way above both our pay-grades opens the box when the need arises and takes us out. Then they put us away when the job is over. Unfortunately, sometimes that person fucks up and uses the wrong tool for the job."

"Yeah, but those fuckers rarely get blamed," Moore said. "In fact, they usually get *promoted*."

"You chose to be in this toolbox, Saint," Gentry replied. "The minute you did you gave up the right to bitch and complain. You don't question, you just go out there and get the job done to the best of your God-given abilities. We don't live in a perfect world. The *enemy* you fight today may just end up being the *friend* you have to work with tomorrow. Sometimes the black and white is going to be just varying shades of gray. When you find yourself in that position you make the best call you can and learn to live with your choice."

"Penny for your thoughts?"

Maguire turned, as the memory slipped away, and saw Sandy Barnes standing in the doorway.

"Let me guess, more bad news?"

Barnes frowned and shrugged her shoulders, as she walked into the office and sat down.

"Has there really been any *good* news during this investigation?" she asked.

"I keep thinking a rainbow has to appear, eventually."

"Well, that's not going to be today," Barnes replied.

"Well, don't keep me in suspense," Maguire said.

"I just got a call from Billy," she replied. "It seems as if our medical examiner is having a change of heart."

"About what?"

"He's updating his findings regarding Amber Skye's death. According to Godwin, after a closer examination he believes that the official cause of death is accidental asphyxiation."

"What about the ligature marks on the neck?" Maguire asked in disbelief.

"In his opinion they were not the primary cause of death and were mostly likely sustained during sexual intimacy *ante-mortem.*"

"Bullshit," Maguire replied angrily. "Do you believe it?"

"Does it matter?" she asked cynically. "I won't lie to you, it comes across as pretty damn convenient, but that doesn't mean it's any less official. It's not like we have any viable option to dispute it."

Maguire knew she was right.

Disputing the findings would cast a light on the investigation, something no one was in favor of and after his talk with Arianna Barone, there was zero chance the family would hire a private pathologist to re-examine the dead girl's body.

"Well, they got their wish, didn't they?" Maguire replied. "What about Ackerman?"

"Too soon, but I'm not holding my breath," Barnes replied. "If I was a betting gal, I'd put the odds at about 80/20 for suicide."

"Varying shades of gray," he said softly.

"Huh?"

"Nothing," Maguire replied.

"It's obvious that someone wants this bag of shit to *disappear* and whoever it is has the power to pull all the right strings to get it done."

"It looks like we've hit the end of the investigative road on this one, Sandy. Have them close out the case and transfer it to Special Services."

"Yes, sir," she replied.

"Oh, and just to let you know, you will have an opening in your office on Monday."

"What do you mean?" she asked quizzically, "Who?"

"Deputy Chief Acevedo is getting promoted," Maguire replied. "He's going to be the C.O. of Detective Bureau Staten Island."

Barnes stared at him calmly, but inside her mind was reeling.

To say that this was *unusual* would be grossly inaccurate. She was the Chief of Detectives, and it was her bureau. Not only was she being told that she was losing her X.O., but that changes were being made without her consent or even her input.

"Staten Island?" she asked, "You know that he lives in the ass-end of Orange County."

"Then he should probably invest in some good audio-books," Maguire replied.

"Is there something you're not telling me, sir?"

"He's been leaking information, Sandy."

"To whom?" she asked with alarm.

"Nydia Flores," Maguire replied.

"The City Council Speaker?" Barnes said, a look of shock on her face. "Why do you think that?"

"I had someone look into the leaks back during the Rosary Bead murder investigation. Turns out Acevedo grew up with Flores."

"Yeah, but that was then," Barnes argued, "and it involved one of the city council member's sister."

"I have reason to believe it is still ongoing, Sandy. As soon as we ID'd Mikala Stevens, he started reaching out to her. I've been dodging direct calls from Flores for the last several days."

"*Sonofabitch*," Barnes said angrily.

"I want you to know that I don't hold any of this against you, Sandy."

"Yeah, but he's my X.O.," she protested. "I brought him in with me. I trusted him to have my back."

"We do the best we can," Maguire replied. "This is his bag of shit to own."

"So you're doing a tactical *demotion* by sending him to Staten Island," she replied.

"It takes him out of the loop, but it also gives him a command. It'll make it harder for him to complain."

"Oh, I am sure he will still find a sympathetic shoulder to cry on," she said.

"Then he can hand in his papers and retire," Maguire replied. "Either way he's marginalized."

"That will not sit well with the Speaker."

"I doubt anything I do will ever sit well with Flores, so I'm not about to concern myself with trying."

"You think that's a good move politically," she asked. "Word is that there may be changes ahead."

"Playing politics has left a bad taste in my mouth lately," he replied. "I'm about done with the game."

"Hey, I'd like you to stick around a bit longer," she replied. "I've got another year left."

"I'll see how long I can tread water," Maguire said with a laugh, "but I'm not making any promises."

"Fair enough," she said, as she stood up. "I'll reach out to Billy and have them refer the case to Special Services."

"Thanks, Sandy," Maguire replied. "try to enjoy the weekend."

"Will do."

Maguire watched her walk out the door before picking up his cell phone. He dialed the number and listened as it rang. A moment later he heard the call go to voice mail.

"Ang, I just wanted to let you know you will have a new case coming across your desk. We'll talk more about it next week."

Maguire ended the call and got up, grabbing his jacket from the coat rack next to the door and walked out into the main office.

"Are we going somewhere, boss?" Jackson asked.

"Yeah, Luke, it's time to go home."

CHAPTER THIRTY-SIX

Sheraton Times Square Hotel, Manhattan, N.Y.
Tuesday, November 4th, 2014 – 10:53 p.m.

"Where are we at?" Cook asked her assistant, as the two women sat on the couch in her suite.

"215," Emersen Lee said, after consulting the app on her iPad.

"And Whitmore?"

"With Florida, he stands at 154."

"They just called Virginia for you," Anderson Clark called out from across the room, where a dozen of her staffers were huddled around the television maintaining a watchful vigil of the latest news reports.

"228," Lee said, revising her count.

Cook did a quick count in her head. There were a total of 538 electoral votes and so far 382 were spoken for. That left only 156 in play, as both candidates chased the magic number of 270 to clinch the election.

She looked over at the digital clock on the end table.

The polls would close out on the West Coast in less than five minutes and with that closing would come the long anticipated result from California and its fifty-five votes.

Deep down inside she *knew*, but at the same time she refused to celebrate prematurely. As much as everyone believed that California would go her way, it was still Whitmore's home state and nothing could be taken for granted. If he took California then this would become a contest all over again.

In the ballroom downstairs there were over two thousand people waiting for her to give her victory speech, if California fell, they would be waiting a long time.

Her inner circle had envisioned a landslide, but it was looking more like a brutal slog through a swamp. Yes, she was ahead, but her dream had been for a decisive victory. The last thing this country, or her campaign, needed was for it to be a close race. She knew that if she did not beat Whitmore, by a statistically significant amount, then the beginnings of her presidency would be mired in what-ifs. As much as the media *loved* her, she also knew that they were a fickle breed. She knew that she would have some uphill battles with Congress and she didn't need or want the pundits on cable news wondering if Whitmore would have worked harder to get things done.

You should have gone to Florida more often, she chided herself.

"It's eleven o'clock," Lee said.

"All right people, this is it," Cook said, as she got up and walked over to join the rest of the team.

"You've got this, Madam Secretary," one of her staff said enthusiastically.

Cook smiled warmly, "From your lips to God's ear, darling."

"Okay, we are being told that we have some new totals coming in to our election desk," one of the news anchors said into the camera. "Paul, where do we stand?"

They watched as the scene cut away from the assembled group of political prognosticators and focused on a single person standing next to the interactive map.

The moment of truth, she thought, as her fingers gripped the back of the chair she was resting on.

"Well, Holly, we've been informed that the polls have just closed in California," the man said, as his hands selected an area of the map and enlarged it. "And the election desk is confident in predicting that California will go to Eliza Cook. That means, with 283 electoral votes, the former secretary of state will now become the next President of the United States."

The room erupted in cheers.

Eliza closed her eyes and swallowed hard, as those around her began to celebrate.

"Congratulations, Madam President-*elect*."

Cook opened her eyes and turned to see her assistant standing there.

"Thank you, Em," she said, as she hugged the woman. "I couldn't have done this without you."

"That's not true," the woman said with a smile, "but thank you for saying it."

"After we get into the White House, you might not be thanking me."

"I'll take my chances," Lee replied.

"You just won Oregon and Washington," Clark said. "That puts you over 300."

Cook took a deep breath, allowing herself to come to terms with the fact that all the hard work, all of the boring meetings, and the countless days spent flying between campaign stops, had finally paid off. Now, reality came crashing in like a ton of bricks.

In a way the campaign had almost seemed surreal; like a never-ending vacation. Yes, she had always known what she was running for, had always kept her eyes on the prize, but till now it was always a theoretical pursuit. It wasn't like you could try-out the presidency to see if it fit you. There was no apprenticeship to groom you for the role or job shadowing. No, you ran for the office and, if you managed to win it, you learned very quickly how to swim or you drowned.

"Ma'am, I have Congressman Whitmore on the line," Em said. "He wants to congratulate you."

Cook took the phone and held it up to her ear.

"Good evening, Duncan," she said.

"Madam President-*elect*," the man said, "I just wanted to call and congratulate you."

"Thank you, that's very sweet of you, my dear."

"Well, it was a hard-fought campaign and I just wanted to let you know that I am a firm believer in all's fair in love and politics, but now that the race is over I will be happy to work with you."

"Thank you, Duncan, I appreciate that. I know there are a lot of issues that California is currently facing and I want you to know that I will be happy to work with you to restore the shine back to the Golden State."

"Thank you," Whitmore replied. "I won't take up anymore of your time. It seems we both have speeches to give this evening."

"You were a worthy opponent, Duncan. Keep your chin up and we will talk again soon."

"Yes, ma'am."

Cook ended the call and handed the phone back to her assistant.

"Well, I guess that makes it *official*-official," Cook said with a smile. "So it must be time to go share the good news."

CHAPTER THIRTY-SEVEN

Sheraton Times Square Hotel, Manhattan, N.Y.
Tuesday, November 4th, 2014 – 11:48 p.m.

Melody watched, from her vantage point off stage, as Eliza Cook delivered a rousing acceptance speech to the throng of supports packed into the ballroom.

"It is time for us to take back our country. For too long, the political establishment has looked down its collective nose at you, the American people. They have forgotten the fundamental rule that they are the *employees* and that you are the employers, but tonight you sent a message that I can assure you was heard *loud and clear*. Change is coming to Washington."

The crowd erupted in raucous applause.

"I promised you that if you elected me, I would be ready to deliver for you on day one," Cook continued, "and that day begins tomorrow."

"She's on a roll, isn't she?"

Melody turned her head slightly to see Maguire standing at her side.

"James," she said, spinning around and wrapping her arms around him.

"Wow, did you miss me?" he asked.

"Oh, God yes," she whispered in his ear, as she clung to him tightly. "I was wondering where you were."

"Well, I just came back from the Waldorf," he replied. "Let's just say the mood is a whole lot different over there."

Melody released him, taking a step back.

"Oh, I bet it is," she replied, "but right now I'm struggling with everything going on here. I mean do you believe that this is all happening? That I will actually be the secretary of state?"

"Yes I can, angel," he replied. "In fact, between you and Eliza, I feel bad for all those world leaders who will get their asses handed to them by a pair of tough-as-nails women."

"I'm glad you have such a high opinion of me," she replied, "but that's not helping. Right now, every ounce of me is trying to figure out a way of saying *'thanks, but no thanks.'* I'm just not sure what scares me more, the job or Eliza."

"I will go with Eliza on this one," he said. "That being said, you need to go easy on yourself and just accept it. You're going to do fine, Mel. You've spent most your adult life battling billionaire boardroom bullies and you've never lost. Do you think they are any less of a threat?"

"No," she replied grudgingly.

"Then why do you worry about this so much?"

"Because I have always been able to fall back on the fact that I know my industry inside and out, but this is a different animal. I know you keep telling me that there is no difference between the two, but I'm just not sure how to be politically correct."

"It's been my experience that people *expect* the politically correct answers, but they really want to hear the truth. Just be you and I am telling you that you will ace this. People are going to quickly know who you are and where you are coming from, just be yourself and make them change."

Melody nodded.

"Just promise me you won't start acting like one of those egotistical, pompous-ass politicians."

"Well, if I do, then you have my permission to spank me," she replied.

"There's a dark and secluded area behind the stage, do you feel like getting in some practice now, so I know if I'm doing it right when the time comes?"

"You're incorrigible, you know that?" she asked with a smirk.

"I've been called worse things," he said, pulling her close and kissing her playful.

"Oh and trust me; I know all about your ability to *get it right* when the time comes," she said.

"Ahem, I'm sorry to interrupt you two."

James and Melody separated, as they watched Alan McMasters walking toward them.

"No interruption," Melody replied.

"I just wanted to come over and say congratulations, Madam *Secretary*."

"Well, I don't want to jinx anything, but same to you Mister *Secretary*," she replied. "I just hope that we can get through our senate confirmations as easily as Eliza got elected."

"She has a way of making it look easy," McMasters replied, "but I don't imagine it will be that hard. We have to remember that we both have James to help keep us on the straight and narrow patch."

"He's not quite boy scout material," Melody said, wrapping her arm around Maguire's, "but he has a very reliable moral compass."

"Yes he does," McMasters replied. "Unfortunately, I'm not out of City Hall just yet, so do you mind if I steal him from you for a few minutes? I have some issues we need to discuss."

"Not at all," Melody said, releasing James' arm. "Just try to have him back before he turns into a pumpkin."

"Yes, ma'am," McMasters replied.

The two men watched as Melody walked off to where a group of staffers had gathered to listen to Eliza's speech.

"You've got an amazing lady there, James," McMasters said.

"Is there something you needed to discuss with me?" Maguire said, doing very little to disguise the annoyance in his voice.

"I just wanted to say thank you for what you did," McMasters replied, "and that I am sorry."

"You don't have to apologize to me."

"But I do," McMasters replied. "I asked you to do something I shouldn't have. That being said, I was at the funeral and Jack wanted me to tell you how happy he was at the discretion in which you handled this matter."

"I didn't do it for you, or for Jack Barone," Maguire replied sharply. "I did it for Mrs. Barone."

"I know you see things different than us degenerate politicians, James, and if the truth is to be told, you're probably right. We should hold ourselves up to a higher standard. It would be preferable to see the world in black and white, instead of the grays we often seem to navigate through."

"Oh spare me," Maguire said with disgust. "Don't hide behind the whole scourge of politics thing. People like you and Jack Barone know exactly what you are doing. You play this half-assed game knowing the system will protect you and you don't give a rat's ass about the victims."

"Under the circumstances, perhaps I should reconsider my recommendation that Jack keep you on," McMasters replied.

"You do whatever you have to do, Mr. *Mayor*," Maguire said icily.

"Look, all I meant was that we both know you didn't want this job and losing Rich was tough."

Maguire stepped in, closing the distance between himself and McMasters, till the two men were face to face.

"Don't you dare bring my friend into *this* conversation. You and Jack Barone are reaping the benefits of my empathy toward a grieving mother. Perhaps it is time you realize that your lifestyle choices can affect the lives of innocent people. I suggest you use the second chance you have been given wisely, because I strongly doubt there will be a third."

"Maybe Melody was wrong about you," McMasters said, as he took a step backward. "Maybe you are a goddamn Boy Scout."

"If I was, then the only cabinet position that would matter to you right now would be the attorney general, because that's who would be investigating you."

McMasters swallowed hard, as he felt his face redden at the not-so-veiled threat.

"Are you two boys having fun?"

Both men turned to see Cook approaching them with her security team in tow.

"Madam President-*elect*," McMasters gushed, as he fought to regain his composure.

"At ease, Alan," she said dismissively. "This is a night for celebrating, so why don't you go and have some fun, but not too much fun. I need to have a few words in private with my *favorite* police commissioner."

McMasters looked at Maguire, then back at Cook, as a sense of dread began to engulf him.

"That means you're dismissed, Alan," she said, waving the fingers of her right hand with a dramatic flourish.

"Uhh,...... Yes, ma'am," he said dejectedly, before turning and walking away.

Cook waited until McMasters was out of ear-shot range before she spoke again.

"I hate politicians," she said, "but I guess they are a necessary evil."

"If you say so," Maguire replied evenly.

"I do," she said with a smile. "Now come with me, because I really do need to talk to you."

Maguire followed her, as she led him over to where a holding-room had been set up. A Secret Service agent stationed at the door opened it as she approached.

"Thank you," she said, "Please give us a few minutes."

Cook and Maguire walked inside and he heard the door close shut behind them.

"Have a seat, James," she said, as she sat down and motioned toward a vacant chair. "Melody tells me you've been busy lately. So tell me, how things are going with work?"

"Well, to be honest, I might be perusing the wanted pages in the not so distant future."

"Why?" she asked, a clearly concerned look on her face.

"Just a difference of opinion really," Maguire replied, "but I'm lower on the food chain."

"Hogwash," she said dismissively, as she opened one of the bottled waters on the table next to her chair and took a drink. "You're not going anywhere. I'll make sure of that."

"With all due respect, you don't have to fight my battles."

"Oh I'm not," Cook replied. "I'm just not prepared to leave my flagship city without you at the helm of the law enforcement ship; at least for the time being. Besides, McMasters knows full well that he takes his marching orders from me."

He stared at her for a moment, as he played a form of mental gymnastics with the myriad of thoughts running through his head. For obvious reasons, the most serious of which was the fact she was the president-*elect*, he had to judge just how far he could go, or should go, in talking with her.

Despite managing to keep his face impassive, Cook could tell that there was something going on in his head.

"Come on, James, out with it," she finally said. "You might be a fabulous police commissioner, but you're a horrible poker player."

"I'm trying to figure out how to say this *diplomatically*," he replied.

"Dear Lord, if I wanted a diplomat running things I would have had McMasters hire someone like that idiot Thornberry. I already have enough fawning sycophants around here; just say what's on your mind."

"In that case, do I have your permission to speak freely?"

"Absolutely, James," Cook replied. "Everything that is said in this room, stays in this room."

"It might not be my place, but are you sure McMasters is the right person for secretary of defense?"

"You don't think his background is good enough for the position?" Cook asked probingly. "He was a highly decorated Marine officer, a state senator and now the Mayor of New York City.

"It's not that I'm questioning his accomplishments, or his military career, but there is more to being a leader. I just wonder if he has the right temperament for the job."

"This is about Mikala Stevens, isn't it?"

Maguire leaned back in the chair, crossing his arms over his chest. One thing was for certain, Eliza Cook never failed to amaze him.

"I'd ask how you knew, but...."

"But I didn't get to where I am today by being stupid or ignorant," she said with a wink and a smile. "Truth is that I know all about the highs and lows of *everyone* I surround myself with."

"Then you know he was having a *relationship* with her."

Cook nodded.

"Alan came to me and confessed his sins," she explained. "Do you have reason to believe that he was directly involved in her death?"

Maguire shook his head, "No, but that doesn't mean he doesn't bare some overall culpability."

"Where are you at with your investigation?"

"We've hit a bit of a brick wall," Maguire replied.

"Keep digging, but do it careful," she counseled. "Alan isn't the first politician to get jammed up because he was thinking with his little head instead of his big one. And he's also not the first one whose paramour ended up dead. Things happen in life that may or may not be connected and I don't want his life to be destroyed over something he *didn't* have a hand in."

"Understood," Maguire replied soberly.

He knew her concern had merit. He recalled the case of a married congressman who'd been having an affair with an intern. The body of the young woman had been found dead and the media, as well as the local police agency, immediately focused their eyes on the congressman. It was a salacious story and it drove the narrative for months. The ensuing scandal cost him his congressional seat, even though he had never been implicated and a potential suspect had confessed early on. Nearly a decade later another man was convicted of the woman's murder, but the congressman's career had already been destroyed.

"Mind you, I'm not opposed to *anyone* having a little extracurricular fun, life is entirely too short to be boring, but from this point forward I demand absolutely discretion from those working for me. I just don't see the point in throwing away an otherwise stellar career."

"That's very generous of you," Maguire replied, "but have you thought about the potential ramifications of what he has already done?"

"You're talking about potential *Guideline D & E* issues?"

"Folks that have had extramarital affairs are viewed as being highly susceptible to blackmail," Maguire replied. "He could have issues with his security clearance."

"I appreciate your concerns," she replied. "I truly do, but what's done is done. Although I don't believe the threat of blackmail will be an issue in this case."

"Oh really?" Maguire asked with a shocked look.

"No, I made Alan tell his wife what happened."

"And she was okay with it?"

"Okay is a very *broad* word," Cook said with an amused laugh, "but Jill McMasters is a realist and she knows that a scandal wouldn't benefit anyone. Let's just say that she grudgingly accepted that he screwed up and that it won't happen again. For the record, Alan knows that his days of catting around are over and that he is cut-off. He also knows that if he fails me again, *it* will be permanently cut-off."

"Well, I felt an obligation to advise you," Maguire said. "I didn't want you starting things off by getting caught in a surprise."

"And that is precisely why you are so important to me, James," Cook replied. "I need someone at the helm who I can trust to keep me informed about both the official and *unofficial* activities going on in the city."

"I appreciate your support," he replied.

"Well, it's the least I can do; considering that I am stealing your soon-to-be wife."

"I will do my best, but I'm just another paid city employee that serves at the pleasure of the mayor and with your win that might change soon."

"Yes and with my help Jack Barone will be the next mayor and he serves at my pleasure. I just need to get him through the next election so I don't have to deal with that dumb-shit council speaker. The last thing I need is for her to come in and re-fuck things up with her idiotic socialist agenda."

"Then what?" he asked.

"We both know this is just a pit-stop for you. The city is filled with self-important people, with grandiose titles, but the only one that means anything to me is the one you have and I need you here, for the time being, but that will change. And when that time comes we will cut-down your travel time to see Melody."

Maguire wanted to press her on the issue, but he knew better. Cook was the consummate political player. It was her game and she would show her cards at the moment she decided and not beforehand.

"Yes, ma'am," he said.

The conversation was interrupted by a knock at the door.

"Come in," Cook called out.

The door opened and Emersen Lee poked her head inside.

"Excuse me, but Moira O'Keefe from Fox is looking to do a quick interview with you and Mr. Cook."

"Harry's still up?" Eliza asked, genuinely surprised.

"I guess he's making an election night exception," Em replied.

"Alas, duty calls, James," she said, as they both stood up.

"Congratulations again, Madam President-elect," he said.

Cook took a step forward and hugged him, holding the embrace as she whispered in his ear, "Remember what I said; this is just a pit-stop."

"Yes, ma'am."

Cook took a step back and smiled. "God, I wish I could clone you, James. I could control the world and I would never have to leave the executive residence."

Maguire watched, as Cook turned and made her way out of the holding room.

When the door closed, he picked up one of the bottled waters from the side table and opened it.

I hate politics, he thought, as he took a long drink.

Maguire waited a moment longer, contemplating everything that he and Cook had discussed, before making his way to the door.

Walking outside, it took a moment for his eyes to adjust to the dimly lit backstage area which caused him to bump into another person walking by.

"I'm sorry," Maguire said, before realizing who it was.

"Commissioner Maguire, what an unpleasant surprise," Dean Oliver said sarcastically.

"Who let you past the Secret Service?" Maguire asked.

Oliver looked at him with a smug grin.

"President-elect Cook likes to keep her *best* assets close by," he said. "You never know when they'll be needed."

"I always thought she was a good judge of character," Maguire replied, "but I guess no one is perfect."

"No, you're right, Commissioner, no one is perfect. Some policemen cannot even catch the killer of a young woman."

Maguire took a step forward, closing the distance between himself and Oliver.

"You're right, Dean, I may not be perfect when it comes to police work, but just remember, I wasn't always a cop and what I was before I *was* perfect at."

"Let us just hope that my former agency will be as good as you when it comes to protecting your lovely lady."

If Oliver had wanted to provoke a reaction, he got it in spades. Without warning, Maguire grabbed the man by the lapels and drove him backward till the man hit the wall; hard enough to illicit a loud grunt.

Oliver raised his right hand to fend to off the attack, but he had severely underestimated his opponent. Maguire caught him by the wrist, pinning it to the wall, as he simultaneously brought his right forearm up to the man's neck for a brachial strike. At the last second, Maguire held back, but it still landed with enough force to stun Oliver.

"You'd better think long and hard before you utter another word; you hear me, *slick*?" Maguire said menacingly.

A second later, the two men where pulled apart by several Secret Service agents.

"Break it up," one agent, who was holding onto Maguire, said, as two others pulled Oliver away.

"No, no, it's all right," Oliver said dismissively, jerking his arms free. "We're fine."

"What the hell's going on?" an agent asked.

"It's nothing," Oliver replied, gently massaging his neck. "The Commissioner was kind enough to show me a useful tactical control move. *Krav Maga*, wasn't it?"

Maguire kept his steely gaze on the man and just nodded.

"Thank you," Oliver continued, straightening out his suit jacket. "I'll do my best to remember it. You never know when it might come in handy. Have a good evening, gentleman."

Maguire and the agents watched, as Oliver turned and walked away. Once he was out of range, the agent closest to Maguire turned to face him.

"What the hell was that all about, sir?"

"A storm warning," Maguire said, as he watched Oliver turn the corner and disappear.

CHAPTER THIRTY-EIGHT

1 Police Plaza, Manhattan, N.Y.
Wednesday, November 5th, 2014 – 4:57 p.m.

Maguire was sitting on the couch in his office, recovering from the post-Election Eve insanity.

It was hard enough trying to oversee the protection coverage of two presidential candidates, let alone one where your other half was playing an integral role. On top of it all, he couldn't get past his little episode with Dean Oliver. Something about the man made his skin crawl. Not out of a personal dislike, but out of a serious professional distrust.

Maguire couldn't get past the fact that Oliver, despite his prior job as a special agent for the State Department, didn't seem to be playing for the same team. No matter who was calling the shots, Maguire had always envisioned that law enforcement was united in pursuing a common goal, justice, but that didn't seem to apply to Oliver.

That's not entirely true, he thought. *Where was his justice for Mikala?*

He took a sip of coffee, as he pondered his role in this fiasco.

But that was different, wasn't it?

Maguire tried to reconcile the dilemma by believing that he was acting in the best interests of Arianna Barone.

She was also a victim this, wasn't she? he thought. *Surely protecting a woman who had just lost her only child had some redeeming virtue?*

He set the coffee cup down on the end table and rubbed his weary face. He was struck by the fact that he had to argue his innocence with himself, and yet he still wasn't entirely convinced of it. The severe lack of sleep he was experiencing wasn't helping matters any.

In Oliver's case he had freed a potential terrorist, putting not only the city, but America at risk. One thing he knew, terrorists never stopped trying. Qaseem bin Khalid might have been put on ice by his friends in the Saudi security services, but he knew that there would always be others to continue the fight.

Who else would Oliver help if the right people asked him too?

Maguire's thoughts were interrupted by a knock at the door.

He looked up to see Amanda standing in the doorway.

"Sorry, boss, but you have a *visitor*."

Maguire was about to ask who when he saw Nydia Flores brush past the woman and enter his office.

Massi was about to reach out to grab the woman, when Maguire waved her off.

"It's okay, Amanda," he said, as he rose up from the couch. "Council Speaker, please have a seat."

"You're a tough man to get hold of, Commissioner," Flores said, as she removed her coat, draping it over the back of the chair and took a seat.

Flores' appearance was deceptive, something she routinely used to her advantage. She was an attractive woman, with long brown hair and eyes, and a bronze complexion that gave her an exotic look. Most men stopped there, which often resulted in their demise. They mistook her for being one-dimensional, when behind the beauty resided an equally formidable mind. It was a mistake that Maguire was intent on not replicating.

"It's been a busy couple of weeks with the election going on," he replied, "Coffee?"

"Please," Flores said, "black."

Maguire walked over to the serving table, pouring her a cup and refilling his own.

"Thank you," she said, as he set the cup down on the table. "I hear you've been busy promoting some people."

"We all go where our talents can best be used," he said, maintaining a neutral demeanor, as he sat back down.

"Indeed," she replied, taking a sip of her coffee. "I'm sure you're happy that the election is now over and you can get back to the more mundane tasks of policing the city. You know, robberies, burglaries,...... murder."

"As much as I would love to believe that you just came by to pay me a social visit, I have a feeling there's something you'd like to discuss with me."

"Does your keen investigative mind tell you that or the phones calls from me you've been ducking?"

"I would never duck your calls, Madam Speaker."

"Let's stop with the formalities, James, we're both adults and we both have the best interests of the city at heart, don't we?"

"I'd like to think so," he replied.

"And speaking of best interests, I'm curious how the investigation into Amber Skye's death is going," Flores said. "Such a terrible tragedy."

"It's ongoing," he replied cautiously, "but since it is an active investigation, I am not at liberty to discuss the matter."

"Well, as we both know I'm clearly not just *anyone*, James. It's a matter that speaks to the issue of safety for the residents of this city."

"Yes, it does, but with all due respect, Madam Speaker, I also don't want to jeopardize the investigation."

Flores smiled at the continued *formality*, as she cradled the coffee cup in her lap.

A part of her had wished that someone else was sitting across from her, but another part also enjoyed this game. Maguire was not like any of his predecessors. They could be threatened, bribed, and cajoled into talking. For the most part they weren't cops, they were politicians, just like her, and they spoke, or at least understood, a common language, but not Maguire and that intrigued her.

Flores took a sip and then set the cup down on the table.

It was time to change tactics.

"Let's cut to the chase, shall we?" she asked. "We both know that the ruse of your *investigation* is just a smokescreen aimed at protecting the public advocate."

"Don't you mean the next mayor?" Maguire countered.

"For the time being," she replied, "but just remember who actually pays the bills in this city. He might run things, but if he, or you, wants to do anything you will have to play nice with me."

"Is that a threat, Madam Speaker?"

"No, James, it's not a threat, it's just a friendly reminder if you want to keep that chair when Jack Barone is gone."

"Well, seeing how you're the likely candidate for the job, I just assumed you would rather have your handpicked person sitting here. Someone who is more inclined to be...."

"What? A yes man?"

"So to speak," Maguire replied.

"Yes men or women serve their purpose, but they have limitations. I don't dislike you, James, and while I might not agree with all your actions, I respect them; even when you are saying *no* to me."

"Duly noted," he replied.

"For the record, I will not get into a pissing match with you over this one. Despite what the mayor and my opponents like to allege, I do in fact have a heart. Jack Barone and his wife have a right to grieve their loss in private, even if she was a little tramp."

"I'm sure they would be moved by your *compassion*."

"I'm not a big believer in sugarcoating things, James, and I only show compassion once; that applies to both them and you," she said firmly. "Remember, there are no guaranteed winners in politics and the person on top today might not stay there for very long. So moving forward I would strongly suggest that you mind how you dot your i's and cross your t's. And yes, that *is* a threat."

Maguire nodded.

"Well then, I guess my work here is complete," Flores said, as she stood up.

Maguire got up and she extended her hand toward him, "It was good to see you again, Commissioner."

"Likewise," he replied.

Maguire walked her to the door and paused, seeing Sandy Barnes sitting at one of the desks. When Flores had left, he motioned her to come inside.

"What was that all about," Barnes asked, as she closed the door.

"The tiger lady was kind enough to pay me a visit to personally inform me that my *get out of jail free* card has officially expired."

"I take it she knows?"

Maguire nodded, as he sat down at his desk.

"How much?"

"Enough," Maguire replied, as he opened the bottom right desk drawer and removed a bottle of whiskey and two glasses.

"You want a drink?" he asked.

"Is the Pope Catholic?"

Maguire smiled, as he opened the bottle and filled the glasses.

"Just please don't tell me you have any more bad news, Sandy," he said, sliding the glass tumbler toward her. "I'm ready to go up to the roof and jump."

"I don't have bad news, but I don't have good news either."

"All things considered, I'd call that a win," he replied, taking a sip of his drink.

"I guess," she replied, staring out the window.

"What's on your mind, Sandy?"

"I don't know," she said, taking a drink.

"It's obvious that something is not sitting well with you."

Barnes took another drink and then set the glass on the desk.

"Permission to speak freely, sir?" she asked.

"There's no other way in this office."

"This case is bullshit," she replied, a tinge of anger in her voice.

"I'm not going to argue that point," he replied, "but what other choice did we have, Sandy?"

"We could have pushed the issue more," she said. "We could have brought Doctor Godwin in for an *interview*, pressed him on his findings, put the screws to him a bit and see where that got us."

"It would have gotten us exactly where we are today, nowhere."

"You don't know that," she replied.

"I wish that were true, but it's not," Maguire said. "This game was rigged from the beginning."

"Why do you say that?"

"Because there's more going on here than meets the eye."

"Well, I know that I am just the Chief of Detectives, but would you mind shedding some light on that cryptic message?"

Maguire took a sip of his drink, as he considered her request. Opening this door was dangerous, he knew that, but he also knew that she deserved an answer and maybe he needed to clear his own conscious.

"Mikala Stevens' death was a cover-up," he said somberly.

"For who?" she asked. "You wouldn't say that unless you had a short list."

"If I had to bet the farm, I'd say the mayor."

"McMasters? What's the connection?"

"He was having an affair with her."

"Do you believe that McMasters had her killed?" Barnes asked, a shocked look gripping her face.

"No, I don't," Maguire replied, "If I did he'd be in cuffs. I actually think McMasters had feelings for her."

"Then who?"

"That's the million dollar question," he replied. "I think someone decided that she was becoming a liability. I don't know if we will ever find out all the names in her little black book, but it's clear that whoever is behind this had enough juice to remove any potential roadblocks; including the initial findings of our medical examiner."

"Isn't that even more reason to investigate?" she asked. "I mean if he McMasters cared for her shouldn't he want to know who killed her?"

"Unfortunately, it's no longer just about him," Maguire explained. "Now that the election is over, it won't be long until the announcement is made that McMasters is going to be nominated for secretary of defense."

"You're shitting me?"

"No, and when he steps down that means…"

"Jack Barone becomes the new mayor," Barnes said with disgust.

"A scandal would end that quickly."

"So you're putting the kibosh on the investigation for political reasons?"

"No, I'm not," Maguire said indignantly, "I couldn't care less about the political ramifications, but I do have to consider other factors."

"Such as?"

"Arianna Barone," he replied.

"I would think she would want to know who killed her daughter," Barnes said. "Surely she'd want justice."

"That's what I thought as well," he replied. "But I had a long talk with her last week. As a mother, she is torn, but she also understands that nothing we do will bring Mikala back. I won't go into all the details, but suffice to say that continuing the investigation would only end up compounding her losses."

Barnes took a sip of her drink, as she thought about what he had just told her.

As a mother herself, she certainly had empathy for Arianna Barone, but she also couldn't imagine living the rest of her life knowing that the killer of her child walked free.

"I'm just concerned about the potential precedent that we might be setting here," she said. "If we establish we have two sets of rules to follow."

"I've considered that as well, Sandy. I'm not happy with it, but I've also concluded that what we are investigating goes well beyond our capabilities."

"Why do you say that?" she asked.

"Because I believe that whoever did this is well beyond our reach," Maguire replied. "If we continue to investigate this we are going to be chasing after a ghost and the only thing that will end up being destroyed will be other innocent lives."

"You really believe that?" she asked earnestly.

"I do," Maguire replied. "It's sometimes hard to believe, but there are things that happen in our society that are decidedly uncivilized. I've seen it first-hand."

"Have you ever.....?" she began to ask

"That's a question I can't answer, Sandy," he replied.

"Don't ask, don't tell?"

"More like don't even hint at it or you'll end up in federal prison."

"I miss my days of innocence," she scoffed.

"You and me both," he replied, "but this is the hand we've been dealt."

"You're the boss."

"That I am," Maguire said somberly. "And, not to change subjects, that brings up something else I wanted to discuss with you."

"What is it?" she asked.

"As much as this incident has left a bad taste in my mouth, I am apparently destined to stay in this chair for the foreseeable future," he said. "Overall I'm satisfied with the leadership of the Department, with *one* exception."

Almost immediately she felt a wave of nausea come over her. For nearly a week she had been struggling with the fact that her own executive officer had betrayed her. It had caused her to second guess herself. The role of an X.O. was a critical one; not only were they required to take over in the absence of the commanding officer, but they were vital in providing the C.O. with support and advice. Acevedo's duplicity had not only shocked her, but it had also caused her to question both her judgment and fitness for her assignment.

Still, she was proud of her law enforcement career and the fact that she was the first woman to achieve the coveted title of chief of detectives.

And maybe now you are going to be the last, she thought.

Barnes steeled herself for the worst.

"And what position would that be?" she asked, aware that her voice had cracked a bit.

Maguire opened his center desk draw and removed a small blue box and slid it across the desk.

A quizzical look came across Barnes' face as she opened the box and peered down at its contents.

"What….. What is this?" she asked.

"If I'm staying I need someone I know I can trust to be my right hand," Maguire replied.

"Why me?" she asked, as she removed the first deputy commissioner's shield from the box and held it in her hand. "I wasn't exactly *sharp as a tack* when I selected Acevedo."

"You didn't fail, Sandy, he failed you, there's a difference. As much as I know you disagreed with the direction this case went, you did your job. Trust me when I say that I know from experience just how difficult that can be."

"What about Tony Ameche? Shouldn't he get the slot?"

"Tony's a good man," Maguire replied, "but you're my choice."

"What about my job?"

"I'm going to put Billy Walsh into the slot."

"I don't know what to say?"

"Say yes, Sandy."

"Yes," she replied, doing her best to control her excitement.

"I'll have the orders drawn up immediately," Maguire said. "Bring your family to work tomorrow and we'll hold the official swearing in at ten o'clock."

The two of them stood up and he shook her hand, "Congratulations, Commissioner Barnes."

"Thank you," she replied, "Thank you for having this kind of faith in me."

"It's not faith, Sandy, you earned this."

"I appreciate that," she replied. "Well, I better get going. I have some calls to make."

"Me too," he replied. "Congratulations again, Sandy."

Maguire watched, as she walked out of the office and then sat back down at his desk. He picked up the cell phone and made a call, listening as it went to voicemail.

"Mother, it's Paddy, call me as soon as you can. Something has come up here and I need your help."

CHAPTER THIRTY-NINE

Southampton, Suffolk County, N.Y.
Thursday, November 6th, 2014 – 8:16 p.m.

Maguire walked into the salon and paused.

Over the course of the day an extraordinary transition had occurred. To his amazement, a majority of the furniture had been removed to accommodate several long tables that now held a variety of phones, computers, and printers, as well as a number of binders. What had once been a place of peace and tranquility had morphed into a political war room with Melody standing in the middle of the room, like a modern day general, talking to Gen, as they planned their next move.

Well, that was to be expected, he thought.

As soon as the post-election party had ended, Eliza Cook held a press conference announcing her selections for several key positions in her administration, including those for secretary of state and secretary of defense; which promptly set off a media firestorm.

Things had gotten so frantic at 1 Police Plaza that Thomas Cleary, Maguire's deputy commissioner of public information, had spent almost the entire day in the auditorium fielding questions from the press about rumors of Maguire's anticipated departure. It seemed as if the press had abandoned their role as investigative journalists and had taken up reading *tea leaves*. Every manner of scenario was given equal time. Some had him leaving the city to take over as head of the FBI, while others pointed to *anonymous* senior administration officials who warned that he would be fired after McMasters left.

Had it not been so bizarre he would have laughed, but now, as he stood at the entrance to the salon, he couldn't help but wonder if it wasn't as far-fetched as he'd originally thought?

"Hey stranger," he said, as he walked toward Melody.

"Hey, cowboy," she said with a big smile. "Welcome to Shangri-La."

"If this is your idea of paradise, we might have to get you out more often."

"I hope you don't mind the upheaval," she said. "It just made more sense to have a dedicated area for me and Gen to work in during the transition."

"Not at all," he replied. "It'll just give me more reason to get off my lazy butt and head down to the gym. Would you girls like to join me?"

"No thanks; I'm good," Gen replied, without lifting her head from the document she was reading.

"I'm shocked," Maguire said sarcastically.

"Ignore her," Melody said, as she took him by the arm and walked him over to the fireplace.

"I miss you, cowboy," she said, when they were alone. "I feel so bad about how crazy things have been lately."

"I miss you too, angel," he said, gently brushing a stray strand of blonde hair from her face.

"Do you?"

"Yes, I do, why do you ask?"

"It's just that…."

Their conversation was interrupted by the buzzing of his cellphone.

"Hold that thought for a moment," he said.

Maguire lifted the phone up, to read the display, and frowned slightly. "Sorry, babe, I have to take this call."

"It's okay," she said. "It can wait."

Maguire kissed her on the cheek and then accepted the call, "Hello?"

"You have a moment, my son?"

Maguire held up his finger to Melody, indicating he'd be right back, and walked toward the patio door.

"I always have a moment for you, Mother," he said, when he was safely outside.

"Sorry I couldn't get back to you yesterday, but, as you can imagine, things are a bit *chaotic* in the swamp right now. By the way, give my warmest congratulations to your lady on her nomination."

"Thank you," he said.

"So what did you need?" Mother asked.

"I need you to do some snooping for me," Maguire replied.

"On who?" the man asked cautiously.

"Dean Oliver."

"Ah, what has Eliza Cook's piss-boy done now?" Mother asked with a slight chuckle.

"He crossed the line from professional *thorn in my side* to personal the other night."

"Oh, well that changes things a bit, doesn't it?"

While their paths had crossed on several occasions, Maguire knew that the man had been operating under orders. It didn't make it right, but it did make it professionally understandable. In their line of work, it was always professional, even the disagreeable things that one often had to do. You learned early on to never *take* anything personal and, more importantly, you never *made* anything personal. But Oliver had hinted at a disregard for that mantra and now Maguire needed to know just how serious he needed to take the veiled threat.

"I have a feeling we will cross paths again," Maguire said. "I just want to know what I am really dealing with; beyond the typical dust-jacket blurb."

In the background, Maguire could hear the sound of fingers tapping a keyboard, as Mother began searching personnel files.

"Hmmm," he heard the man say gruffly on the other end of the phone.

"That doesn't sound positive," Maguire replied.

"Your man is bit of an enigma," Mother replied.

"How so?"

"His file has been cleaned," the man said. "He was an Army grunt, more specifically, an 18F snake eater."

"Special Forces?"

"According to this he was. Last entry in his 201 says he was an intel sergeant."

"What else?" Maguire asked.

"Nothing, just the prerequisite school information, but that's about it," Mother replied. "Either he was the laziest *rear-echelon mother fucker* there ever was, or someone decided to make his folder a mystery."

"Any medals?"

"Just the usual, Marksman, National Defense, Good Conduct," Mother replied.

"I'm actually quite surprised the fucker went three years without screwing up," Maguire scoffed.

"Or he just didn't get caught."

"How long was he in for?"

"It says eight years, which coincides with his employment with the State Department."

"Anything in that file?"

"It's pretty damn vanilla; just a posting to Virginia and New York."

"When did he separate?"

"According to this it was around the same time that Cook left the State Department."

"You have any connections down at Bragg?"

"I may or may not have a buddy who still owes me at JSOC," Mother replied, referring to the Joint Special Operations Command.

"Can you see if you can entice him to part with some scuttlebutt?"

"Great," Mother said sullenly. "Now I get to hear him tell me how 'when the President dials 911, the phone rings at Fort Bragg,' for only the four thousandth time."

"I owe you," Maguire said.

"Paddy, if you lived to be as old as Methuselah you still couldn't pay back all the shit you owe me."

"I don't have to live that long, Mother, I just have to outlive you."

"I'll call you as soon as I know something," the man said, ignoring the light-hearted dig. "But in the meantime I would suggest that you *assume bad-faith* in any dealings you might have with him."

"Thanks, I plan too," Maguire said, and ended the call.

He made his way over to the railing and leaned on it.

It wasn't unusual for a special operations member's folder to be sanitized of certain information. He knew that his own folder had *a lot* of missing information in it, but this particular one seemed a bit *too clean* and that troubled him.

"Hey there, are you okay?"

Maguire looked back over his shoulder to see Melody standing in the doorway. "Yeah, babe, I'm fine, why?"

Melody adjusted the collar on her coat, as she made her way over to him.

"I don't know," she said hesitantly, as Maguire draped his arm around her shoulder and pulled her close.

"What's wrong, Mel?"

"It's nothing, I'm just being silly."

"If something's bothering you, you need to tell me."

"Are we okay?"

"Of course we are," Maguire said. "Why wouldn't we be?"

"It's just that you've seemed so preoccupied lately and I know this whole election thing hasn't helped. Now, with the campaign behind us, I just want to make sure there are no problems."

"Oh, Mel, no, it's not like that at all."

"Then what is it?" she asked.

"It has nothing to do with us, angel," he said. "It's just this case I've been working on."

"What's wrong?"

"Have you ever had to make a decision that you knew in your head was wrong, but in your heart you did it for the right reasons?"

"Yes, I have."

"Did you ever second guess yourself?"

"Yes, frequently," Melody replied. "I don't believe that anyone in a position of authority hasn't struggled with that dilemma from time to time."

Maguire turned around, his back toward the railing, and gazed up at the house. "Do you know what the protection detail call-sign is for this place?"

"No, what?" she asked, turning around.

"Castle," he replied.

"Sounds fitting, considering that was the look I was going for when I had the architects design it."

"Yeah, but a castle is supposed to be strong, impenetrable," he replied. "But sometimes I cannot help but wonder if it is all just some grand illusion. That instead of stone and steel it's made of glass and if we aren't careful, it will all shatter into pieces."

"Is that a metaphor for us?"

"No, I'm just thinking about the dangers we face from the outside world."

"Please don't hold anything back from me, James. If there is something I need to know about I want you to be upfront with me."

"I know you're not naïve, but you shouldn't trust everyone you're going to D.C. with."

"You know something, tell me."

"McMasters was having an affair with a young woman who turned up dead," he said. "It was made to look like an accident, but I don't believe it was."

"Did he kill her?"

"No, but my gut instinct is that she was killed because of what they were doing."

"A cover-up?" Melody asked. "Does Eliza know?"

"Yes, to both questions."

"And she's okay with it?"

"I get the feeling that she doesn't want to sacrifice him on the altar of political correctness for something he didn't do," Maguire said. "She just asked that I proceed with discretion."

"Wow," Melody said, shaking her head. "It's moments like this that make me question everything we're doing."

"I get that," Maguire said, "but if we don't do it, who will?"

"Yes, but why us?" she asked. "Why can't we just pack it all in, buy a place in Bora Bora and spend the rest of our lives in the pursuit of happiness and pleasure?"

"Because in the absence of good, evil will prevail," he replied. "Or as Edmund Burke so eloquently said, '*The only thing necessary for the triumph of* evil *is for* good *men to* do nothing.' I've given too much of my life to this country to see that happen."

Melody stepped in front him, wrapping her arms around his neck and kissed his cheek.

"I love you," she whispered in his ear.

"I love you too, angel."

"Enough with this insanity for one night," she said. "Come to bed."

"You go on ahead; I'll be up in a minute."

Melody smiled at him, "Don't keep me waiting, cowboy."

"I won't," he replied, giving her a kiss.

Maguire watched, as Melody turned and walked back toward the house.

She was an amazing woman and he was deeply in love with her, but in his heart he also wrestled with the fact that he still had *feelings* for Tzviya. What made matters even worse was that she obviously still had feelings for him; the meeting in Brooklyn had proven that. Even now he could remember the way the warmth of her lips had felt on his, as she had kissed him. In the heat of the moment it would have been so easy to allow that smoldering ember to re-ignite, and yet he hadn't. It shouldn't have been as difficult a decision as it had been, but it was.

It wasn't the past which troubled him now; it was the realization that their paths would one day cross again. Would he be able to control his feelings for her, when that day inevitably came?

He pushed the thoughts from his mind.

There were other far more pressing matters that he needed to focus on and he couldn't shake the feeling that there was an unseen enemy looming on the horizon.

Maguire gazed up at the house, as he made his way toward the patio door, and wondered whether their *glass castle* would be strong enough to withstand whatever threats might lie ahead.

CHAPTER FORTY

The White House, Washington, D.C.
Tuesday, February 10ᵗʰ, 2015 – 4:23 p.m.

Melody stared out the window of the SUV, taking in the sights of her new *home*, as the motorcade made its way west along Constitution Avenue.

Despite all the assurances that she was a highly qualified nominee, her confirmation hearing hadn't gone as easily as anticipated. Sadly, it was everything but her abilities that had been brought into question. Melody was accustomed to the routine grandstanding, that many of the senators engaged in, but this seemed more personal, as if it had been their goal to hurt her.

Going in she knew the odds where in her favor, but the vote was still close enough to make her wonder just how much they could get done, if Congress was that divided.

"You okay?"

Melody turned to see Maguire looking at her.

"Yeah, just taking it all in," she replied, squeezing his hand tightly. "It's real now. It's happening."

"Yes it is, Madam Secretary of State – *designate*," Maguire said cheerfully. "Relax and enjoy the moment, angel, you earned this."

"I feel like a Christian being led to the lions."

"Actually, that feeling will probably be more appropriate on your first foreign trip," he replied. "That's when the real knives will come out."

"You make it sound so damn *appealing*," she said sarcastically. "I can hardly wait for the festivities to begin."

"Well, you won't have to wait very long," he said, pointing to the White House off to their right. "You're about to get your marching orders."

The motorcade made a right turn onto 17th Street and headed north.

"*Trader* Actual to *Crown*, please be advised we are one minute out," the State Department, Diplomatic Security Service lead agent in the front seat said into his radio.

Melody looked at Maguire and smiled, "Are you ready for this, *Trident*?"

The Secret Service had assigned them radio code names; both of which paid homage to their past lives.

"As ready as I will ever be, *Trader*," Maguire said, before leaning over and kissing her cheek.

A moment later the motorcade turned off 17th and was waved through the vehicle checkpoint at Pennsylvania Avenue by the Uniformed Division officer, while several others, armed with Heckler & Koch MP-5 rifles, monitored the area. A moment later the motorcade headed through the NW checkpoint and made its way toward the White House.

"I guess it's show time, angel," Maguire said, as the vehicle came to a stop.

They watched as the agents began exiting from their vehicles and took up a defensive perimeter around the motorcade. Once the lead agent received the all clear, he opened the rear passenger door and Melody exited the vehicle. Maguire then got out on the other side and walked around to where she was waiting.

"I guess this is it," she said, as Gen and Gregor joined up with them.

A young female staffer was waiting in front of the portico and extend her hand out to Melody, "Madam Secretary, it's my honor to welcome you to the White House. President Cook is waiting for you."

"Thank you," Melody said, shaking the young woman's hand. "Please lead the way."

They followed her to the door, which led to the West Wing entrance, where a Marine stood watch. As they approached, he opened the door in precise military fashion.

Once inside the lobby they were met by Vice-President Vernon Mays and his wife.

"Congratulations, Melody," he said warmly, and gave her a hug. "Allow me to introduce you to my wife, Penelope."

"It's a pleasure to meet you, Secretary Anderson," the woman said, shaking her hand.

"Thank you very much and please, call me Melody. I'd like to introduce you to my fiancé, James."

"Actually, we already know James," Vernon said.

"You do?" she asked, with a quizzical look.

"Senator,... I mean Vice-President Mays was kind enough to help us out during the terror investigation," Maguire interjected. "And Mrs. Mays was a gracious host during my visit."

Melody looked at him, a little smirk on her face, before turning back toward Mays.

"James certainly gets around, but he has a tendency to forget the details," she replied. "I can't wait to *not* tell him what I do at work all day,"

"I have a feeling you will be even busier than you might imagine," the Vice-President replied.

"Well, that's why I have my big-gun with me," she replied. "Please allow me to introduce Genevieve Gordon and her boyfriend, Gregor Ritter. Gen is going to be my chief of staff."

Once pleasantries had been exchanged, Mays took Melody by the arm.

"Please, come with me," he said, as he led them down a corridor. "President Cook wants to hold the swearing-in ceremony in her office."

For a moment the comment didn't register with her, but then she realized exactly what office he was talking about and she could feel the butterflies in her stomach take flight.

Mays led them past the Cabinet Room, which would soon include her own personalized chair, and into the Oval Office; where Cook stood up from her desk and walked around to greet her.

"There's *my* Secretary of State," she said ebulliently. "God, you gave them a helluva fight, Mel. I'm so proud of you."

"Thank you, Madam President," Melody replied. "I thought they had me on the ropes a few times."

"Nonsense," Cook replied, "I can tell you with absolute certainty that the world was watching your performance and now they know this administration means business."

"I appreciate that vote of confidence."

"You earned it, my dear," Cook replied, as she turned slightly to greet Maguire. "Ah, James, how is my favorite policeman?"

"I'm doing well," he said, as Cook gave him an unexpected hug.

"I'm coming up to the city next month," she said. "We need to have dinner and you can bring me up to speed on how Jack's running things."

"I'd be honored," he replied.

"Good, it's a date then," she said, as she turned toward Gen.

"I haven't forgotten you, my dear," Cook said with a conciliatory tone and a warm smile.

"Thank you for inviting us, Madam President," she replied. "Please allow me to introduce Gregor Ritter, my stubborn other half."

Gregor came to attention, performing an almost *half-bow*, as he accepted her hand. "It is my honor, Madam *Präsident*."

"Well, you're certainly not from around here," she said with a smile.

"No, ma'am," Gregor replied. "I'm German."

"Gregor is the head of Peter Bart's security detail."

"Ah, my dear friend Peter," she said. "Well, I'm glad to know that both he and Gen are in good hands."

"Thank you," Gregor replied. "That is very kind of you to say."

"So where is the little one I keep hearing so much about?"

"Wolfgang is with the nanny for the week," Gen replied. "We thought it might be nice for a little parental R&R before things get crazier."

"You're a very smart woman, Gen," Cook said with a smile. "Enjoy your family when you can, but never forget to enjoy some *alone* time as well."

"I couldn't agree more," Gen replied.

"Well, I guess it's time to get this show on the road," Cook said, before turning to face the gathering.

"Well, as much as I am sure Melody is dreading this moment, I think it's time we administer the oath of office, before she makes a mad dash for it and I have to put the entire White House on lockdown."

The staffer motioned for Gen and Gregor toward the side of the room, while Cook led Melody and Maguire over to her desk. As they were getting prepared, the Press Secretary led in a small group of reporters and photographers.

"Do you have the Bible?" Mays asked.

"I do," Maguire said, holding up the leather bound family Bible that had once belonged to his mother.

"If you would, Melody, please place your left hand on the Bible, raise your right hand, and repeat after me.

Melody did as directed, following along with Mays as he administered the oath of office. In the background she could hear the rapid-fire sound of photographs being taken to record the moment.

"I, Melody Anderson, do solemnly swear that I will support and defend the Constitution of the United States against all enemies, foreign and domestic; that I will bear true faith and allegiance to the same; that I take this obligation freely, without any mental reservation or purpose of evasion; and that I will well and faithfully discharge the duties of the office on which I am about to enter. So help me God."

"Congratulations, Madam Secretary of State," Mays said, as he shook her hand.

"Thank you," she replied.

"You will do great things for this country, Melody," Cook said, as she hugged her newest cabinet member.

"Thank you for this opportunity, Madam President," she replied. "I won't let you down."

"I know that," Cook said reassuringly, then turned toward the assembled press pool to give a statement.

"Having someone of Melody Anderson's talent and intellect leading the Department of State will be an incredible asset for our country at a critical time in history," Cook said. "She is prepared to take the message, to both ally and adversary, that America stands resolute to support freedom and democracy, both at home and abroad. To our friends she will be a steadfast reminder of America's pledge to always be there, but to our foes she will serve as a warning that we will be watching and willing to take any action that threatens to undermine peace. She has my complete trust and support. Today, she has my sincere congratulations on becoming America's newest Secretary of State."

Cook waited until the press pool had been removed, before addressing Melody.

"Well, now that we have one major event down," she said, "Tell me, when are we planning the wedding?"

Maguire smiled, as Melody looked over at him.

"We've decided on the end of May," she said, looking back at Cook. "Just a simple ceremony."

Cook waived her hand dismissively, "My dear, you're the Secretary of State; simple went out the window five minutes ago. Your marriage will be the social event of the year, so you had better prepare for a venue that can host a few hundred *close* friends. If you'd like, I'll have my people reach out to Washington Cathedral. I'm sure they will be more than accommodating."

"That's very kind of you," Melody said, somewhat stunned.

"We'll discuss it over lunch later in the week," she replied, "but for now there is something more pressing going on in Eastern Europe that I need to talk to you about, so I am going to have to steal you away from James for a few minutes."

"By all means," Melody replied.

"They've set up a small reception in the Roosevelt Room," Cook said to Maguire, "I promise I won't keep her too long."

"Take your time," Maguire said, as he leaned over and kissed Melody's cheek. "Congratulations, angel."

Maguire watched as the three of them walked out the side door, which led to the President's study, and then walked out of the Oval Office.

"Well does this make you a kept man now?"

Maguire pivoted to see Mother standing in the hallway.

"I thought this place frowned on people like us?" Maguire said, as he shook the man's hand.

"They keep renewing my pass; I think they consider me *gifted*."

"I hear they have special schools for that now," Maguire replied.

"After putting up with all you *froggie* little shits there's nothing more I need to learn," he said. "Let's take a little walk."

The two men made their way down the same hallway, that Maguire had come through earlier, until they reached a stairwell and headed downstairs. A few moments later they arrived at the Navy Mess, which was only a stone's throw from the Situation Room; the same room that Maguire had been in just over a year earlier.

The memories of Rich's death flooded back as the two men took their seat in the empty room.

"This is the only place in the building that feels like home to me," Mother said, "and they even serve great coffee."

"Well, you chief's always got the better stuff."

"Rank does have its privileges, son."

A moment later a Navy steward appeared and laid a steaming mug of hot, black coffee in front of Mother, before turning to look at Maguire, "Coffee, sir?"

"No thanks, I'm good."

Maguire waited till the sailor had departed, before looking at Mother.

"Are they recruiting directly from elementary school these days?"

"How the hell do I know?" Mother replied. "*All* of you look like your twelve to me. Hell, half the time I thought I was going to have to send your squad out with *floaties*."

"We were young, weren't we?" Maguire asked, laughing at the mental image.

"We were all young once," he replied, "and blissfully ignorant."

"So what do I need to know," Maguire asked.

"The details you were looking for on Oliver," Mother replied, handing him a thumb drive, "but you didn't get that from me."

"Get what?" Maguire asked, as he slipped the device in his jacket.

"Exactly," Mother replied. "What you might find even more interesting though is what I found out about the thorn in your side."

"I'm all ears."

"First off, he's no joke, so deal with him accordingly if you ever have to," Mother said. "My buddy says he was an overachiever, even by their standards. Our spooky brothers over in *Christian's in Action* took a liking to him and rumor is that he did a lot of *freelance* wet work for them under official cover."

Maguire frowned at the news. It was that he didn't already have a gut feeling about the man, but he wasn't particularly thrilled about the confirmation.

A lot of bad things happened to bad people around the world and the use of special operations personnel, including SEAL's, was not all that uncommon, especially by the aforementioned CIA. The only real issue was ensuring that the *right* people were sent to meet their maker; a line of distinction which sometimes got blurred in the planning stages.

"Just another tool in the tool box," Maguire muttered. "Ain't that right, Chief?"

"I'm afraid so, Paddy," he replied. "But you and I both know that once you get a taste for that shit, your moral compass becomes a bit *skewed*. Normally someone like him will chase the money; parlay their government skills into a private sector gig or become a *gun-for-hire* in some third world shithole."

"And yet here we are in good old *CONUS*."

"Threats are everywhere, my son," Mother replied, as he took a sip of his coffee, "but not all are visible."

A dark look came over Maguire's face, as he contemplated what he had just been told.

"I know that look and it's not good," Mother asked with apprehension. "What are you thinking?"

"How did he hook up with Cook?"

"Officially, when he was working for DSS," the man replied. "He was a liaison to some senate committee. When Cook became secretary of state, his star apparently rose. Why do you ask?"

"Like you said, normally folks like him chase after the money," Maguire replied. "Freelancers don't last long. Folks get paid to do a job their *told* to do and can you think of anyone with a bigger bank account than the United States?"

"You think *she* is pulling his strings?" Mother asked, couching his words.

"I think she knows exactly what she wants and isn't about to let any *inconsequential* details get in her way."

"If that's the case, then you had better make damn sure you stay on her good side."

"It's not *me* that I am concerned about," Maguire said somberly. "I'm worried about *who* I potentially just served up to her."

Mother's jaw clenched tightly, the muscles in his cheek rippling, as the *meaning* of what Maguire had just said set in. For him politics had always been a messy game, but it was always professional. Now it appeared as if it may have crossed the line.

"Well isn't this just *another fine Navy day*?"

"Indeed," Maguire replied, wishing he had a choice of something stronger than coffee right now.

"All I can tell you is to tread lightly, Paddy, but you already know that," Mother cautioned. "Like the man said, if you have to act, '*Let your plans be dark and impenetrable as night, and when you move, fall like a thunderbolt.*'"

"Hooyah, Chief," Maguire replied.

EPILOGUE

Needles, California
Saturday, February 21st, 2015 – 7:33 a.m.

A bulky, obsolete 27" television set sat on top of a dresser that had long ago seen its better days; much like everything else in the run down El Ranchero Motel on the outskirts of town. The dull image on the screen showed Eliza Cook talking to reporters at a press conference at the White House.

"For too long the United States has engaged in a convoluted Middle East policy which claimed to bring about change, but did very little to foster a climate that would nurture that change. The principal goal of my administration will be to bring about that peace. Whether those countries accept the proverbially carrot or the stick is their choice, but our resolve will not waver."

The screen switched to a news-studio where a panel of dour-looking pundits was sitting around a large table.

"Are we perhaps looking at a fundamental paradigm shift in U.S. foreign policy, Burt?" the host, John White, asked.

"I think we are, John," retired U.S. Army Colonel Burt Asher replied. "It seems to me as if President Cook is intent on throwing away all the progress President Behre had made in fostering an environment for peace."

"With all due respect, Colonel, I have to disagree," national security analyst Cassandra Samuelson chimed in. "You're saying Cook's *big stick* policy jeopardizes progress when in fact the only reason that any of these countries have even come to the table was for the lavish bribes Behre has been handing out like party favors."

"Bribery is a strong word, Cass," White interjected. "The United States has a long history of providing aid to numerous Middle East countries and I don't think it is appropriate to call them bribes."

"Really?" the woman asked. "And just what have we gotten for all that generous aid? The modern conflict dates back a century and estimates put the death toll at three million or more. Can you actually define this as *progress*?"

"I understand that you feel the need to further the Cook *agenda*, seeing as you were a member of her advisory team," Asher said, "but I'd caution you to look beyond the talking points. We need to progress these talks before we expend anymore precious blood in the region."

"The *reality* is that our enemies don't fear us," she said tersely. "They only put their swords away just long enough to line up for the freebies we hand them. Perhaps it's time we embrace the old adage, '*Si vis pacem, para bellum.*'"

"Spoken just like someone who has never actually faced the scourge of war," Asher replied dismissively.

"And on that note we're going to take a short break and allow our panel to cool off," White said.

The man lying on the bed turned the television off and threw down the remote in disgust.

He'd grown weary of all these talking heads discussing things that they had absolutely no clue about. Asking some thirty-something, *think-tank policy wonk* about actual war was like asking a nun how to field strip an M-4 rifle. Sure she could talk about the importance of it *theoretically*, but until you held it in your hand during a firefight, and it jammed, you could not comprehend or appreciate the actual need for that knowledge.

He swung his legs over the side of the bed and sat up. The colonel was right. There were too many folks in D.C., who'd never set foot in a combat zone, who were chiming in on military issues that they knew nothing about. He'd learned the lesson the hard way, as an E-5 infantry grunt who'd served two combat tours in Iraq.

He'd enlisted for what he believed were all the right reasons, including honor, pride, and patriotism. It didn't take too long for him to realize that none of those mattered to the politicians who sent him into harm's way or the academy ring-knockers who command soldiers, but did not understand how to fight a war.

The final blow to the *illusion* of his military career came when he'd almost lost his life in an IED blast. While the professionalism and bravery of the front line medics were unquestionable, they'd brought him back from deaths door several times before he made it to the hospital, the apathy in which he was treated when he finally got back to the states brought an end to the deception.

Left alone, he had a choice to either wallow in his misery or to do something to effect a change from within.

He chose the latter.

The man got up and walked over to the dresser. Next to the antiquated TV he picked up his wallet, keys and a Glock 43, which he slid into the holster in the small of his back. Then he grabbed his leather jacket, which lay on the chair next to the bed, and slipped it on, before picking up his helmet.

Outside the sun was shining brightly on this crisp, February morning. It was a perfect day for a cruise, especially when the route would take him through the desert, but he knew that pleasure wasn't his final destination today.

He put on his helmet and got on the blacked-out *Harley-Davidson Fat Boy* and fired it up, listening to the throaty growl of the exhaust. An older couple, walking out of one of the adjoining rooms, frowned in displeasure at the rumbling sound. The man smiled behind the tinted face shield, revving the throttle one more time for effect, before pulling out of the lot.

He made a left on J Street and headed north until he jumped onto Interstate 40 heading east. It only took about fifteen minutes before he crossed the Colorado River and entered Arizona. He looked down at his watch. It was a leisurely two-hour ride to his destination, which would get him there with about twenty minutes to spare. More than enough time to scout the area and make sure he had no *friends*.

To call this stretch of Arizona road *desolate* would have been kind. For a city-boy like him, the Mojave Desert had more in common with some distant alien landscape than it did to a country with over three hundred million residents; still there was something incredibly peaceful about it.

Endless miles of desert scrub dotted the landscape; while off in the distance mountains rose up to meet the cloudless blue sky. It was easy to get lost in his thoughts, but he also mentally reprimanded himself to focus on his training. During the ride he made sure to adjust his speed at differing times, enough so that any tail he might have had could be spotted; even though he didn't think it necessary. At times it felt as if his only company was the occasional semi-trailer which was often heading in the opposite direction.

Still, the solitude gave him ample time to think about the choice he was about to make.

Just outside Seligman he pulled off the highway and made his way along a lonely stretch of two-lane road. Seligman had gained the title *Birthplace of Historic Route 66* and was dotted with a number of tourist locales that catered to sightseers and souvenir shoppers, but those places didn't interest him. His focus was on an old, rundown bar, frequented by bikers, just on the outskirts of town.

He pulled into the parking lot just before ten-thirty and found a spot, away from the front door, that was next to a vintage 1949 metallic green Panhead. Stenciled on the side of the gas tank was the familiar eagle, globe and anchor of the United States Marine Corps.

The rider was older now, probably in his mid-50's, sporting a beer belly and a chest length beard. He was wearing a pair of faded jeans and a beat-up black leather vest over a t-shirt. It was a far cry from the spit and polished man he once knew, but he instinctually knew that he was still a man to be reckoned with.

He pulled up and then carefully backed his bike into the spot, removed his helmet and turned off the ignition.

"Good morning, Sergeant Aikens," the man said, after the engine turned off. "I was wondering if you would show."

"Morning, sir," the man replied. "You know I'm a man of my word."

"Indeed I do."

"Besides, technically speaking, aren't you the one who is early?"

"Early is on time; on time is late," the man admonished him.

Aikens scanned the area with a trained eye, looking for anything that might seem out of the ordinary; both on the ground and in the air.

Aikens had to hand it to the man; it was the perfect place for a covert meet.

The bar sat out in the middle of nowhere with a great *line-of-sight* visibility, in either direction, for miles. Even if there was some form of *fluid* surveillance, they wouldn't be able to get close enough to monitor what was going on or being said without being seen.

"It's a far cry from Fallujah, isn't it?"

"Sand is sand, sir," Aikens replied, "and I have had my fill for a lifetime."

"Well, at least no one is shooting at us over here."

"Not *yet*," he said somberly.

"The needs of the many, son," the man replied. "We swore an oath to protect and defend the constitution from enemies both foreign and *domestic*. Last time I checked there was no expiration on that oath."

"I understand, sir," Aikens said. "But are we sure that this is the right path to take?"

"I appreciate your concerns," the man said. "I had the same ones at first, but I'm afraid we don't have any other choice. People in this country have become so polarized that they would vote against their own interests, even their very lives, if it ensured that the other person didn't win. Regrettably, we saw this play out in November."

"But this seems a bit excessive."

"Maybe," the man replied, "but when you have a cancer growing sometimes you have to take radical action. I had hoped that all the rhetoric was just that and when the election was over things would return to some semblance of normalcy. Sadly, the latest appointments within the administration point toward a policy of escalation in hostilities, not peace, and our elected representatives don't have the backbone or the willingness to push back. If we don't take action now, it just might end up being too late."

Aikens nodded.

He'd become somewhat of a news *junkie* over the last several years and it was impossible not to see the precarious direction that this new President wanted to take the country in. To be fair, the world had always been a very dangerous place, but you didn't make things better by making it *more* dangerous. Even worse, none of the political cheerleaders, who were rooting for the more aggressive posturing, had any kids who would have to pick up the sword to defend those policies. No, that work was ultimately left to the patriotic grunts like him.

Aikens glanced down at his disfigured hand.

"So have you made your decision, son?"

"Yes, I have," Aikens replied. "I'm in."

"I'm glad to hear that and I know the Lieutenant Colonel will be as well. We need more folks over at *The Company*."

"How many are on board?"

"Enough, for now," the man replied, "but we expect those numbers to grow shortly."

"What do you need me to do?"

"For now, *HUMINT*," the man said. "This is going to be one of those ops where we will only get one opportunity to bring the entire system down in one fell swoop, so we need to make sure we have all our pieces in position before the green light can be given. This will be a surgical strike, so we need eyes and ears to know where the players are at all times."

"I can do that," Aikens replied.

The man looked around cautiously, before reaching into his vest pocket and removing a USB thumb-drive, which he then passed over to Aikens.

"This is a list of our targets," he said. "Commit the details to memory and then destroy it. I don't want anyone to get burned on this op over a stupid mistake. Is that understood?"

"Loud and clear, sir."

"From now on, all contact will be through onetime use burner phones, make sure you don't leave a purchase trail behind you. Always use cash and never buy from the same place twice."

Aikens nodded.

"Here's a number," the man said, handing him a piece of paper. "Once you have information, on any of the targets, you call this number and let me know."

"Are there any contingency plans if the op gets compromised?" Aikens asked, slipping the paper into his jacket pocket.

"Son, if this op goes south we're all going to hang for treason," the man said dispassionately. "So I strongly suggest that you don't screw up."

"*Ooh-rah*, sir," Aikens replied sharply.

Aikens watched as the old man stood up and kick-started the motorcycle; bringing it to life with a loud roar.

"*Ooh-rah, Devil-Dog,*" he replied. "Semper Fi."

Aikens watched as the motorcycle pulled out of the parking lot and headed down the road.

Operation Medusa had begun.

ABOUT THE AUTHOR

Andrew Nelson spent twenty-two years in law enforcement, including twenty years with the New York City Police Department. During his tenure with the NYPD he served as a detective in the elite Intelligence Division, conducting investigations and providing dignitary protection to numerous world leaders. He achieved the rank of sergeant before retiring in 2005.

He is the author of both the James Maguire and Alex Taylor mystery series' and has written several non-fiction works about the New York City Police Department's Emergency Service Unit and the aftermath of the September 11th, 2001, terror attack.

For more information please visit us at:

www.andrewgnelson.org

ANDREW G.
NELSON

CPSIA information can be obtained
at www.ICGtesting.com
Printed in the USA
LVHW020324140921
697765LV00019B/425